CHARLIE

NORTHERN GRIZZLIES MC
BOOK FOUR

M. MERIN

Charlie: Northern Grizzlies MC (Book 4)

ISBN: 9781790442133

Copyright 2018 Maura O'Brien

Cover Art by Madelene Martin www.madbookdesigns.com

Edited by Edits by Erin

Formatting by Dark Water Covers

CHAPTER ONE

May 2018

CONNAL

"ROYCE!" I YELL, SEEING THE SPRAWL OF papers all over my desk.

"Yeah," he says as he ducks his head in. "Ahh, sorry about that. Um, Janine needed to use the washroom."

"Tell me you did not fuck that skank on my desk, asshole!" She's a damn townie who isn't even welcome at the MC's parties anymore.

"No! Betsy said she thought Janine was trying to get one of us to knock her up, so I just let her blow me when I finished her car." Royce looks pleased with himself for thinking up that solution.

"Let me be abso-fucking-lutely clear on this. You keep your dick secured in your pants in this...in my garage, and especially in my goddamn office!" I am fuming. That's all we need is for that woman to tell people she has to blow the mechanic. Shit.

"Alright! Chill, I won't do it again." He shrugs and turns to go.

"Go get the bleach and clean any and all surfaces she touched or breathed on, then find that fucking stack of applications. I need someone hired, yesterday!" I yell out to his back.

"Oh! I forgot," Royce says, turning back to me. "Some old dude, Mike or Mack? He called earlier. Said he knew someone who had applied and he wanted to talk to you about it."

I growl in frustration. Mack was in the MC way before my time. He lost a leg in an accident and now teaches an advanced certification auto and motorcycle mechanic course for a small school in Boise. Fuck, he wouldn't just recommend anyone. And at this point, we're so behind I'll hire anyone he tells me to.

Looking up his number, I'm reaching out to him minutes later.

"Hey, Mack! I heard you called. Tell me you have someone for me!"

"Yeah, I called yesterday. Fucking took your sweet time," he grumbles.

"I just got the message!" Royce is such an asshole, I think again. I'm knocking papers aside in the mess, looking for the applications to see who Mack has for me. "Look, I'm desperate here. Who you got for me?"

"Charlie Scott. Young kid, best I've seen come through here in a long while."

"Charlie's ok with the move? I don't pay Boise rates," I confirm.

"Yeah. Charlie knew I was from that way and just told me there hadn't been any word from you, so I called to make sure you were still hiring and give you my two cents. The ASE exam is today, I don't think passing that will be a problem. Not for Charlie."

"Got it!" I yell, excited to finally find the Charles Scott application. "OK. Yeah, looks like what? Twenty years old? High marks all around, and been working at a local garage part-time for three years? I can start him with a month probation period, as soon as he can get here."

"Um, well, actually." I hold the phone away to stare at it, trying to figure out what the fuck his hemming and hawing is all about. "Yeah, never mind. I'll call Charlie with the good news. I'd guess a day or two to pack and get there? Can you send details, including a temp place to stay, to whatever email is in the application?"

"No lease or anything to worry about on that end?" I am juiced at having someone here in a couple days, but that seems quick to me.

"No, Charlie's been living out back, above my garage. Doubt there's much to pack up. Uh, Charlie was in the foster system a while. Mainly raised by a grandfather, he was a mechanic and a drinking buddy of mine. He died about seven years ago."

"Don't care about that shit, just him getting here that fast would really help me out. Will start him out with tires and basic oil and filter changes until I get caught up with the bigger projects, then I'll work on some bigger tickets alongside him," I say, looking up as Royce ducks his head in letting me know I have a delivery of parts to go check in.

"Glad this works, Connal. I appreciate it and am relieved to have Charlie with someone I trust." He clicks off before I can remind him I'm hiring a mechanic not adopting a pet.

JAKE

"Hey, tall, dark and quiet, how you been?" Betsy wraps an arm around me in a half hug, before taking the seat next to me at the bar.

I nod at her, leaning away to get out of range of her perfume; that stuff always makes me sneeze. I turn back to the story Roy and Vice are telling. Vice is the shortest brother here, not a lot taller than Betsy actually, but no Napoleon complex there. Roy's his uncle and would have knocked that shit out of him years ago if that'd been the case.

Vice has had me working on the build out for a new spa that's going up down the road from Rusty's Bar. Nice having the steady work this time of year. I never gave much thought to what I'd do after the Army, but while in, Connal became the only real friend I ever had and he told me to look him up when I got out. Now I'm working on Vice's construction crew and doing runs for the MC.

Cash in my pocket, brother's by my side, meals, and

a room, plus girls when we want them. Not a bad life. Just been getting restless. Again.

Prospect comes around with fresh drinks for all of us. This kid doesn't have a road name yet, but with the last name Madda, guessing it'll be Madman or something like that.

Gunner strides into the clubhouse. Back from the latest run, he'll be in and out though. Stopping to report in before going home to Riley. Lucky motherfucker.

Didn't think much of it when Jasper announced he was taking Emma as his Ol' Lady. They were married and having kids before anyone could blink. Flint was next with Bree, minus the kids.

We started drifting a bit with Jas and Flint so eager to be with their Ol' Ladies. Gunner shocked the shit out of all of us when he hooked up with Riley. Her family is majorly connected and, although her grandmother has a soft spot for Gunner, her parents are working to get the whole MC arrested and disbanded.

It was Riley who really brought us back together in a different, stronger way. Flint is older, but Jasper, Connal, Gunner, and Vice patched in about the same time. When I made my way here a few years later, I just hung out with that group, 'cause of Connal.

No one was pleased about Gunner's match until he started bringing her around. You can't not like Riley. She knows that I don't talk much and she can sit calmly near me without fidgeting or babbling. That's pretty fucking rare, especially for a teenager. Then she started having our group over for Monday night dinners, and man can she cook. I've eaten at a lot of high-end joints, but nothing like what she does. So now, as long as we're in town, Monday nights the nine of us are around their table.

As great as that's been, it's hard sometimes. It's been making me want a serious relationship more and more. I know Connal feels the same, just feels like slim pickings around here most days.

"Jake, Vice, get back here," Gunner calls from the hall leading back to Jas' office.

He turns back, not waiting for us. We follow and close the office door. Flint and Jas are already seated and I can tell from their faces something went down on Gunner's run.

"The State Police were waiting for us," Gunner starts. "They moved too soon and picked up the diversion. The Russian let me know in time for me to get off the road with the package."

I tilt my head to the side as Vice starts swearing and Gunner continues.

"I made the drop and took the long way back. Lawyer just let Jas know that that Russian'll be released this afternoon. He's gonna head to the cabin for a few days, bore the shit out of any tail he might have."

"So where does that leave Jake, Royce, and prospect for their run next weekend?" Vice asks the question forming in my head.

"Lot of unknowns right now," Jasper says. "I may move the timeline up a little. Jake, you three need to figure out alternate routes or consider riding in a couple cages set with traps. I don't want any chatter about this over any line or in front of anyone who doesn't have a patch, is that understood?"

After agreeing, Vice, Gunner, and I hit the bar.

"Russian was clean right, Gunner?" Vice starts in. "Nothing *recreational* on him?"

"Didn't pack his fucking bag, Vice," Gunner growls back. He throws back the whiskey that prospect brings him and motions for another. "Fuck."

"Hey, Betsy!" Vice calls. She looks up, I image pleased that he's called for her.

"Yeah, baby?" She crosses quickly to us, sidling up to Vice.

"You know where the cabin is, right?" he asks, oblivious to the smile she gives him as she nods. "Good. Grab some petty cash, hit the grocery store for a few days' worth of food and go keep Russian company. All right, sweetie?"

She quickly tries to hide the hurt that flashes across her face, knowing he's sending her off to be with someone else. I see her spending more time with Russian nowadays than she does with Vice, so it's not like she's getting a shit assignment. Fuck, it could have been Frank.

Betsy nods, grabs a few bottles from behind the bar and heads back towards her room.

Once she's out of sight, Roy leans over to slap his nephew upside the head. "Damn, Vice! That was fucking cold!"

"What?" Vice turns towards us with a confused look on his face. "Not gonna leave our brother yanking his own dick for a week!"

"You know that Girlie's carried a torch for you for years," Roy responds, getting in his face. "Don't gotta return feelings you don't have, but don't be a dick about shit like that. I could have handled it quiet like, without getting her hopes up that *you* were gonna take her away."

"Shit, Betsy knows I enjoy her. She knows I enjoy lots of girls," Vice smirks back. "Not that she has much to do with me anymore anyway."

"Show respect, Vice," I surprise myself by talking, the other three are staring at me with their mouths open.

"Yeah, Jake. I getcha," Vice finally says, before heading out.

I'm surprised a moment later when it's just Gunner and me left at the bar, thinking it's odd he hasn't headed home already.

"You doing alright, Jake?" he asks. I tilt my head and nod, trying to figure out where this is going.

"Riley was worried about you after the dinner the other night. I don't know. I promised her I'd check in with you." He looks as embarrassed as I feel right now.

"Might take a ride after this next run. Clear my head a bit," I say. His hand clamps down on my shoulder, as he finishes up his drink.

"Let me know if I can do anything." He grins at me, before tightening his grip. "Don't you make my sweetheart worry."

I just nod again, my throat feeling oddly tight.

CHAPTER TWO

CHARLIE

SITTING ON THE BUS TO ROWANSVILLE, I CAN'T help but smile as I scroll through the emails from Connal. Mack didn't tell me much about him, but I'm picturing someone close to his age. Fifties, maybe? Connal got a discounted rate for me at a small motel within a couple miles of the garage. I'm sure it'll be a dive but I insisted I wanted to be close to the shop. I didn't want to tell him I don't have a car, but I had to pay for school and I couldn't afford both. According to the maps app, there's a diner and gas station with a mini-mart nearby. That should take care of food.

By the time the bus has rolled into town, I've read all the Yelp reviews for the garage, motel, and diner. My leg is bouncing from excitement as I wait to get off the bus. A few blocks past the stop, I come up to the motel that meets my very low expectations.

Oh, well, it's temporary. And, honestly, not the worst looking place I've ever lived.

"What do you want?" The man in the motel office asks when I open the door. Alrighty.

"Um, reservation for Scott?" I mumble.

"How long you staying?" Is his next question.

"I don't know yet, I'm just starting a job here…"

"You gonna whore for those bikers?"

"WHAT?! NO!" I feel like I've walked into an alternate universe.

"Better not think about bringing tricks back here. I'll toss you out, even if it pisses them Northern Grizzlies off. Hear me?"

When I head out to find my room, I'm much paler than when I walked in. My hand with the room key is shaking as I walk down the line, finding number eight. Quickly locking the door behind me, I slide a chair under the doorknob. Turning I get a look at myself and halfway understand the manager's question.

I'm not wearing one of my usual tight sports bra/oversized shirt combinations today. With a regular bra and t-shirt on, my camper's backpack pulling my shoulders back, the only noticeable thing about me is my boobs. I am height and weight proportionate everywhere but my chest. Freshman year of high school they started growing and within months I was a D. Yep, four inches over five feet and I have stripper boobs. Grandpa would have had a heart attack if he hadn't had the big one a year earlier.

By the time I got to a C, I starting binding them and wearing baggie tops. Living in a revolving door of foster homes, I never wanted any of the men to notice me. I'd heard enough horrible tales from other girls in the group home.

After checking the bed for bugs, I am soon climbing in. Eager to get to work tomorrow.

––––––

"Excuse me?" I call in through the bay door.

A man, probably ten or so years older than me, rolls halfway out from under a Range Rover. His face is obscured by oil but his long body looks very well defined from this angle.

"Just leave the keys in it and go fill out the form on the clipboard in the office. Won't get to look at your car for an hour or two," he calls out, annoyed at the interruption.

"Um, I'm looking for Connal?" I call back.

"Yeah, I'm busy, honey. Leaving your car or not?" he growls from under the SUV.

"Not." I bristle at being called *honey*. "I'm Charlie. Charlie Scott? You hired me?"

There's a clatter as he drops his multipliers and rolls the full way out from under the SUV this time. Standing up, and grabbing a towel, he squints at me, still not speaking. I unroll my overalls from the top of my tool bag and shrug at him.

I open my mouth to talk and he holds up a finger to silence me, pulling a phone out and dialing.

"Mack," he growls. "What the fuck is this? I'm seriously backed up and you're fucking pranking me?"

"What the hell?!" I yell out.

Turning his back to me and storming towards the reception area, he yells. "A goddamn girl is here!" I'm standing there furious and unable to decide whether or not to follow him over the next few moments.

"Are you a stripper? That'd be fucking awesome if Mack sent a stripper," I spin, seeing another guy has come up behind me. He's stockier than the first guy and not nearly as tall, with shaggy brown hair and eyes. Reaching out, he moves to grab my braid. I've had it with the men in this town so I kick him in the shin. Hard. With my steel-toed work boot.

"FUCK!" He roars, clutching his leg and falling to the ground. "Fuck. Fuck. Fuck."

"Goddamn it!" Connal yells from behind me. I turn to see him pocketing his phone as he walks towards us.

"I'm not a stripper or a whore, I'm a goddamn MECHANIC!" I yell up at him. It's when we're standing toe to toe that I notice he's nearly a foot taller than I am. And totally hot.

The corner of his mouth twitches. Still silent, he looks over my shoulder to where the other guy is slowly standing up.

"Your name is Charles?" he confirms, taking a deep breath, he looks back down at me. His full lips still twitching.

"My dad died before I was born, mom named me after him," I explain.

There's a low chuckle from the guy behind me. "It's like 'A Boy Named Sue' in reverse."

I turn, narrowing my eyes at the man I can only imagine is another mechanic.

"Hey, hey! Don't kick me again!" He waves his hands in front of him and backs up.

"Royce, get that carburetor finished. *Charles*, my office." Connal looks to each of us. "Now."

This time I follow him as he turns and quickly heads back past the reception desk. He's behind his desk when I catch up and I place my toolset in the spare chair before sitting.

"I need this job, Connal. Mack was my instructor and I thought you would have checked my other reference?" I will work hard here..." I start before he holds up his hand, staring at me.

"What was the tool I dropped back there?"

"It was a torque multipliers. I don't have one of my own," I stumble out, shrugging. "They're expensive."

"They are expensive. When you use my tools, you don't fucking drop them. Got it?" he responds. And I'm thrilled at his meaning.

"I hire you, you pull your weight. I'm backed up and don't have time to babysit. You'll get the shit jobs at first and I don't want any bitching about that."

"No bitching. Got it." I nod at him, trying to suppress my grin.

"Fuck. Another goddamn smartass," he growls, pulling out and lighting a cigarette from a pack on his desk. "Royce has been making the coffee, it's always watered down. You make it now. And that's not cause you're a chick, so stop rolling your eyes at me."

"After coffee, where do I start?" I ask, holding his

eyes with mine and trying not to seem giddy over starting the job.

"There are two cars in the first lane, worksheets are on the driver seat. Always check the license plate number on the forms to the car itself. Basic work for you this first week or two. There will be a couple more drop-offs for oil changes and stuff around lunch time. Some of the customers may give you some shit. Be polite. No kicking."

"Got it," I say, biting down on my lower lip. He squints at my mouth as if waiting for the next smartass comment from me. Growling again, he continues.

"You're pretty. Royce is a man whore." I raise my eyebrow at him. "You fuck around with him, even on your own time and I will fire you." My jaw has dropped. "I don't need that shit in here and he's in the MC with me, I ain't firing him."

"Got it," I repeat, shrugging more to myself than him. I held on to my virginity this long, no sense losing a job over it.

CONNAL

She isn't fucking pretty. The more I look at her, the more I notice. Her long neck, with her light brown braid over one shoulder. Her blue eyes that originally flashed ice at me are now warmed by the laughter in them. The old scar, running along her hairline, from her temple to her ear. Her small hands, which look almost delicate, even though I can see her picking at a callus on her palm. She fucking does it for me.

"You need to change, lock anything up, use the locker in the bathroom behind me. Customers aren't allowed back here." I'm going to regret this. I just know I'm going to regret this. I think as she walks into the bathroom to change.

As she emerges, she has her overalls on over that large shirt of hers. Just as well, it's still cool up here this time of year. Plus, she looks bulkier so the guys won't check her out. Yeah. Right.

She stops as we get to the coffee machine in the reception area and starts in on that while I get back out to the Rover. Once she finishes up the first car and moves to the second one I slide under it to make sure everything looks right. Royce grabs his mug and walks back to reception.

"FUCK!" I hear him yell for the second time today, before a thundering crash.

Charlie and I look at each other before moving to the door. There's coffee all over the floor with Royce flat on his back, looking like he's gasping for air.

"Shit, you ok?" I look down at him, not sure what he needs.

He reaches out to me, so I pull him into the nearest plastic seat. "Charles, get a mop from that closet and some towels."

She looks annoyed that I'm still calling her that but moves quickly, and I turn back to Royce who is still trying to pull air into his lungs.

"She's trying to kill me," he finally croaks out. Charlie looks at each of us with big round eyes.

"What did I do?" she finally asks.

"I didn't knock the coffee. It was all over the floor." He points to the machine and there really is coffee everywhere.

"Charles, you have made coffee before, haven't you?" I ask, pinching the bridge of my nose together.

"Nooo," Charlie admits. "I just...well, I just put the measurement from the can into the top part and the water in the back?"

"Did you use a filter? Take the top of the coffee pot off?" Royce growls at her, and I find myself wanting to defend her when I see the embarrassed look on her face.

"Honest mistake. Won't happen again." I start, cutting Royce off and trying not to smile. "Are you hurt?"

He shakes his head at me, "No? Good, show her how to use the coffee machine then."

"Fuck! Do we even know if she used oil for the goddamn oil change?" he yells, standing up. I quickly push him against the wall before remembering that he did fall pretty hard already. Charlie is cleaning every bit of coffee off the floor and keeping her eyes away from us.

"She had shop classes, not home ec. Show her how to use the fucking machine then we all get back to work." I stomp off, not wanting either of them to see me smile.

"I'm sorry, Royce," she whispers before he crosses over to make new coffee. His grousing is cut off by a siren out front.

"What the fuck now?" I ask as I head out.

CHAPTER THREE

CONNAL

SHERIFF MICHAELS WALKS TOWARDS ME, HIS car is blocking the entrance and there are two state police cars behind him.

"They have a warrant, Connal," he starts. "I got a call they were on their way here and called Jasper. He's en route with the MC's lawyer. Meanwhile, these guys get to check your inventory and any vehicles you or Royce... Who's that?"

Michaels cuts off when he sees Charlie coming out, so I introduce them. The MC more or less has an understanding with Michaels. He doesn't like us, but he's happy as long as crime and drug busts are low. We monitor that, not wanting our bigger contracts affected. But the look he's giving Charlie right now has nothing to do with professional interest and anger shoots through me.

"New hire. She doesn't have a car," I state. "Charlie,

you go on now, get back to work, like I said." I gently nudge her as some bureaucrat approaches me and starts listing what they're looking for.

Royce and Charlie keep working while the State Police go through yesterday's delivery with a fine tooth comb. Our lawyer eventually arrives and keeps an eye on them, muttering about the Maddock family targeting MC businesses. Gunner's Ol' Lady's parents have appointed positions with the governor and they are more determined than ever to bring us all down.

The shop gets slammed with oil changes after lunch, so I move Royce to work with Charlie on getting them all done. There are no further complaints between those two, just some hostile glances thrown each way.

I cut Charlie loose after five and confirm she'll be in by eight the next day. Watching her walk out, I think about asking her what her dinner plans are, but best leave that alone.

JAKE

Leaving the worksite after some overtime, I turn towards Ray's Diner to avoid meatloaf night at the clubhouse. Fucking hate that shit.

A bit past the garage, I see a young woman with a long braid down her back, walking near the side of the road. Not the best area to be walking, so I slow down to see where she's heading. She turns at the sound of the bike and stumbles when she sees me. Pulling up beside her, she's quickly back on her feet and shooting me an embarrassed little grimace.

I tilt my head, patting the seat behind me in invitation. Her blue eyes dart from the seat to my face, and I am pretty surprised at the disappointment that hits me when she quickly shakes her head and continues on, her shoulders hunching forward, without a word.

She's tiny and beautiful. Watching her continue towards the diner, I move up past her and pull into the gas station to top off my tank at a pump where I have a clear view of her progress. Grinning, I see her go inside Ray's and take a seat at the counter.

Parking my bike, I quickly join her.

She has a glass of water in front of her and is studying the menu and the specials board like her life depends on it. Finally looking at me, her eyes widen when she recognizes me. Shit, she looks scared. And young.

"Hi," I say, trying to figure out what to say next. Not sure of how to engage her.

Margie, the waitress, swoops in.

"Jake! How are you? Is Connal coming also?" Marge asks, babbling on without waiting for an answer. "Riley and Gunner were in for breakfast. Could they be any cuter? I would never have matched those two up." She pauses long enough to fill my mug.

"How about you, hun? Want anything other than water?" She raises an eyebrow at the waif beside me.

"Just a cup of today's soup, please." The woman orders. Margie nods then spins towards the kitchen.

"Did you hurt yourself?" I ask her when we're alone

again. Knowing she fell onto the grass near the road, but still wanting to check on her.

Her eyes don't make it up past the tattoos on my neck, but she pulls her eyebrows together and shakes her head.

Without thinking, I lift a finger and smooth the slight crease in between her brows. She immediately starts at my touch, her blue eyes finally meeting my grey eyes.

"Here you go, hun." Margie has returned with the cup of soup and a couple packs of crackers, pulling the girl's attention back away from me. "What do you want to eat, Jake?" she asks, quickly looking between the two of us.

Without thinking, I randomly order, just to get rid of Marge.

I open my mouth to ask the girl her name when the doorbell sounds and Connal calls out, "Jake. Charles."

She quickly turns around, nearly spilling her soup. The asshole doesn't sit beside me but on the other side of the woman next to me. Boxing her in between us, she looks even smaller than before.

"Hi, Connal." She quickly acknowledges him, and then gives me another look before digging back into her soup.

"How do you…" Connal and I burst out at the same time. His eyes widening at the fierceness in my voice, until he realizes he sounded the same.

"Charles?" I ask, looking at both of them.

"It's Charlie," she says, looking up at me with a lopsided grin on her face.

"My new mechanic," Connal drawls out, staring back at me. "She just started today. Imagine my confusion at Charles being a female."

"Mechanic?" I ask. Getting a dirty look from her, I quickly hold my hands up in surrender.

"Don't question her on that. I'd say Royce has learned his lesson, but probably not, cause its Royce." He laughs to himself.

"Royce?" I prod, trying to figure out why her cheeks are flaming red.

"It was an accident," she firmly states, glaring up at Connal.

"And his shin?" He winks down at her before grinning over her head at me.

"He called me a stripper!" she grinds out. "It's 2018. There have been female mechanics for a long time!"

Coffee shoots through my nose. I don't know whether to laugh at her belligerent tone and facial expression, or go finish Royce off for her.

"How'd you two meet?" Connal asks next.

"Wait, what else happened to Royce?" I ask. Not remembering the last time I enjoyed a conversation this much.

"He slipped on some coffee," she says firmly. Her ears are bright red but the corner of her mouth is twitching. It's adorable.

"Charles here was to make the coffee. But while she can crank out a dozen oil changes in an afternoon, her kitchen skills must be lacking. Royce landed flat on his back in a lake of coffee," Connal is laughing and I can't catch my breath.

Marge comes over with my plate and Charlie asks for her check. Margie takes in Charlie's red face and starts glaring at the two of us as she pours coffee for Connal.

I grab Charlie's check when Marge holds it out to her. It instantly rips as she tries to wrestle it out of my hand. Glaring at me, Charlie lays two wrinkled one dollar bills and two quarters on the counter and moves to leave. As I reach for her wrist, I hear her stomach growl and realize that although she's tiny. That cup of soup was too.

"Nice to meet you," she says, tugging her wrist back as she heads out. "See you tomorrow, Connal."

My eyes dart to the tattered state of her dollar bills and notice she must have pocketed the crackers. I immediately turn to see if Connal noticed.

"What did she have for lunch?" His eyes widen as soon as my meaning registers.

"Shit, I don't know." He watches her walk across the parking lot to the motel. "She got to town yesterday, just finished her certificate courses with Mack in Boise. There was a fucking warrant served on the Garage today so I wasn't paying attention."

"What else do you know? I saw her walking when I was heading here, we didn't get to talk." He nods at me, knowing that's not my strong suit anyway.

"Mom named her Charles for her dead father. She gets annoyed at me calling her that, so I'm sticking with it. Grandfather raised her, he died and she went into the system." He pauses to steal fries from my plate as he moves into her empty seat. "Mack knew her grandfather. She recognized him when she signed up for the courses and he took her under his wing."

"What are we going to do about her?" I ask, acknowledging the fact that we both want her. "She seems pretty fucking innocent."

"She's twenty," Connal shrugs, realizing that doesn't have much relevance. "She *is* pretty fucking innocent."

I sit and eat, while we each think this through.

"She's got a temper," he suddenly speaks up. "And she's a smartass. She doesn't miss details and she keeps a neat workstation." Connal continues to list attributes that he spotted during the day.

I finish eating in silence and wait until Connal is finishing up before I order a sandwich and chips to go. He trails behind me as we mount up. Riding across the street, I knock on the door we saw her go into. While I want to lecture her when she opens it without checking who's there, I freeze up and just shove the food container at her before turning back to my bike without a word.

Looking at her in my mirror, she's still standing there with a bemused expression on her face as I ride away.

CHARLIE

I've been starving all day. Turning away from the hot, but kind of odd man, whose cut indicates he's in the

MC with my boss, I can barely help but rip into the food container. I know I should be embarrassed that he saw through me so easily, but without a hotplate to make ramen on, my diet has been suffering.

Chips! Something I can eat later. And a fully loaded ham sandwich with a pickle on the side. I slowly eat half the sandwich, then carefully wrap the rest and put it in the mini fridge for another day.

Jake. He's dark to Connal's light. Dark hair, grey eyes, well over six feet tall with skin slightly darker than my pale shade. Well, the skin that isn't covered with ink. Kind though, besides the food he brought me. I could see it in his eyes as he sat beside me, unsure of what to say. Connal's shaggy hair is much lighter and well matched with green eyes. He's not as bulky as Jake but close in height.

Finally sated, I head off to shower all the grease and oil from my body. Enjoying the feel of having my breasts free for the first time all day, I rub the rough bar of soap around my body, trying to erase the pressure lines. Closing my eyes, I reach further down, picturing the men I've met today and wondering how each would touch me. Thoughts of Royce are quickly dispelled. I can't imagine him as anything but selfish.

Alternating between thoughts of Connal and Jake, I slide my finger between my folds and quickly bring myself off. Groaning softly, I finally step out of the water, throw on a light shirt and panties, and crawl into bed.

CHAPTER FOUR

CHARLIE

THE NEXT MORNING, I LOCK MY ROOM BEHIND me and turn to see Connal waiting on his bike.

"Hop on, Charles," he says, holding a helmet for me.

"What are you doing?" I ask, my jaw nearly on the ground.

"Jake's worksite is in the opposite direction from the clubhouse and he had to be there thirty minutes ago. He got the helmet for you last night, though." Connal smiles at me. "Don't make me late now."

I move forward, captivated by the helmet as much as his smile.

"I owe him for the sandwich and now this," I say, trying to figure this all out. I always insisted on paying Mack some rent for the space over his garage. That plus school and transportation didn't leave much after my part-time job. There was a small inheritance from my grandfather that I got after I graduated from high school. That's long gone though, and until Connal pays me, I only have enough for another week at the motel and soup at the diner.

"Naw, I should have made sure you were square yesterday," he pats the seat behind him again. "Just, you threw me off a bit."

I finally get the chin strap adjusted, and awkwardly straddle the seat behind Connal.

"Lean with me, but not too hard," he says, reaching back for my wrist. "Hold on tight, now."

And we're off. The ride is over before I can catch my breath from the feel of his hard abs beneath my hand.

"Hop off now, Charles." Connal reaches a hand back to help me. "Better get used to this."

"I don't mind the walk, Connal, really." I try to hand the helmet back, but he ignores me.

"Get that coffee brewing then start in on the first lane again," he says, walking in to meet Royce, who's watching us closely.

After stashing my helmet and throwing on my overalls in the back bathroom again, I don't have a moment to spare in the next few hours. The shop really has been backed up, so Connal has stacked appointments for oil and filter changes. Halfway through the morning, I trip, knocking into the used oil bin and some sloshes out. I look around for the guys, who are both under cars; before I rush off to the closet with the cleaning items.

"FUCK!" Comes Royce's roar. "Fuck. Fuck. Fuck."

Rushing to the door back out to the garage, I see

Royce flat on his back near the oil spill and Connal has just rolled out from under the car he was working on.

I'm standing in the doorway holding the *Caution: Spill Area* triangle, a container of sawdust, and some towels. Connal takes in what just happened and simply rolls back under the Shelby he's working on.

I walk towards Royce, knowing no matter what I say he won't be happy. I plop down the Caution sign first.

"Can I help you up?" I ask, shifting the other items in my hands.

"Get the fuck away from me," he growls and I swear I hear a chortle from under the Shelby.

"Um, if you have oil on your boots…"

"Give me the goddamn towels, then start spreading the sawdust. Don't say another fucking word to me." I do as he says, then turn back to Connal's office.

Bringing an ice pack from the employee fridge, I lay it down on the table near where Royce is stretching. A moment later, I jump as it smacks the wall over my head.

"Enough!" Connal bellows. "Don't fucking treat Charles like that."

"She's trying to fucking kill me!" Royce roars back. "You might not care since you banged her, but her screw-ups are painful!"

Every word he says is bad enough, however, new customers have arrived and they're looking between us like a tennis match.

"We didn't," I weakly say, realizing Royce misunderstood Connal giving me a ride to work.

"I didn't. Now back to work," Connal voice drowns

mine out before he storms over to see to the customers.

CONNAL

Goddamn Royce. I didn't even think of what it looked like, riding up with her like that this morning. He can get fucking used to it though, cause it felt damn good. Jake was right about her not eating enough though. The bulky clothes she wears covers up the fact that there's not a lot of meat on her bones.

Finishing up with the customer, I place an order for a couple pizzas to be delivered for a late lunch. Should be enough left over for her to eat tomorrow. Don't want to be too obvious about this.

Jake and I talked things through last night and we're going to try to get Charlie to accept us as a package deal. Ever since the first time we had a ménage during a drunken night our unit was on leave, it's just always been something I—and he—enjoyed more than going back to one on one.

We've played with the idea, over the years of setting up house with one woman. The last woman we had an ongoing relationship with turned into a disaster, but we both feel so drawn to my new mechanic that we want to give it a try again.

Before I make it back out to the garage, my phone is ringing.

"Hey, I found a company in Michigan that makes custom-sized mattresses," Jake starts. "I think eighty five inches wide would be good, what do you think? A king is seventy-six."

I think that's more than Jake spoke all last week.

"Putting the cart before the horse there, aren't you?" I ask, closing the door to the reception area.

"I have a feeling about her," he says, more subdued. "Besides, we have to get an order in with Gunner to build the bed frame, so it'll take time."

"I think eighty would do it. She's tiny, Jake," I sigh, hoping he's right. "Hey, she liked the helmet. Good call on that."

"Yeah?" I can hear him smiling through the phone. "Did she bring lunch?"

"No, I'm handling that. You'll pick her up when she's done?" I ask.

"Yeah, just give me a twenty-minute heads up." He disconnects after that.

Standing there holding the phone, I shake myself as I realize I'm staring at her legs under the car. Grinning, I go and grab my own creeper. Sliding in next to her, her startled eyes inches from mine.

"Wasn't this a tire rotation and alignment?" I ask.

"Yep. I was just going to come get you." She directs my gaze up to the transmission mount, "The mounts are all going, Connal."

"How'd you figure that out from a rotation?" I smile, wanting to test her a bit.

She rolls her eyes at me. "Sheet said the car was pulling to the left, so after I did what I was supposed to, I got in and changed gears a bit. If you want, I can show you, but the engine clearly moves when you shift from reverse to drive and back again."

"Miller's a cheapskate, he won't be happy about this," I tell her, gaging her response. "You good to explain it all to him, when his son brings him back?"

"Suuure," she says, biting that plump lower lip of hers.

All I want to do is lean over and take it in my teeth. She must see my intent because her eyes widen and her...

"OUCH!" I end up yelling in her face as Royce kicks the shit out of my leg.

"Hey, your pizzas are here. I ain't paying for 'em," he announces, walking away before I can retaliate.

"You're not fucking eating them then either, I guess?" Rolling out and heading towards the delivery kid in the reception area. "Come and get it, Charles. Feel free to do another of your ninja attacks on Royce later also," I add, louder than necessary.

"Not fucking cool, man," he growls. I turn to see him giving Charlie another dirty look, nearly tripping when she sticks her tongue out, mocking him.

Good thing Royce is leaving on that run later this week. He needs the time to chill the hell out about Charlie's mishaps.

After she moves the car she was working on and cleans up the lane a bit, she wanders in, filling up her water bottle but eyeing the pizza.

"Help yourself," I tell her, indicating the other plates.

"Can I chip in?" she asks, making my jaw drop.

"Royce, how come you never offer to chip in?" I look at him shoveling his second or third piece into his mouth.

"Cause you're a cheap bastard and it's like a bonus," he responds with his mouth full, smirking at me.

"Huh," I smile at Charlie. "Better get to it before he eats your bonus then."

This seems good enough for her and she eagerly dives in. When she nearly matches the slices Royce consumes, my stomach twists around the pieces I ate. She's trying to eat slowly, I can see that. But more than anything, I can see how hungry she is and doubt she had much for breakfast, hoarding whatever was left from what Jake got her. When she slows down, I ask her to put the leftover box in the back fridge.

"Shit, man," Royce speaks up from right behind me as I watch her walk to the back. "When do you think she last ate?"

"Nothing regular, that's for sure," I answer as quietly as he asked, surprised he caught on. "Trying to figure out how to move up her payday."

"I'll pick up bagels in the morning. Those'll last a few days," he says, before heading back out to work. With that simple statement, he redeems every negative thought I've ever had about him.

I walk back to my office and see Charlie coming out of the bathroom, arranging her overalls over her bulky shirt.

"I'll order you a couple uniform shirts, need your size," I say, walking in. "And I need you to fill out some forms, should have done it yesterday. Do you have a bank account? That's the easiest way for me to pay you."

"Oh, yeah, I have a checking account," she shrugs, looking down. "I meant to ask, what days we get paid?"

"Every other Friday. I'll pay you this week in cash though. Otherwise, you'd have to wait another week."

"Is that a problem? I'd appreciate it if you could," she looks up at me, relieved. "Do you need me on Saturday? I wanted to start looking for an apartment nearby."

"Could you work until one?" I volley, looking forward to extra time with her. "Will switch off Saturday's between you and Royce, but he's got other business this weekend."

JAKE

I ride up to the garage a bit early, just to make sure I catch Charlie. She's standing outside dealing with Andy Miller and his son. For once those assholes are smiling, so my hackles go up.

Parking around the side of the building from them, I hang back to eavesdrop. I listen to her answer questions about the timing to get his engine mounts replaced. Then he confirms that she'll be the one doing the work.

"Oh, I'm not sure, Mr. Miller. Depends on the schedule when the parts arrive. Now can I just get your signature here that you'll pay for the parts and I'll get them ordered today?" She nicely spins the part where

Connal has her on shit work during her probation period.

"I'll only sign it if you do it. You found it. I doubt that other slacker around here would have noticed," he says, finally sounding like the grumpy asshole the whole town knows him to be. "Connal! Get your ass over here," Miller bellows over Charlie's head.

Meanwhile, his son actually leans in to smell her hair.

"Back the *fuck* up, Junior!" I yell, halfway across to them before I realize what I'm doing.

"Jake?" Charlie turns to look at me but not knowing how close Miller's son had stepped toward her, she knocks into him.

The next moment seems to play out in slow motion. She bounces back from him but catches herself before landing on her ass; he's not so lucky. His foot slides and he reaches out, trying to right himself but gets his father's wrist and nearly pulls him down on top of him. Junior's head makes a sickening crack on his bumper on the way down.

Momentarily dazed, Junior is bleeding pretty well from his scalp.

"Dumbass," his father berates. "Didn't you learn anything from smelling that waitress last year?! Get in the car."

Royce is quickly there with a couple hand towels, applying them to Junior's scalp. Miller signs the document for the parts before apologizing and driving off.

"What just happened?" Connal speaks up for the first time, still not entirely sure what he just witnessed.

"Well for one, you seem to have hired the only person who can get Old Man Miller to spend money without throwing a hissy fit," Royce says while laughing.

"What's funny?" I ask him.

"I'm just happy she didn't hurt me this time!" he says, heading back to the car he was working on.

"He was smelling my hair?" Charlie's nose is scrunched up, as she looks to me for confirmation. "That's so creepy."

"Well, I'd say he learned his lesson," Connal drawls. "Why don't you go clock out for the day?"

"Charlie?" I finally speak up again. "Can you grab your helmet? I'd like to take you for a ride."

She takes a moment, looking back and forth between Connal and me, uncertainty clear as day across her face. She finally nods and moves inside without another word.

"Did you place those orders, Jake?" Connal asks me, although his eyes follow her path towards his office.

"Yeah. With delivery, it'll be about five weeks for both items."

"Gotta find a place for us to live. She's apartment hunting on Saturday. You have any objection to me making that difficult for her?" Connal finally looks over to me.

I shake my head, beaming as she heads back to us. Taking the helmet from her, I fasten it on her head; ensuring the strap is the right length.

"See ya later," Connal says, as I help her get on behind me.

Right after I blow by the motel, I feel her tugging my cut. "Where are we going, Jake?" she shouts out when I slow at a Stop sign.

"Thought I'd show you the town. You're new here, right?" I call back.

"That's nice, but it's probably kidnapping if you don't explain that first!" she yells back, laughter in her voice.

I shrug, enjoying the feel of her behind me. We ride through and around town, and I occasionally point out places of interest. Finally pulling up to the overlook past Rusty's Bar, I help her off. She immediately removes her helmet and walks towards the viewpoint.

"It's beautiful here!" She smiles back at me. "Is this where you brought girls when you were in high school?"

"I'm from back East," I let her know, enjoying her smiles. "Met Connal in the Army and kind of followed him here when I got out."

"Oh? No family left?" She reaches for my hand, looking sympathetic and I remember what Connal told me about her upbringing.

"Big family. They're loud and in everyone's business." I use her hand to pull her onto my lap as I sit on the stone ledge.

"That doesn't sound so bad?" She looks up at me.

"They wanted me to be a lawyer," I raise an eyebrow as her giggle washes over me.

"Jake, I met you yesterday and it doesn't seem like you talk nearly enough to want to do that." She blushes and looks down to our intertwined fingers.

"Loud people never really stop to listen though, do they?" Moving our hands upwards, I tilt her chin. "I really want to smell your hair, but don't want you accidentally knocking me off the ledge here?"

"I haven't showered since last night," she says while scrunching her nose up. Before another moment has passed, she has leaned back into my chest until her head is under my chin.

We stay that way, quietly passing the time until I notice the light starting to fade.

"Come on, we'll meet Connal for dinner," I say, nudging her off my lap.

"What? No, I haven't showered and…" She starts looking nervous.

"Please Charlie? On me?" I lead her to the bike, "Besides, I didn't have time to shower after work either."

CHAPTER FIVE

CHARLIE

I FEEL LIKE I'M CAUGHT UP IN A WHIRLWIND.

I sit on the bike behind Jake, one arm around his waist, the other on his back between our bodies. I could have sworn Connal was thinking of kissing me earlier. Although not completely decided on that matter, I was surprised when he didn't say anything about Jake taking me on the ride after work.

Although not nearly as surprised as I was to find myself on Jake's lap, enjoying the view, feeling comforted for the first time in a long time. As we ride away, it occurs to me that was the most romantic thing any man has done for me.

Since I've graduated from high school, I've just been working and studying. A time or two, at parties I found myself kissing and getting groped by some guy who was never comfortable enough to look me in the eyes again. So, I pretty much gave up on that.

Now I'm off to dinner with two guys, and not appropriately dressed. Even if I had showered first, I'd be mortified to show up in a different top what with *the girls* and all. I start to relax a bit when the restaurant seems to be a mid-range hamburger place. Jake parks next to Connal's bike and ushers me in. We find Connal waiting in a U-shaped corner booth, I'm quickly sandwiched between the two of them.

As nervous as I am, I'm happy to discover how easily the conversation flows. Connal takes the lead guiding the conversation. I sit back and listen to their stories, some from the military and some of Connal's childhood, then of the time he went to Jake's parent's house for Christmas. Apparently, they were shocked that he, a Utah native, had never been to any of their favorite western ski resorts. And finally, his misadventures on his ride across America that led to him settling down in Idaho.

Jake knows these stories as well as Connal and occasionally jumps in with his own version of events. Before I know it, they are ordering dessert, unconcerned that I cannot eat another bite. While they dig into pie, I tell them about my first foster home.

Laughing about the hoarder with several cats, how I had been there a day before I realized there was another foster child living in the maze of junk and how the foster parent kept saying, "Look out for Harold, he's around here somewhere." I thought she was talking about a cat, but Harold was actually her dead husband who was decomposing in a spare bedroom. I was out of there the day I happened upon him.

I always considered this a funny antidote about my first weeks as an orphan. As I stop giggling, I notice the look of horror on Jake's face and pure sadness on Connal's.

"I'm so sorry, baby," Jake whispers, leaning his forehead down and pressing it against mine. "I'm so sorry you had to live like that."

Being pulled in the other direction, Connal anchors me against his side in a tight hold. Lightening up after a moment, he looks to Jake, then back at me.

"We'll find you a good place to live, OK, Charles?" He's staring so intently, I nod at his words without considering his meaning.

"I'm sorry," I say, trying to blink back tears. "I didn't mean to..."

"Shhh, Charlie," Jake says, taking my hand again and giving me his beautiful smile. My mouth pops open and his smile widens, showing off dimples I would kill for.

"Show off," Connal mumbles, waving for the check.

As we head out, I pause to put on my helmet.

"Ride with me, Charles?" Connal calls from his bike.

Before I can say anything, Jake starts his bike and says, "I'll pick you up from work tomorrow." Leaving me to Connal and my head spinning again, he peels out without another word.

Feeling suddenly shy, I quickly mount up behind Connal and hold on to his hips as he heads back to the motel. Pulling into the lot, I'm getting the *glare of death* from the motel manager.

"What's his problem?" Connal asks as he helps me get off before following me to my room.

"Well, he decided I was a whore the day I got here and he doesn't seem any more impressed with me now," I say, opening the door. "Thank you for dinner, and lunch, Connal."

"Thanks for joining us." He pecks my cheek so quickly, I wonder if I imagine it. "Lock your door now."

I turn and follow his advice. When I don't hear his bike start up, I peek through the curtain to see him stalking towards the motel office.

CONNAL

Slimy motherfucker that runs the motel won't be saying much to Charlie anymore, I can guarantee that. I notice her curtains swaying and smile to myself as I mount up, eager to get to the clubhouse and talk to Jake. I know we agreed to go real slow with her, but I'm curious to hear what he did when they were together.

Pretty full house in the bar area, Diamond immediately comes up to me with one of the newer Girlies in tow.

"Connal!" she squeals. "You and Jake haven't double teamed Stacy yet! He says he's not interested but you'll convince him, won't you?"

"Please!" Stacy whines. "It's not fair! I've been here three months now and didn't even know that was a thing with you two! Even Ana didn't know about it, but I get a turn first."

"Step the fuck back. We aren't interested," I growl, moving back to where Jake is sitting off to the side.

"Did you kiss her?" I ask by way of greeting.

"No. Sat her on my lap up at the lookout point though. You?"

"Pecked her cheek," I fess up, pouring a beer from the pitcher in front of him. "She's confused about what's going on, Jake."

"I know. Just wait until next week, though. Get her used to us being around?" I nod along, thinking that's the right tact.

"God, but that fucking story she told, Jake." I slam my hand on the table.

"I almost lost my shit, brother," Jake's hand tightens around his mug. "Do you know how she got the scars?"

"She has more than one?" I raise an eyebrow at him.

"When she was getting off my lap, I saw another scar on her shoulder, the same side, going down her back." He smirks at me.

"Let's ask tomorrow? Can't be much worse than tonight's tale," I answer, hoping I'm right.

We both turn as a cheer goes up across the room, Diamond has pulled another Girlie up to the small stage and they're dancing while playing with each other's titties.

"A year ago, I would've hit that," Jake says, tilting his head towards the stage with a sour expression on his face. "Lately man, I don't even care enough to give any of these girls a glance."

"I worry though, we just met her and we're pretty fucking invested…"

"That's the best thing, boys." Flint slides into the chair beside me. "When you wake up one morning and there's only one woman on the whole fucking planet that matters."

Putting down a fresh pitcher, he sizes up both of us. "You two were looking pretty serious over here."

"I remember that day you first saw Bree." I smirk at him. "We look that way now?"

"Wedding's coming up fast. Got your dates picked out, boys?" he answers back.

"One." Jake firmly answers. "One date for us."

"Don't suppose this is that new mechanic Royce swears'll be the death of him?" Flint quirks an eyebrow at us.

"Oh, Jake, I forgot to tell you! She took him out again today, it was hysterical," I tell them both about Royce and the oil slick then continue to tell Flint about her charming Miller while wrecking her own special brand of havoc on his son. Both of them are in tears laughing and we're starting to draw attention from others.

Shortly, we're finishing off the last of our beers and Flint's checking the time. "Bree'll be getting off soon, gotta run. You two take it easy on this girl of yours? Might be a lot for her to process."

"We will, boss," Jake speaks up. "I think Bree would like her," he adds, knowing the weight Bree's opinion holds with Flint.

Flint stares at Jake for a moment before nodding,

knowing how careful Jake is when he speaks. Clasping my shoulder, he heads out.

We turn, heading up to our rooms on the second floor. Ignoring the sounds of my brothers' partying and fucking in other rooms, I boot up my laptop and start searching for a house. A home that we can make with Charlie.

––––––––

The next morning, Jake is knocking on the bathroom door that connects our rooms. Most of the upstairs rooms in the clubhouse have Jack and Jill bathroom configurations and it made sense for us to get adjoining rooms.

"I think I found it," he says walking in. "Check this out."

Handing me his laptop, the page is open to a three bedroom, two bath ranch. It's on a few acres and right up the road from Jasper.

"Look—the best part?" He clicks through the pictures. "There's a second living space, with a fireplace and double doors that head out to the backyard."

He looks expectedly at me, but seriously, I haven't had coffee yet.

"We can make that the master. The bed will fit and we can build in a closet and a bathroom to make it an ensuite." He gets frustrated as I continue to stare at him. "What's wrong?"

"Jake, I've known you for twelve years. You've

spoken more since meeting Charlie than you spoke in the first year or two I knew you."

He shrugs.

"I mean, downright fucking *chatty*, Jake." I try to reemphasize my point.

"I'm excited."

"I get that, brother. I really do." I run my hand through my hair and get up, grabbing and lighting a cigarette from my dresser. "But if she doesn't go for us, then what?"

I hate the thought of Jake being this worked up and everything going to shit.

"If she only wants you. Then, I walk away," Jake says, surprising the shit out of me. "She's amazing Connal. She's had a lot of shit go down, then she comes here and almost gets turned away, but she's good, and sweet, and funny. She doesn't give up. She doesn't snort powder up her nose, like so many of the women around here.

"She is hungry, but she doesn't take the easy way. You see what she looks like, it never occurred to her to trade on that. If she'll only take one, I'll go. But brother or not, I will. Fucking. Kill. You. Slowly. If you ever hurt her." Jake's face backs up his last sentence.

"Ok, Jake. Make that more words than the first five years I knew you," I say, dodging the empty beer can he picks up and throws towards my head.

At that moment, I know what Plan B is.

If she won't accept us both. I will be the one to cash out. Jake once took a bullet for me and saved my ass more than a dozen times, both overseas and on runs for the MC. We have been to hell and back, but he's never been animated about anything or anyone. Not like he is about Charlie. If the last act I can perform as a friend is to ghost out, that's what I'll do.

Though I hope it doesn't come to that. I hope, for the first time in years. I hope that this woman can find it in herself to do the unthinkable.

To love and tie herself to two men.

JAKE

Getting to work early, I get started on the steam room that was slated for today. By the time Vice rolls in, I've got the plumbing sealed up and ready for inspection.

"Need to leave a bit early, Vice," I say as he looks around.

"Fuck, Jake," he laughs. "You work this fast and we'll lose money."

I move towards the next area slotted for a steam room.

"Hey," he calls. "You and Royce'll be in cages for this trip. Leave tomorrow just after lunch."

I raise my eyebrows, surprised they're moving the run up rather than pushing it back.

"Trucks'll be ready by then?"

"Royce and Connal are handling that," Vice says, surprising me that they would do the work in the garage, what with the raid that went down the other day.

"What about Charlie?" I ask, suddenly worried about her getting caught up in this.

"Who?" Vice pauses. "Ha, I heard there's a chick down at the garage now, that her name? Connal gonna bring her by the clubhouse to part…"

His sentence is cut off, along with his oxygen. My hand clenching his throat until his eyes are at the same level as mine, his feet dangling, and his hands scratching at my wrists.

"Don't," I growl at him. "Don't," I repeat, shaking him, so angry at the picture that formed in my mind that I can't form any other words.

I'm ballistic at the thought of Charlie unprotected in the clubhouse. It's only Hawk barreling into me that loosens my hold on Vice's larynx.

Next thing, the three of us are in a pile. Vice is gasping for breath. Hawk is yelling at me, though I can't make out the words. And all I can do is close my eyes, trying to block out the red I see and picture Charlie's perfect blue eyes.

The three of us finally take a breath and focus on Vice when he speaks.

"Head on out, Jake. Come back after your run, but…"

"Vice. Don't fucking think about her," I growl, getting up I reach a hand down to help Vice up before I leave.

I text Connal as I head out; need to let him know what went down, that I exploded and will have to make it right with Vice. I ride straight there, having him meet me out back because I know once he hears what happened he'll let me take Charlie out for a ride. He'll know that I'll need her near me to soothe my anger.

When I pull up, he's waiting, smoking out behind the garage. I can't forget that he's my brother first, so I lead with my need to be around Charlie right now before explaining what I did.

"Fuck," he laughs. "Remember Gunner? I think he knocked Frank's tooth out or broke his nose that first time Riley came to the clubhouse. This shit happens. Vice'll let it go."

"I lost it, Connal," I admit, motioning for one of his smokes. "I fucked up," I say, before inhaling a mess of chemicals that work to calm me down. We stand out there smoking, but the cigarette is almost repulsive to me today. I just want to see and touch her.

"I need her to finish up another car after the one she's on." He shrugs. "She knows her shit well enough to get the requested job done then inspects everything else. She uses every crap job I give her to learn more, Jake. It's fucking awesome to have someone like that here."

"She really loves it, doesn't she?" I smile at him.

"Yeah, but more than that. She has the knack for the work and the customers," he laughs, tossing his butt away. "I mean, shit, we don't lock her down and Miller's gonna be coming by with flowers soon."

"We won't take this away from her, Connal. That's got to be something in our favor, right?" I ask.

"Why don't you run her out to that house you want to see? Tell her you want a female perspective?" He grins at me. "Maybe swing by Jasper and Emma's place afterward, so Emma can meet her?"

I nod and hang back as he gets back to work.

Calling the real estate agent, I arrange to have her meet us. Next, I text Jas and ask about stopping by his house with a friend for Emma to meet.

I have no fucking idea what all the emoji's are that he uses in his response, but I'm pretty sure what the eggplant is supposed to be. Jesus Christ.

CHAPTER SIX

JAKE

Before long, I'm heading in to ask Charlie for her help. She looks over to Connal who gives her the thumbs up, so moments later we're heading out.

We beat the agent out to the property giving us time to walk around the house. Charlie points out a few things worth considering before letting out an excited scream. Next thing I know I'm running behind her as she takes off towards a tire swing.

"Jake!" She pants, climbing into it. "I read about these and saw them in movies, but... Oh wow, push me, please?" She looks like a kid at Christmas, and I know I'll never say no to her.

Fifteen minutes later, the agent makes herself known and by then Charlie is pushing me on the swing. No matter what I said, she didn't want me to miss out on the tire swing once she made me admit I had never been on one.

Walking back to the house, we're breathless from laughing, but best of all, I'm holding her hand.

The place needs updating, but the second living space I had scouted online is perfect for a master bedroom for three adults.

Once the agent leaves us to wander the empty home a little more, Charlie starts to open up about what I could do with different areas. I commit each comment to memory, only discarding her ideas for the second living room.

Asking Charlie to check for my phone near the tire swing, I tell the agent what my starting cash offer is and ask that an inspector meet me out there early the next morning. Luckily, Charlie finds my phone right where I let it slip and we're soon off to Emma's.

CHARLIE

Being whisked away from work was unexpected but after walking through the house Jake wanted to see, I'm suddenly shy as we pull up to his friend's house. Even more so, when a tall, striking redhead emerges, a child held in one arm and her belly slightly rounded with the promise of another one.

"Jake! Jas said you might stop by!" She calls out to him while smiling at me.

He simply nods at her, so she introduces herself. "I'm Emma and so happy to meet you! Charlie, right?"

I laugh but eagerly return her one-armed hug.

"Well, Connal won't stop calling me Charles." When she raises an eyebrow, I continue, explaining my birth name.

Welcomed into her home, she darts off to put her son down for his overdue nap explaining that his twin sister is already asleep. Jake comfortably makes coffee for himself in the kitchen; getting me a glass of water. Then we sit in the living room quietly awaiting her return.

Emma heads straight towards the coffee when she returns. Inhaling the scent, I can see how much she enjoys her caffeine. Before we start to chat, she swears Jake and me to secrecy over having coffee while pregnant. Jake just sits back, holding my hand and occasionally refilling their mugs.

After realizing my connection to Mack, Emma absolutely lights up.

"Jasper was hospitalized in Boise a while back, Mack was wonderful! He whipped the nursing staff into action, calmed me down, and sat with me until Flint, Connal, Jake, and Russian could get there," she gushes. "I had Jasper send him a fancy bottle of whiskey as a thank you, but...he really helped me keep it together that day."

I cannot remember the last time I had a girlfriend to talk to and the time with Emma goes so fast. I'm truly saddened when one of her children start fussing, ending our visit.

"Charlie, give me your number. Jake, I'm calling Riley. I want her at Monday's dinner!" she demands of both of us.

"I might still be out of town, but Connal can take her," he replies, looking at me with a flash of his dimples. I don't miss the startled expression that briefly crosses Emma's face.

As I'm fastening my helmet, I ask him about the dinner and he explains the new tradition and concisely tells me about their group of friends. Riding back towards the garage, I can't help but be flattered that she wants me there, but nervous about why they are so readily accepting me.

"Let me get your phone, Charlie," he says as we pull up behind the garage and I'm sliding off his bike. I unlock it and hand it over watching as he quickly programs both his and Connal's cell numbers. "I'm leaving town for a few days, I won't be able to reach out but call Connal if you need anything."

"Royce is going with you?" I ask, cocking my head to the side.

"Yeah, Connal and I usually go together, but Royce has uh, something he wants to do," he shrugs, looking off to the side. His meaning clicks pretty quickly.

"You mean, he has *someone* he wants to do? Wherever you're going?" I clarify, getting a sheepish grin and a nod from Jake. My voice drops and I look away while asking my next question. "Is there someone there for you, Jake?"

He quickly cups my face with both his hands, lifting my head up so I'm looking into his eyes, taking in the earnest expression I see reflected there. "No, Charlie. No one there for me."

I'm slowly leaning up to him when the back door

swings open and Connal sticks his head out. "Getting backed up in here, Charles!"

My face flames red and I quickly run in past Connal as he holds the door. Getting back into my overalls, I race to make my way up to my usual lane. Coming around the side of a van, I trip and fly into Royce's stomach.

My hand shoots out and I grab the van to keep from falling. Royce however, falls back onto a tire that is on the ground behind his feet.

"Goddamn, son of a *bitch*!!!" he howls, and I can't help but get annoyed at how dramatic he can be. I mean he fell onto a tire, not the cement. "Fuck. Fuck. Fuck."

I stick my hand out to help him up but getting a glare from him, I turn to get the ice pack out of the fridge in Connal's office. Jake and Connal are wedged in the doorway, both having run toward the commotion.

"Is he alright?" Connal asks, only able to see Royce's feet from where the two of them are standing.

"Yeah, there was a tire…" I start before I see the expression on their faces, right before they burst out laughing. "It was an accident!" Is all I can think to say, pushing past them to get that ice pack.

Walking back a moment later, Jake is leaning face first into a wall, his shoulders shaking, while Royce spews obscenities about me to Connal. I don't think the big grin on Connal's face is helping the situation, but I maneuver past him to offer up the ice pack.

"She's like a hundred pounds soaking wet, Royce. I

doubt she tackled you on purpose." Connal tries to reason with him.

"I tripped." Trying to explain, but that just gets another glare from Royce and a chuckle from Connal. Royce finally takes the ice pack from me though.

"See? She tripped. She didn't intentionally tackle you, Royce." Connal actually gets this out without laughing but Jake starts howling again.

"Four times since she's been here, Connal! It's not fucking funny. What the hell is she going to do to me next week?" he yells, glaring at me.

"Wait, the first time was intentional. You called me a stripper and tried to touch me." Royce lets out another growl and Connal steps between us with a hand extended towards him.

"Charles, back to work. Now. Royce, if you aren't hurt, clean this shit up and get out of here. I'll see you next week. Jake, just get the fuck out of here!" We all turn at his tone. It's easy enough to realize when Connal is near his breaking point.

CONNAL

Jake waves his longest finger at me and heads out the back, I can still hear him laughing over the mumbling coming from Royce behind me. Charlie is on her creeper and sliding under a car. I head back to finish up the work on the Shelby and just pray for a couple hours of quiet.

———

Wiping down my work area when I finish up, I finally look around long enough to see that Charlie cleared the cars she needed to get to and is in the reception area with a child hanging off her back, another one around her leg and is holding car keys out, to whom I can only guess is the mother. The thought of her with our kids playing like that gets me fucking hard, so I stay standing with the Shelby between me and the picture window while the mother helps to disengage her children.

Jesus Christ. I'm still standing there moments later when she locks the door behind them.

"Anything else tonight, Connal?" she asks from the doorway.

"Nah, grab your things. I'll give you a ride, Charles." She smiles and nods, heading to my office. I secure the bay doors, stopping myself from following her back there.

"There's a meeting tonight at the clubhouse, so we can't do dinner," I explain as she's walking towards my bike.

"I know, Emma mentioned it earlier." She smiles up at me.

"How'd you like her?" I ask, hoping she'll get on well with Riley, Bree, and Emma.

"She was great. It's been a while since I've had 'girl time' and I'm sure Jake was bored to death." She blushes as she gets her helmet on. "Where are Royce and Jake heading anyway?"

"Club business, Charles. Never gonna discuss that with you," I reply, rubbing her leg as she gets on behind me, wanting to take the sting out of my words. "Don't take it personally."

The ride is over to soon and as she's getting off the bike, I bring up what I'm most worried about.

"You set for dinner?"

"I'm fine, Connal," she snaps, quickly turning towards her room. I'm off my bike and behind her in a flash. Pinning her between me and the door, I lean down, my mouth against the shell of her ear.

"Don't be like that, baby girl. I just need to know you'll get something to eat tonight, Charles," I whisper, enjoying the feel of her as a shiver rolls through her body.

Using a finger to turn her face back to me, her expression softens and she's focusing on my lips.

"I still have half the sandwich Jake got me," she admits, then grins moving her eyes from my lips to my eyes. "You two have been stuffing me all week, so it's been in the fridge."

"Better get used to that," I grin down at her before pressing my lips into her hair. "I'll be here in the morning, Charles."

As I walk back to my bike, I hear a quiet sigh from her and smile to myself. That's enough for now.

The bar of the clubhouse is packed when I get there. Everyone is taking it easy before church, but most will turn that up a few notches afterwards. Nearly tripping over Diamond's feet from where she's giving Frank head, I push aside and growl at the prospect who's standing, enjoying the display and make my way back to where Gunner and Flint look decidedly pissed off.

"What's going on?" I grab a spare glass from the table and fill it from the pitcher.

"Word is Frank wants to make it official with Diamond," Flint growls out. "But somehow the dickwad still thinks it acceptable to have her tits swinging out while he face fucks her in front of everyone."

"How the fuck did she wrangle that out of him?" I ask while angling away from the scene across the room.

They both shrug, probably more concerned about how their Ol' Ladies are going to take the news. While Betsy's always toned it down around them and gone out of her way to be respectful, Diamond doesn't know the meaning of *toned down*.

"Flint, how long has that kid been a prospect now?" I change the subject. "Madda? You gonna nominate him?"

"Ain't been a year yet, he's solid though. Hell, he ain't even eighteen for another week or two." Flint flicks his eyes to the kid in question. "He did well on his GED exam and has been working with Wrench a bit. Seems to like technology. Huh, well at least once he got over Wrench's complexion."

That gets a frown from all of us.

"He'd never seen a black person before, if you can believe that. Emma figured that out when she was working on the test material with him," Flint shrugs. "Once Wrench got him talking, he really took a liking to the kid so I just stayed out of it."

"Get back here. Clear out if you ain't patched," comes Vice's call from the hallway. Gunner goes to stand near him as everyone files down the hall for the meeting. "Joey, you stay up here. Mick, head up to the gate."

The meeting covers what steps Gunner and Wrench are taking to find and plug the leak that caused Russian to get picked up and other local items. It gets interesting when Frank speaks up at the end.

"Jasper, brothers, I've been real fond of Diamond for a while now…"

"Yeah, most of us are too!" Royce calls out, to laughs from the younger guys.

"I want to make her my Ol' Lady," Frank continues, silencing the room.

After a moment of silence, Jas finally speaks up. "You're older than I am, but considering what you were just doing, I'm not sure you realize what that means."

"What the fuck?" Frank raises his voice, "She's been blowing me out there since she stumbled in a few years back."

"Stupid motherfucker," Flint roars. "Was that meant to be a fun, little last hurrah before claiming her? Think I'd ever treat Bree that way? How about you Wrench, how many times did you have Amy swinging her titties out there as she put on a sword show?"

"It's fucked up, Frank," Wrench quietly agrees, his dark eyes showing his disgust.

"You want her as an Ol' Lady?" Jasper jumps back in. "Show us that you and she can act like it. Go exclusive for a few months then bring it back to us."

"This is bullshit and you all know it," Frank growls at Jasper.

"You want a vote, Frank? I'll give you exactly one try. If it comes out Nay, my trial period offer is revoked and we won't consider it again," Jasper calmly responds. "I'm giving you that much out of respect for your years as a brother."

Frank looks around the room considering it. Apparently, he notices what I do—too many brothers inspecting the table in front of them. He'll never get the numbers.

CHAPTER SEVEN

CONNAL

I HANG BACK AS THE MEETING IS ADJOURNED, waiting to talk to Jake.

"Charlie alright?" he asks by way of greeting.

"Yeah, she got a lot done, then I got her home. She wasn't pleased when I asked if she was set for dinner. How was the house?"

His smile makes an appearance. "Perfect. Real close to Jas' home and Gunner's shop, so that's a plus. There's a huge old tire hung up as a swing in back. She loved it, had me pushing her on it. I'm meeting the inspector out there before I get on the road tomorrow."

"I got money saved up, Jake. I want to contribute to this also."

JAKE

"Your name will be on the title next to mine, Connal. But I got this," I shrug. My trust fund can cover the property a thousand times over. Not common knowledge that I have one, but I know Flint and Jasper are aware of it, having checked me out. Connal's seen my parent's home, so he knows more than most and hasn't ever betrayed that confidence. "Why don't you run by it this weekend, make sure you're ok with it?"

He nods and gets the agent's number from me before heading up to his room. I head out to the bar to apologize to Vice.

He sees me coming and smirks, "You just had to say it, man."

"We good?" I grunt back. That was easier than I thought.

———

The run over the next few days goes smoother than any of us expected. I decided to immediately head back, rather than stay over at that Club like prospect and Royce will.

Happy to have the silence during the ride home, I push through the long drive instead of stopping, eager to be home to pick Charlie up for work the next morning. Finally pulling off the highway, my stomach drops as I see flames shooting up a couple miles down the road.

"What's up?" Connal answers, his voice fuzzy from sleep.

"Motel's on fire. Get here," I pocket my phone and park the truck next to the perimeter the cops set up.

Grabbing a cop's arm, I pull him around to face me. "Short girl, long brown hair. Room eight, where is she?" I yell at the startled officer.

Looking at his clipboard, he finally says, "Oh, Charlie Scott, right?" As I nod frantically, he simply points and I run in that direction.

Cutting around a couple parked ambulances, I stop suddenly. She's right in front of me, covered in soot with an old blanket wrapped around her, fighting the oxygen mask a paramedic is attempting to put on her.

Seeing me, she reaches out her hand, the paramedic finally tells her to wear the mask before storming off. As Charlie stands, her blanket falls away and Holy. Fucking. Hell.

I run towards her reaching for the blanket to wrap her back up.

"Jake?" Her voice is rough but she has a little smile on her face until she realizes all I'm interested in right now is making sure the blanket is fully covering the front of her nightshirt. Her breasts are huge and the shirt does little to hide their shape or the outline of her nipples.

"You ok, baby?" I whisper, pulling her into my arms. She nods, but I look down and see tears in her eyes.

"Baby, where you been hiding these?" I whisper in her ear, shifting my body to put emphasis on her breasts.

"I lost my clothes, Jake. I just got my pack with pictures and papers before the bedspread caught fire," She hiccups, holding tight to my cut. Keeping her close, the feel of her chest pressed into me causes my cock to harden. I adjust the blanket again and can see she just has a thin, long t-shirt, shorts, and her unlaced work boots on.

"We'll take care of that, don't you worry," I assure her; reaching behind her with a thought to get her to wear the oxygen mask. "Come on now, just catch your breath, baby."

I gently get her to sit back down, kneeling in front of her.

"I don't need that, Jake." She brushes the mask aside. "I had it on for like twenty minutes. I'm not hurt. I just couldn't think of where to go."

"Charles!" Connal bellows from behind me. Shit, I forgot to call him back.

He's upon us and pulling her into his arms in seconds, but is just as suddenly holding her at arms' length.

"Charles?" Ok, so I'm not the only one who didn't know about her generous boobs. He pulls open her blanket, takes in her bounty before looking at me like he's pissed off. "How the fuck have you kept these hidden?"

He might be asking her but he's still looking at me, I shrug.

"I'm not hurt at all, Connal, thanks so much for asking." Charlie's eyebrow is raised and she's smirking at us both.

I sit, pulling her onto my lap. "Baby, it's just not something we expected so much of..." I flounder and look at Connal for help.

He starts pulling her blanket over her chest and since he's trying not to touch her chest, doesn't do much better than I did. "He's right, Charles, we didn't realize you had so much, you know..." It's when his eyes get cartoon character big that Charlie tries to get off my lap.

"Enough." She rolls her eyes. "I have boobs. Really big boobs. I get it. I keep them wrapped so I don't have to deal with what you two are doing right now."

Both of our eyes snap up to hers, guiltily.

"Sorry, baby girl," Connal says, cupping her soot-stained cheek. "Doesn't that hurt though?"

"I was in the foster system when they—when they popped up." She shrugs but has leaned back into my chest. "It was better keeping them under wraps, so to speak."

My arms tighten around her, angry for the years she wasn't protected.

"Come home with us?" I ask. Connal's head shoots up and I know we're going to be moving faster than we planned. "We have two rooms and our own bath at the clubhouse. I'm working on that house, Charlie. But will you come with us for now?"

"I can stop and get you some clothes, maybe from Riley?" Connal adds, looking at me. "Then we'll do some shopping in the morning. Let us take care of you, baby girl?"

CHARLIE

This past week has been a roller coaster like I've never imagined. I finished my course, moved across the state, met two men that interest me, another who thinks I'm trying to kill him, and while I'm nearly penniless even after Connal paying me in cash on Friday. Now my motel room and my clothes are ash.

"Charlie?" Jake whispers again.

"I'll be safe there?" I ask. If I hadn't met Emma last week, I'd be a lot more intimidated at the thought of them taking me to a motorcycle club's headquarters.

"We'll always keep you safe," Jake promises, and Connal quickly drops a kiss on my forehead.

"Jake, get her back there. I'll swing by Riley and Gunner's to get some clothes for her," Connal directs. "Riley's about your height," he explains when I look confused.

"Um, my boobs," I burst out awkwardly. "Can you get me an ace bandage to wrap them? I'm guessing my chest is larger than hers?"

"Oh, man, is it ever," Connal chuckles. "Don't get mad at me! You brought them up!" He lifts his arms in surrender when I glare at him, dramatically backing away. Jake's chest is also shaking behind me.

"I think there's a bandage in the First Aid kit at the clubhouse." Jake grins down at me, carrying me to his truck. "You don't wrap them at night, though do you?"

He sounds appalled, so I just stay silent.

"When'd you get back to town?" I ask next.

"Just now, Charlie. Saw the motel the moment I

turned off the interstate. Fucking scared ten years off my life. Called Connal as I was pulling over but I didn't breathe again until I saw you." He squeezes my hand and brings it to his mouth. "Then I saw your boobies and nearly had a heart attack!"

I groan and playfully smack him for that comment.

"Jake?" I pause, not sure how to continue.

"Yeah, baby?"

"I'm confused. You and Connal are great...I just don't understand..." I stutter, completely unable to voice what I want to ask.

"Let's wait till Connal is with us, ok? Don't worry about anything, we'll talk it out," he whispers, reclaiming my hand.

Shortly, we're pulling through a gate and around a large T shaped building, until Jake parks near the door. I barely have time to pull my bag onto my lap before he's opening the door and lifting me up.

"I can walk!"

"Hush now, baby. Let me get you upstairs, alright?" He enters quickly and nearly runs up a flight of stairs. I hold him tightly until he's opening another door and gently sets me down. The bedroom is sparsely furnished with just a bed, nightstand, and dresser. A large TV on one wall, but no personal items in sight. Much like how I've lived since my grandfather died.

"Here are some towels, you go ahead and shower." He tugs my pack away, putting it on the dresser before giving me the towels. "You can sleep in this tonight." He digs through the drawers for a black t-shirt and drawstring shorts.

I head through the door he indicated and almost start crying again when I see myself in the mirror. I quickly remove the smelly, dirty clothes I'm in and jump in the shower, enjoying the cool water until it starts to heat up.

Since there's no conditioner, I shampoo my hair twice, hoping to get the smell of the fire out. Rolling up my ruined clothes, I shove them in the trash can before pulling on Jake's clothes.

Nervously walking back into his room, Jake's sitting on the end of his bed and Connal is leaning against the door. I walk over to check out the pile of woman's clothes that Connal points to on the dresser, and while the t-shirts will be a little snug, the jeans are my exact size and taste.

"Thank you," I whisper, just staring at the clothes, not knowing what to do or where to look. Jake, reaches out and draws me towards him.

"You feeling better?" he asks, settling me in between his legs, my waist is clasped in his hands. I nod, unsure of where to put my hands and very conscious of Connal watching us.

Jake cups my cheek and very slowly pulls my face towards him, gently placing his warm lips against mine. A shudder goes through me and I sway into him. He pulls me tighter into our kiss and I run my hands through his hair until he slowly pulls back.

"We won't push you, Charlie." He strokes my face. "We won't hurt you and don't want to scare you, but we do want you to consider *us*."

I've barely registered Connal crossing over to us

until he is pulling my face towards his and leaning down. "Consider us, all together, baby girl," he grounds out before kissing me. He is much more forceful than Jake. His tongue takes immediate possession of my mouth but I find myself returning his kiss without thought.

Shock at their meaning flows through me, but I can no more pull away from Connal than I could from Jake. He finally pulls back from me.

"I know we're a lot to take, and like Jake said we'll keep this at your pace." Connal caresses my cheek, as Jake rubs my back. "But will you try this with us?"

"The three of us?" I slowly reply, still attempting to process what I'm hearing; getting a nod from each. Turning away from them, I start pacing the room as they stay frozen in place, watching me while I try to sort this out in my head.

Finally, I stop and crawl into the middle of the bed, pull the blanket over me and lean back against the wall.

"Explain it to me. All of it."

CHAPTER EIGHT

CONNAL

JAKE AND I look at each other for a split second, then he spins to sit near her knees and I yank my boots off before sitting on her other side.

"It's something we've done casually in the past, but not casual with you. I don't mean that. We want a real relationship..." Jake starts, disastrously.

"Shut up, Jake." Words I never thought I'd speak. "Slow down."

Reaching to take one of her hands, he looks at her and smiles. "Ask me anything, Charlie. I don't know what to say, what's too much." He frowns in my direction. "We won't lie to you."

She takes a deep breath, looking between us both.

"So, you two hook up with one girl?" We both nod then I elaborate.

"The first time it happened randomly. It was years ago when we served together. We just really enjoyed it.

We've had separate experiences since then. It's just for something long-term—you know, permanent—we always kinda thought we'd go it together." She takes a deep breath and I know what her next question will be, but Jake beats me to it.

"Nothing physical between Connal and I. Never been about that. I mean we aren't going to freak if we accidentally cross swords, but we aren't more than friends. Brothers really," Jake tells her. "I don't know how to explain how it feels, but it really becomes about giving you more and more pleasure."

"And you've tried a long-term before?" she asks, studying her hands.

"Once. It was less than two months and we ended it. She kept trying to put a wedge in between us. 'No, do it like Jake does it.' Or that kind of crap when the other wasn't around," I explain.

"She ended up saying two was too hard for her to deal with, that she just wanted to be with me," Jake picks up the story, it's his to tell after all. "Couple nights later, I walk into the room to find her stabbing a needle through my condoms. Put her and the condoms in the hallway and she ran off with a trucker a few days later. I kept tabs on her just long enough to know I hadn't gotten her pregnant."

"Wow," Charlie breathes out. "Others would know…if I was with both of you," she says more to herself than to us, frowning.

"Again, we'll protect you. We'll keep it slow and as discreet as you want for starters. But behind closed doors, not anyone's business what we do," I insist. "No one here's gonna judge you; not so long as we're all respectful of each other."

"I would want a relationship, guys. Not just a hookup," she says, continuing to stare down at her lap. "And we can wait a bit before we do everything?" she adds, hesitantly.

"All at your pace, baby girl. We want to keep you happy." As she frowns again, I add in, "Jake and I won't touch anyone else. We'll get tested, so you can be sure we're clean, but we always keep it wrapped up."

"Oh!" She looks surprised and more skittish than when I kissed her. "I'm not on birth control. Umm."

"Charlie?" Jake questions at her uncertain expression. "What is it?"

"Nothing, it's just that I've never…" Jake and I lean back.

"You're a virgin?" I whisper and her face bursts out into a full blush before she nods and covers herself with her hands.

"I just spent a really long time hiding. Then with the courses I was in, well, I was the only girl and didn't want the guys there talking about me or about them!" She adds the last part while indicating her very, very ample chest. She grabs a pillow a moment later and swats both of us as our eyes can't seem to move from the damp shirt covering her tits.

Laughing at us, she then pulls us closer.

"I'm really tired and this is kind of a lot right now," she starts.

"Do you want us to go?" Jake asks, and I'm pretty relieved when she shakes her head.

"Can we just sleep though?" Her eyes tentatively dance between us.

"Yeah, shit, don't know what I would have done if you kicked us out, baby girl!" I grin at her before walking towards the bathroom. "Don't know if Jake mentioned it, my room is on the other side of the bathroom. Be right back."

Hauling ass, I change into sweatpants then wait on Jake, while he's using the bathroom. Once I'm done in there, I eagerly slip into bed. Jake is already on one side of Charlie and she's lying on her back, yawning.

Jake leans over her to give her a thorough kiss and I reach for her hand, bringing it to my mouth. She giggles and flicks her eyes, looking shyly at me, her other hand is wound through his hair. I smile, and then lean in to nibble at her neck. When my teeth reach her earlobe, a shudder runs through her again and she lets out a sigh.

"Like that?" I needlessly murmur, moving over I kiss her swollen lips. Pulling back, I can see Jake gently rubbing her stomach and watching us with a grin on his face. "Get comfortable now, Charles."

I lie next to her, rolling onto my side, as Jake reaches over to turn off his lamp. Curling back to her, he starts talking about the coming day.

"I gotta meet with Jasper in the morning. I'll let Vice know I'm taking the day off. We'll go shopping for some clothes, ok, Charlie?"

"I have work. And the clothes Riley loaned me..." she whispers.

"Nope, it's almost dawn. You and I are taking the

day off, Charles," I tell her. "We'll get some rest then we can all go shopping."

She nods, barely able to keep her eyes open. A moment later when her breathing has evened out, Jake whispers, "This'll work."

JAKE

My mind is moving too fast to sleep much the next few hours. After finally sinking into a deep sleep, I wake up spooning Charlie. My cock is so fucking hard it's painful and I lightly groan into her hair.

"I hear you, brother," Connal whispers from her other side. I lift my head to see the blanket tented over his morning wood and Charlie's head resting on his arm.

"I gotta take care of things," I whisper back, easing myself from the bed. She's hasn't moved, so I quickly grab my clothes and head out.

Knocking on Vice's door, he opens it widely when he sees me. I'm immediately hit with the smells of sex and weed, nearly knocking me backward.

"Not working today," I say, looking over his shoulder to the outline of a couple girls in his bed. "Be back tomorrow."

"You're back early from your run anyway, not a problem," he calls out to my back.

Next, I knock on Jas' office as I'm walking in. Flint is there, going over the books.

"How was the run?" he immediately asks.

"Good," I respond. "Give this to Jasper?" I toss him the envelope from the run then turn to go.

"Stop!" Flint yells. "Turn. Sit."

I want to growl in frustration but follow his commands.

"What the fuck are you up to Jake?"

"Motel burned down," I say.

"Yeah, four dead, no working fire detectors." Flint looks at me appraisingly, before filling in the news I hadn't yet heard and I'm nearly shaking all over again. I know how bad the fire looked last night, but that others died and Charlie could have, infuriates me all over again.

"Charlie stayed there," I say, by way of explanation.

Flint pinches the bridge of his nose. "Jake, you know I respect you but this is one of those times I need extended sentences, paragraphs, even. Now tell me what the fuck is going on?"

We stare at each other a moment.

"Charlie is Connal's new mechanic? The woman you two were talking about the other night?" he asks, getting me started.

"Yeah. We brought her back here last night," I explain.

"She's here now?" I nod in reply to his question. "Bring her down. I want to talk to her."

"No." At Flint's frown, I elaborate. "She's sleeping, she needs it after last night."

"She's in your room? Anything in there she shouldn't see?"

"Connal is with her." I don't want to say much more about that right now.

"How long?"

"We're buying a house, will try to get in there later this week," I respond.

"You've known her a week and you are buying a *house*?" Flint says very slowly, looking dumbfounded his eyes suddenly widen. "Fuck, tell me she isn't here against her will?"

"What!? No, boss," I say frustrated. Then Jasper enters the room and I hope I'll be spared more questioning.

"Hey, Flint, Jake. Emma said she invited Charlie to the dinner tonight," he says as Flint moves from his seat.

"Yeah, here's the envelope from his run," Flint starts. "Charlie's upstairs in bed with Connal right now and they're all buying a house together."

"What?" Jas looks surprised.

"Took me ten fucking minutes to get that much from this closed mouth bastard, see if you can do any better?" Flint mutters, leaving the room.

"So, um, the three of you?" Jasper asks, trying to keep a blank face.

"Look, she was in that motel fire last night. We brought her back here and explained what we wanted to her. She seems open to trying something with us but doesn't want attention over it until we're all sure." I fume, pissed I have to explain our business.

"One of you two have to be with her while she's

here. I'll put the word out that no one touches her. Get outta here." Jasper concedes after a minute.

"Thanks, Prez," I say, striding towards the door.

"And stop fucking with Flint! We all know you can talk," he yells after me.

CHARLIE

As I slowly start to wake up, I stretch my back then my arms. Embarrassed by a wet spot under my mouth, my eyes suddenly snap open and I'm very much awake.

"Morning, baby girl," Connal drawls, wiping my drool off his arm.

"I'm so sorry!" I squeal. The first time I sleep in bed with a man and, oh God.

Men. Two men! I look around for Jake. At least I doubt I drooled on both of them.

"Shhh, give me some sugar to make up for it?" He grins wickedly, pulling me towards him. Even knowing my breath must be rough, I lean into him. Quickly pressing my lips to his, I then move my lips along his jaw and down his neck. Just as he's pulling me closer, the door opens and Jake enters.

"Sleeping Beauty just woke up," Connal tells him without looking up.

Jake returns putting a bag and a drink holder down on the nightstand, he slides in behind me. "Hmmm, I brought breakfast but you look better, Charlie."

"Oh! I'm starving," I murmur, turning my head to smile up at him. He cups my chin and softly kisses my forehead, nose, and mouth.

"Everything good?" Connal asks him after Jake tosses the bag on my lap.

"Yeah," he grunts, handing Connal a cup of coffee and me a bottle of water. "Baby, what do you like other than water? I've never seen you drink coffee."

"Water is good. Diet Coke sometimes and green tea when I don't feel well," I say, before taking a bite out of my breakfast burrito.

"Noted," he says with a mouth full of food. "We can meet the agent at the house for a final walk-through then go to the mall."

"Wait! You're buying the tire swing house?" I ask with wide eyes, looking between Jake and Connal.

"We are. Closing Wednesday." He takes another gulp of coffee.

"We want you with us," Connal says, tugging a strand of my hair. "We want to try, the three of us, altogether, right?"

"It's just," I slide to the end of the bed, to face them standing up. "I've never even been on a date and you want us all to live together?"

"We took you on dates last week, Charlie," Jake says, looking confused.

"It doesn't count as a date if the girl doesn't know it's a date, Jake! Connal!" My voice is getting louder. "Living together shouldn't be the first step."

They look at each other, silently communicating. I turn away. Grabbing the clothes and ace bandage, I storm into the bathroom.

Another shower later, I slowly get dressed. My mind is buzzing with thoughts of how we could possibly make this work. And the thought that frightens me, what if I do go all in then it explodes? Logically, I know that could happen in any relationship, but then living and working with them makes it more intense and much more complicated. Especially with the humiliating fact, I barely have the money to stand on my own right now.

I sigh and try to wrap my breasts with the ace bandage. The elastic is pretty shot and I finally give up, knowing there's no way I can do this without help.

Fastening the jeans and holding the towel against my chest, I finally open the door to face them.

"Guys? I need some help." Both of their eyes perk up when they see my nearly naked state. I hold the ace bandage up. "I can't get this to stay up long enough to wrap it..."

CHAPTER NINE

CHARLIE

THEY LOOK AT EACH OTHER AND THEN TRY TO push each other out of the way to get to me first, yelling that they'll be the one to help me. Sighing, I just drop the towel, standing before them.

I mean, they were going to see *the girls* at some point. They stand absolutely still with their jaws hanging down. It's adorable. Then awkward.

"Maybe you should both help me?" I innocently ask, enjoying my power trip. "You know? So I don't have to go out without any support?"

I slide between them, edging Connal back to give me more room; holding the end to one of my nipples, I hand the rest of bandage to Jake. He shakes his head then groans as I raise my arms over my head. He wraps the bandage around my back then hands it off to Connal, letting him wrap the side he's on. Around and around they go until it runs out.

At which point, my borrowed panties are completely wet and I can feel a boner pressing into each hip.

"Fuck, baby," Jake finally groans. "No more of this, ok? I'll buy you however many bras you want, but I hate to see them all smushed like this," he says, tracing his hand down my back.

"No way!" Connal disagrees. "I want them wrapped at the garage and when we're here. No need for anyone else to know about…" He trails off, hopefully realizing how he sounds.

"A couple bras and sports bras, maybe?" I suggest, hoping for a compromise. Reaching back for the T-shirt Riley sent sparks the next debate. It is too tight, even with my breasts snuggly wrapped. Connal goes to get one of his short sleeve work shirts. I gladly put that on over the T, tying it in front.

With that, we're off.

"Guys? I do need some clothes that fit, but can we agree it's just a loan?" I ask, sliding into the middle of the back seat.

"Sure," Connal says, grinning at Jake.

"Absolutely." Jake quickly agrees, winking at me in the rearview mirror.

Hmmm. That was too easy.

"And rent? I want to pay rent." I push my next demand, getting dead silence in return. Connal turns to look at Jake full-on, the latter opens and closes his mouth several times before speaking.

"How about you put a few hundred a month into a savings account? When there's an emergency expense, we can use that money towards the problem." This idea earns Jake a slap on the shoulder and quick agreement from Connal.

I open my mouth to lay out more boundaries but Connal cuts in.

CONNAL

"Baby girl, neither Jake nor I think you're trying to use us or rip us off. We understand where you're coming from with this. Let's just not stress over it." I reach back to hold her hand, stopping her from nervously picking a callus. So far, we've agreed to a loan that we'll never call in. And the day that Jake has an *emergency expense* that his trust can't cover, we're all up shit's creek, but she doesn't know about that.

"The agent's here already. Can we table this until we're back in the car?" Jake asks, getting nods from both of us.

Though I had meant to, I hadn't been by to see the place yet and was pretty happy with it. Jake's idea of using the second living space as our bedroom would not only save us from tripping over each other but leave plenty of room for any children that came along. We could shift our living areas around in the coming weeks when we made arrangements with Vice to handle the updates we wanted in different rooms.

The walk-through quickly becomes a game of secret groping. It started with Jake or me 'accidentally' touching Charlie's hotspots whenever the agent wasn't looking. Charlie quickly joined in though, turning the tables on us. Our girl is a handful, in more ways than one.

Charlie looks deep in thought as we drive away, staring out the window, her eyebrows knitted together.

"You okay back there?" Jake asks.

"Connal, we can't mess around at the garage," Charlie states out of nowhere. Leaning forward between the seats, she goes on.

"I don't want people to think I'm there because we're in a relationship. Plus, it's a lot of time together without Jake, so it isn't fair to him. *And,*" she continues, noticing I was about to talk. "If we break this off, I don't want to be out of a job."

I wait to see if she has anything else to add.

"I agree." She smiles, happy with my statement and Jake grunts. "I really like that you're worried about balancing everything with Jake because we will have like, fifty hours a week there. And you know the business. Shit could go seriously wrong if we're not paying attention."

"But if I stop by for lunch, can we mess around?" Jake smirks at us, showing off his dimples that seem to melt her resolve. "Please?!"

"Maaaybeee," comes her coy response.

Hitting the mall, we pay close attention to her sizes in the first store we go to. After some everyday clothes and weekend wear, we hit the shoe store before we finally drag her into the lingerie shop. Entering, I clap my hands together and rub them in anticipation, drawing a frown from a nearby sales lady.

"No!" Charlie is trying to push me back towards the entrance. "I will do this myself, thank you."

Leaning down to her ear, Jake whispers something I can't make out. Charlie's cheeks flame red and she quickly looks down and away, nodding after a moment.

"Come on, look around real quick. We get to point her towards the ones we like then we got to wait outside." Jake grabs me like we're being timed.

Not pushing our luck, I make a lap around the store. Beating Jake back, I quietly tell her which pieces I like hoping she'll remember the list of colors and styles I like. I figure it's my turn to pony up for her purchases so I slide five large bills into her hand and say a quick prayer in my head.

Jake meets me at the benches outside the store a couple minutes later.

"So, I told her I hate boy shorts and which bras and nighties I'd kill to see her in," I quickly tell him. "Which pieces did you want her to look at?"

"Only one," he says.

"What? One? Which one?" I pester him, once I realize he isn't saying anything else.

"Cupless. Babydoll. Nightie." He looks at me with a 'cat who ate the canary' grin.

"Fuuuuck," I say, starting to walk back to the store before he grabs my arm. "I want to change my answer."

He shakes his head at me.

Thirty minutes later, she emerges. I quickly take her bags but notice every goddamn thing is wrapped in tissue paper. She laughs at me and slides me the change.

"Hey, we can wait if you want to buy more?!" I call, waving it at her and getting an eye roll in response.

"Can we head out?" she asks. "I'm kind of tired and um, are we going to that dinner tonight?"

"Yeah, about that..." Jake and I exchange another look before I start telling her about everyone on the way to the car. After talking about tonight's group, we get into a longer talk about the club girls, Girlies, and parties that has me cringing at her every question.

It suddenly hits me how Jas, Flint, and Gunner felt bringing outsiders into our life. I make a mental note to pull Gunner aside and get his advice on how to navigate some of this. The only thing I know for sure is that I feel that possessiveness that they all demonstrate with their Ol' Ladies and that none of them have looked at another woman since meeting their match. Good a place as any to start.

Getting back to the clubhouse, Jake immediately circles around toward the back entrance without saying a word. Neither of us seems very eager to walk her into whatever may be going on in the front room, but I know we'll have to deal with that soon.

"I have to talk to Jas," I let them know after carrying my share of bags upstairs with them. I pull Charlie into my arms and start to softly kiss her. As she relaxes into me, I slowly stroke my tongue in and out of her mouth. God, the feel of her chest up against me is enough to make me lose all control. "Later, baby. Get some rest now." I breathe into her ear, while slowly disengaging her arms from around me.

"HEY! Get out of there!" I yell, laughing at Jake. He

used our distraction to start peeking into the bags from the lingerie shop.

"Jake!" She reprimands him. "Any more of that and I'll wear nothing but large shirts to bed!" Laughing at the look on his face, I head back downstairs. Jas is in town meeting with some group but I chance upon Gunner so drag him into the bar.

"I need help," I start, causing him to sit up straight. Besides Jake, Gunner has long been my closest friend in the MC. "When you explained about the Girlies to Riley..."

"Was she thrilled that we'd be hanging out around women I'd fucked? That I'd be going on runs without her and there'd be whole other sets of MC groupies on the road?" He gives me a wry grin over while he sips his beer. I shrug and he continues. "Look, I told Riley from the beginning that I can't change my past. She asked for my word I'd never cheat on her, and I fucking won't, Connal. She's it for me. I show her that every day and that's the only thing I can do."

I nod, drinking my own beer and trying to figure out what to ask next. Gunner brought Riley's truck into my garage the day they met. I didn't understand what I was witnessing at the time, but he never wavered since then. No matter the time apart.

"You and Jake going to try this for real?" he asks, looking for something in my eyes.

"We tried before..."

"Shit, that didn't count. That bitch was looking for money and blow. Best thing she did was show you and Jake how you don't need to be treated," Gunner cuts in.

"Charlie is willing to try, and honestly, Gunner, she…" I'm cut off by the sound of a thud and the floor vibrating, hard, before I hear an all too familiar roar.

"FUUUCK!"

"Oh, shit," I go running down the hallway, followed by a few others.

"Fuck, goddamn, son of a cocksucker!" Royce is in a heap at the bottom of the backstairs.

I look up the stairs, seeing Charlie standing halfway up as Jake comes flying out of his room with a towel wrapped around his waist. She holds her hands up as if to calm me. "I left something in the truck, Royce was looking at his cell phone and I startled him when I said 'hello'."

"No, Connal, she can't fucking stay in the club-house!" Royce yells, putting it together.

"It's done, Royce," I respond calmly, reaching a hand down to him. "Just for a few days. You ok?"

It takes us all a moment to register the rumbling noise, we turn in unison as we pinpoint it. Gunner. Laughing like I never heard him before.

"*This* little woman is the one you've been bitching about, Royce?" He finally gets out between deep breaths.

"I just know my Riley's gonna like you," Gunner says after introducing himself to Charlie.

Turning back to Royce, he lifts him up and moves him in the direction of the bar. Words like 'dignity' and 'pride' come drifting back to us, as Gunner lectures him.

"Toss me the keys, I'll get your phone. Jake…" I

signal to him to wrangle her back to his room and I hear Charlie squeal, then giggle as I head out the back door.

Right in time to see Frank fucking Diamond over near the dumpster.

CHAPTER TEN

JAKE

"I told you I'd get your phone, baby," I whisper down to her, showing off my dimples.

"You two are doing everything for me, Jake." She sighs and reaches up to rub one.

"Come on, let's get this bandage off and let you take that nap you wanted," I remind her, as selfish as that sounds. I really do just want her to be comfortable and there's no way she is with that thing on. I place her on the bed, kneeling on the floor beside her, I unlace her work boots. She reaches her hands under her t-shirt and shimmies the wrapping down, starting to unwind it once it's near her waist.

"Here, let's just do this," I say, grabbing a knife from the night table. I carefully slice through it, never wanting to see it on her again.

Pulling a blanket over us, I lie down and pull her into my chest. Rubbing her back and waiting until she sleeps, it's not until Connal returns that I realize I'm trapped. My arm is under her head and her leg has slid in between mine. I can't move without disturbing her.

"Royce alright?" I ask, getting a shrug in response. God knows if Royce will survive till the end of the week at this point. I start to laugh to myself, stopping when I realize he really could have broken his neck this time. Placing a kiss on Charlie's forehead, I'm suddenly pleased we're buying a single level home.

Dozing off while holding Charlie tight, I wake up alone but can hear someone in the shower. Connal walks into my room from the hallway entrance while I'm still stretching.

"Hey. Charles wanted a Diet Coke, you got ten minutes till we need to hit the road. I'm gonna..." His jaw drops and my head swings around to see Charlie at the bathroom door. FUCK.

She looks between us but I'm unable to do anything but stare.

"What's wrong?" she asks. Her wet hair is in her usual braid, but it's the first time we're seeing her in a T-shirt with a bra under it.

"What are you going to wear over that?" Connal asks, crossing his arms across his chest. Charlie's face immediately tightens.

"Baby, you look beautiful," I say, trying to diffuse this, I cross over and cup her cheeks. "We're just not used to, um, all this, yet," I explain, looking down then up as fast as I can. Well, I mean, I'm still looking at her boobs when Connal speaks again.

Connal is quickly beside us. "Baby girl, you have to

know I think you're beautiful. It's just that I wouldn't mind keeping you under wraps."

"You picked this shirt out, Connal," she tries to reason.

"Yes, but for us. Not for everyone. Maybe wear it with a sports bra?" He's digging himself in deeper, I just don't know what to say to help him.

"But I'm wearing something else you picked out also," she adds, in what I'm quickly pegging as her sarcastic tone. Seeing that he's about to dig his heels in, she raises a finger. "I am all covered up. I have boobs. I am wearing this or one of Riley's shirts."

I elbow him when he opens his mouth again.

"Come on, we don't want Jas and Flint to demolish the appetizers before we get there. Connal, go grab Vice. You're driving," I say and he finally nods, knowing he won't win. She grabs his hand, pulling him back and stretches up on her toes for a kiss.

Connal's hand goes behind her neck as he moves the kiss from a peck to a deeper one. Pulling back he looks at her straight on.

"Ours," he growls and she quickly nods in agreement. He exhales, leaving to get Vice.

"Thank you, Jake," she says looking up at me, leaning over to kiss the tattoo that swirls in between my collarbones. Tilting her head up, I level with her.

"For the record, don't ever doubt that we are both gonna be possessive when it comes to you. I don't like that others will be staring at what we are now considering ours, but I think dressing in anything that doesn't confine your gorgeous tits is new to you and healthier.

"Just don't be surprised the first time either of us knocks the shit out of anyone who says anything to you or looks at you the wrong way. God help them if they touch you," I explain and immediately feel guarded after sharing all this, expecting to see a flash of anger in her eyes.

"I'd feel the same way about any woman who would try to touch either of you, and I think that makes me horribly selfish. I don't know, greedy?" She wraps her arms around my neck. "The two of you are so different, but you balance each other and me also. I promise I'm not dressing to impress anyone but you and Connal," she says this earnestly, before pressing her lips to mine.

"Come on, baby," I groan, quickly pulling on some clothes and tugging her out of the room.

Connal is standing next to the truck, smoking. Vice is already in the passenger seat. "We good?" he asks her, getting a big smile from her in return as I help her into the backseat.

"Holy Shit!" Vice explodes, when he turns back to introduce himself and sees her. Well, not her so much as her boobs that he hasn't taken his eyes off of.

"Not a fucking word, Vice," Connal spits out, while I just growl at him. "Not a fucking word."

"Uh, hi, Charlie," Vice says, looking out the windshield.

"Hi, Vice." Charlie acts like Vice's eyes didn't nearly fall out of his head. "Royce has mentioned you around the garage a bit."

"Um, yeah. Um, he told me about you but, um,

never described you." Vice is now staring out the passenger window, anywhere but her.

Connal and I share a look in the rearview mirror. His face finally softens when she leans against me. Minutes later, pulling up to Riley and Gunner's apartment, Vice nearly sprints from the car. Getting her upstairs and introduced becomes a whirlwind for us.

"Wait! She's staying at the clubhouse now?" Bree demands. "What the hell is wrong with you two? I've moved into Flint's house. Take the apartment above Rusty's."

We look at each other and shrug.

"Oh, is that the place near the lookout? Jake drove me past it last week," Charlie asks her.

"Yes, it's furnished and, here." Bree goes to her purse, pulling out keys and wrestles two off. "I'll call Rusty and let him that y'all will be around. The gold one opens the back door, the silver opens the apartment, there's an extra set in the drawer next to the sink. Seriously, you two! The clubhouse?"

"We bought a house, Bree," I try to defend our decision to bring Charlie to the clubhouse for more than a couple nights, but really am psyched at her offer. Getting Connal's elbow in my rib, I frown at him.

"Right, but it takes time to get furniture and then you can't live, covered in dust, while you make changes," she reasons, getting a shy smile from Charlie.

"Thank you, Bree. We really appreciate it," Connal accepts. That settled, Riley calls us all to the dinner table.

"Charlie," Jasper starts in a serious tone after everyone has had a few bites. "I understand you're trying to kill Royce?"

Next to me, Charlie starts choking on her wine. I hand her a glass of water, while Connal rubs her back.

"No," she says firmly. But Gunner and Flint have already started laughing so each story gets retold to the ladies. It's when the story involving the Millers is told, that Bree and Emma start to applaud.

Charlie's face is red, but she's laughing along in good humor.

"Can you imagine if she wanted to hurt someone?" Riley giggles. "I mean, they'd be toast." She sounds in awe of the woman between Connal and me, which gets the ladies all laughing again.

Once dinner is finished, Emma and Bree head back to the bedroom, while Riley tugs Charlie along with her. I stand watching them go, trying to decide whether to follow when Flint slams a hand down on my shoulder.

"Let 'em go, son," he nods to them, handing me a whiskey. "They all took to her right away. Now you gotta let 'em be."

"The one thing I can't figure," Gunner says as he starts to load the dishwasher. "Royce is almost as big of a man-whore as Vice here. He never mentioned those... Well, I mean, the *elephants in the room*, so to speak..."

"We didn't know about them," I say, getting a raised eyebrow from everyone but Connal. He takes over for me.

CHARLIE

Following Riley back to her bedroom, Bree is opening another bottle of wine and pouring glasses for everyone but a pregnant Emma.

"Okay. You have to explain that," Emma says, giggling and swirling her finger in the direction of my chest. I was coming from work when she and I met the other day so *the girls* were pretty tightly bound.

I tell them, and it must be the wine because I pretty much tell them everything about me. Everything except the accident that killed my mother, and left my scars as a reminder. I haven't spoken of that since Grandpa picked me up in the hospital.

After I finish, I find that Riley is holding one of my hands and giving it a squeeze. She tells me about meeting Gunner, then waiting nearly a year to turn eighteen. From there, Bree and Emma share their tales and by the time they finish we've all laughed and cried multiple times. All I can think is that I've not only walked into a really warm but strange family unit. And they seem to want to include me. That by taking a chance in a town hours from all I've known, I may truly have found my home.

Emma rubs her belly and says, "I think your career choice is awesome. Jas and I always wanted a big family but we'll be outnumbered after this one, so it's probably a good place to stop. It's been great tutoring people for the GED test, but I want to be in a classroom. You know? Make use of my degree at some point."

"Just think," Bree quips. "Charlie would have to have four kids before they'd be outnumbered!"

We all explode into good-natured laughter, and at that moment all my nerves of what people will think of me being with two men evaporate. These women just accept it. Just accept our ménage. With them around me, I can't imagine anyone being able to make me second guess myself anymore.

There's a tentative knock at the door and Jasper sticks his head in. "Sorry, Ladies. Emma, I just don't want you getting too tired, darlin'."

She says her goodbyes. Bree and Riley exchange phone numbers with me, with Riley and I making plans for lunch in a couple days. Moving back to the main room, Bree and Flint take their leave also.

"Charles can't be late for work tomorrow, so we'll cut out too," Connal says, in the sternest voice he can muster. Riley has food containers at the ready for Jake, Connal, and Vice causing Gunner to mumble about *sharing his cookies*.

Then Gunner turns to me suddenly, giving me a bear hug that takes me by surprise. "You hold them tight, little girl. Don't matter what no one else thinks," Gunner whispers in my ear. When he releases me, I give him a big nod as my promise.

Work goes smoothly the next day, I'm back in a sports bra with a baggy top. Royce apparently must have heard something from Vice cause I keep catching him checking me out from different angles.

Towards the end of the day, Jake comes by with his truck and the three of us head to the Superstore about an hour from town. They insist we'll need things for the house anyway, so we end up loading three carts with household goods before heading to the apartment Bree is loaning us.

After walking through the apartment above the bar, I immediately text Bree my appreciation. It is light and airy with a fantastic bathroom. Connal lets me know that Jake did the work on it the previous year, making his ears go red. They leave me to start unpacking and setting up our purchases while they go back to the clubhouse to pack their clothes and pick up my bags.

By the time they get back, I've decided we're going to do more than light petting tonight. They've treated me like fine China since the fire and while I appreciate that, I'm just horny as hell from being around them constantly. By the time I hear the truck and Connal's bike pulling up, the sheets in the dryer are nearly done and I've watched a couple videos about giving head to two guys at the same time.

Basically, I'm wet and scared shitless, all at once.

CHAPTER ELEVEN

CONNAL

GREETING US WARMLY AS WE TRY TO GET IN the door with the first load from the truck, I can tell something's up with Charlie. Dropping the things in the bedroom and heading back downstairs, I start to speak but Jake nudges me forward.

"She wants more tonight," he says, once we're outside.

"You don't know that," I reply, trying not to get my hopes up.

"She was like a shark with blood in the water," he says, grabbing his second duffle and her knapsack that survived the fire. "Oral only and we get her to the clinic tomorrow. I want recent tests showing her that we're clean, and then we'll do what she wants regarding birth control or lack of it."

This is the Jake I know as my commanding officer, but it's been years since I've heard him like this.

Picturing how Charlie was with the children in the garage last week, she was a natural and it really struck a chord with me. I'm hoping she won't freak at the idea of having our children sooner rather than later. The two of us are eleven years older than her, so it may be something we want now, more than she does.

Getting back upstairs, Charles is taking the new sheets and towels out of the dryer.

"Oh, can you two give me a few minutes?" she asks. I nod, grabbing a towel and heading for the shower. Jake moves out to the kitchen.

As I quickly finish up, Jake hurries in for his shower, and I find myself pacing in the living room.

"Connal? Jake?" she calls from the bedroom. I'm just in shorts and Jake exits the bathroom, with a towel wrapped around his waist. Walking together down the hall, he opens the door, enters and steps aside for me to follow.

"Goddamn," I groan.

She's wearing her new blue, cupless, babydoll nightie. If I didn't already, I'd owe Jake my eternal loyalty.

"I watched some video clips earlier, but I have no idea what to actually do..." she starts, wringing her hands together.

Jake walks determinedly across the room to her. Sitting on the edge of the bed, he takes each of her hands. "No need to be nervous with us. We do this at your pace." He's a better man than I am, cause with her chest so close to his face his focus is still held on her eyes.

He looks to me and I walk up behind her, putting a hand on each of her hips. She leans back, looking up and smiling at me. Taking her chin, I start kissing her gently, groaning as I see Jake lean forward to lick her nipple. She moans loudly, arching her chest further out.

Jake doesn't need to be asked twice. He shifts and suckles her left tit, while I shift my right hand from her hip up to her other breast.

"That feels amazing!" she whispers, breaking our kiss.

"Sit down on the bed, baby." Jake guides her to his side. "I got to taste you now."

He scoots her up, kneeling between her thighs before lifting the hem of her nightie up. I move further up, kissing her mouth again before trailing down her neck to her chest. Looking down, I see Jake place a kiss on each of her thighs before licking his tongue up through her slit, grinning as her hips buck upwards.

Shifting, I take in her face to see how she is, her mouth is open and her eyes are tightly closed. Not. Good. Enough.

"Open your eyes, baby girl. Look at us?" I ask her, wanting her completely involved in this. She immediately complies, wrapping one hand around my neck and the other she reaches down to Jake's head. Charlie's eyes are half-mast as she semi-smiles at me for approval.

"Here, Charlie," Jake says, taking her hand and dipping one of her fingers into the slit he had just been licking. "Let Connal taste your sweetness, too."

Once she's lifting her finger to me in offering, he

leans down to focus on her clit. Pulling another gasp from her, he digs in.

She's watching him, as I'm licking her juices off her finger. Her breathing is more and more ragged and as much as I want to push him out of the way, he's earned this orgasm. Nibbling on her lips again, I alternate between lightly pinching and massaging her nipples, helping her along.

"Come for Jake now, Charles," I whisper against her lips. She grips my shoulders, kissing me frantically until she hits that peak, crying out and shuddering through her orgasm. Jake moves up to join us, I tilt her head in his direction, and teasingly tell her to say 'thank you'.

Hesitating at first, knowing her juices are covering his mouth and short beard; she's soon deepening the kiss. I slide a finger into her wet core, eliciting a surprised squeal from her.

"You didn't think we're done yet, did you, baby girl?" I ask, kissing her shoulder. "I want your sweetness, too."

Licking and kissing my way down her body, I'm soon situated in front of her lightly throbbing pussy. Dipping my tongue into her wetness, I thrust it in and out. Holding her lower lips open, my face is soon coated with her juices. Pulling back at her increased wiggles, I smirk when I see she is nearly wrestling Jake to get her hands on his cock that is standing at full attention.

"Tonight's just about you, baby," he tells her, securing her wrists above her head in one of his hands. Kissing her nose, he puts his other hand flat on her belly. "Now lie still and let Connal get his fill, huh?"

"Wait," she says in an amazingly husky voice. "I want to make you both..."

"Hush, Charles. This right here?" I say, sliding a finger from her core up to her clit before lightly tapping it. "This is what we want tonight. Ok?"

At her tentative nod, I sink my finger deeper into her pussy, swirling it around before running it back towards her rosebud. At her sudden intake of breath, I focus my mouth on her clit while lightly pressing the tip of my finger into her tightest hole.

JAKE

As Connal settles his face back down between her creamy thighs, I lean over and nip her earlobe, running my free hand up and massaging her breasts. Her nipples are hard, red points; not surprising what with all the attention we've given them tonight.

"Let us take care of you, baby," I whisper into her ear. "Show Connal how wet you get when you come. How much you're enjoying this."

"I am, Jake." She smiles over at me. "You both are just..." Her sentence is cut off by a whimper as Connal begins to lightly finger fuck her back entrance.

"Connal, I'm almost...oh, God, YES!" she calls out before leaning over and biting my shoulder as she squeezes Connal tightly between her thighs.

"That's it, Charlie. We got you," I murmur into her

hair. She threads a hand behind each of our heads, pulling us down towards her neck, sighing contently.

A moment later, a snore slips out. Smiling, I pull back and see Connal looking up at her. I know I've never seen him look at anyone that way and am certain that I haven't, not until Charlie.

"We good, brother?" I ask.

"Oh, yeah. More than ok. And, Jake?" Connal glances between her swollen nipples and me. "You can pick out all her lingerie. You're a hell of a lot better at it than I am."

I laugh a little too hard, getting a sleepy grunt from Charlie before she turns on her side and snuggles into me, unconsciously pushing her ass back into Connal's crotch before I pull a blanket over us.

The rest of the week continues on like this. Connal brings her to work and I pick her up, running whatever errands we need. He has no interest in furniture, appliance, or fixture shopping for the new house, or at least he swears it, giving Charlie and I time together in the early evenings before meeting him for dinner.

On Friday afternoon, Charlie lays down the law.

CHAPTER TWELVE

JAKE

"Enough," she growls when I show up at the garage and try to give her a kiss. "You two, in the office now," she demands before leading the way.

Standing in front of the desk, halfway out of her overalls, she motions for us to lock the door.

"I want your dicks out. Now," she starts without preamble. Getting a blank look from both of us, she continues. "Neither one of you are touching me until you let me get you off."

She actually stamps her foot. Connal manages to keep a straight face until he looks at me and we both bust up. He leans on my shoulder for support. Charlie is not amused. A frustrated growl bursts from her before she's trying to get around us. Connal grabs her by her waist and pulls her between us.

In between peals of laughter, he manages to get out, "That was righteous."

I can barely catch my breath, but rather than let her get angrier, I reach down and undo my buckle and jeans. As soon as I tug my dick through the slot of my briefs, Charlie drops to her knees.

"Winner, winner, chicken dinner," she proclaims before taking my sleeping cock into her mouth, working it quickly with her tongue.

As soon as her lips wrap around my thickening cock, Connal stops laughing and starts yanking at his pants, in a fucking hurry now.

"Fuck, baby!" I call out.

Within seconds, I'm completely hard. She's holding the base of my thick cock in her small hand while sucking and licking what she's able to get into her mouth. Hearing Connal's jeans hit the floor, she reaches back to him, circling the base of his dick with her hand before she starts to rub it up and down.

"Tell me what to do?" she pants, pulling herself back from my dick. "Do I alternate?"

"Sure, Charlie," I moan, wrapping my hand around the one she's using to stroke my dick, guiding her motions. "Get him nice and slippery, too?"

"I won't be able to take much," Connal calls out, at the first touch of her mouth. "That's it, oh shit, baby girl, that's so good…"

Connal continues his litany until what sounds like a sob comes from his lips when she leans back over to swirl her tongue around the head of my cock. With one hand still on Conner's dick, she looks up, flashing me a smile then goes to town, bobbing up and down the portion of my length she can take in her mouth.

After a few months of nothing but my own hand, I'm more than willing to give the lady what she wants. "Choose now! Are you swallowing?" I yell with more force than intended. She seals her lips more tightly around me, so I let go, shooting streams of cum into her mouth as she swallows as fast as she can.

Whatever videos she'd been checking out were great, 'cause she kept up the suction, pulling back with a pop, before giving my sensitive head one last, tender lick.

"Um, do I..." She looks anxiously up at Connal, looking for direction.

"I need you, baby girl," he pants heavily as he works his hand up and down his shaft. "Please?"

Learning that it's alright for her to go straight to him, she turns and focuses solely on his cock. My legs are lightly shaking as I tuck my dick back into my pants. Turning to the fridge, I get a water bottle for when Charlie finishes up Connal. Leaning against the desk, I watch her, ignoring Connal's words of praise and pleading.

What she lacks in experience, there's no denying how eager she is to please us right now. And fuck, thinking of her lack of experience is another huge turn on for me. God knows I don't deserve that, not after the women I've been with.

Connal signals that he's ready to blow and she secures each of her hands on his ass cheeks, showing him where she wants him to come. He wraps his fist around his long cock, stopping her from taking too much and gagging on his spunk. Shit, let's hope there aren't any customers up front, 'cause there wouldn't be any doubt Connal blew his load.

When she leans back, I slide an arm around her, lifting her up and giving Connal a moment to collect himself. Holding her against me, I hand her the water bottle and kiss her forehead.

Sitting in a chair close to us, Connal rubs her back. "Baby girl," he starts, then doesn't seem able to proceed.

"I've never felt anything half so good," I try to compliment her. Tilting her chin and kissing her lips. "We didn't want to push you, have you move too fast then regret it."

CHARLIE

"On my death bed," Connal picks up, leaning in to kiss my shoulder. "I'll be thinking of you demanding, 'I want your dicks out. Now.' And I will die with the biggest fucking smile on my face."

I instantly feel all the blood flow from my face and I reach out to tightly grip both their hands.

"But not for a *very* long time? Connal, Jake?" I can't keep the tremble from my voice. "I can't lose you, either of you. I'm not an idiot. I know. I know what you do is dangerous, but please? Please be careful."

Connal immediately slides forward, and he and Jake wrap their arms around me in an equally comforting and awkward hug. They both whisper assurances to me, although I notice they make no promises.

Jake tugs my braid after a few moments.

"We've got that party at the clubhouse tonight. You still up for it?" he asks and I nod. I've been texting Riley half the day. She's a little younger than me but has been around the MC enough that she is great for advice. I've got to have Jake run me by her apartment for a pair of boots she offered to loan me when we were talking clothes, then I want to chill out a bit as it sounds like it'll go late.

Emma's going to stay home, but Bree will be there and I can't wait to spend more time with both of them.

———

"No," Jake says. Leaning against the door.

"Absolutely not," Connal backs him up.

"It has long sleeves," I exclaim.

"Yeah, no one gives a flying fuck that you have arms," Jake contributes from his post at the door.

"Too much fucking cleavage," Connal adds.

I open my mouth, ready to fling an ultimatum at them when there's a knock on the door. Narrowing his eyes at me, Jake turns to open it.

"Hey!" Bree exclaims. "I was just checking in with Rusty...oh! Charlie, what a darling top!"

"Thank you," I respond, giving both of the guys a glare. "It's not too much for tonight, is it?"

"Not at all. I mean, let's face it, men would notice your chest if you were in a burka, but that shows less than my shirt." Bree gives me a wink once Connal and Jake throw up their hands in disgust knowing they have no chance of winning their inane argument now.

"Well, then, I think we're ready to go." I move towards the door, hoping there won't be a scene. Bree is still standing there and gives me a hug.

"Are you feeling better?" she asks. "I know the fire took a toll on you."

"I'm good. Thank you for your text earlier," I say and she smiles warmly at me as she starts back downstairs.

"One of us by your side all night, understand?" I'm not sure if Jake is saying this more to me or Connal, but I ignore it.

"Burka's not a bad idea," Connal mumbles. Jake squires me into the passenger seat, climbing in the backseat behind me. I wave to Bree as she gets into her own truck.

"Charles," Connal starts.

"Enough," I cut in. "I wanted to look nice and spend time with your friends in a place you've spent a good portion of your lives. You told me to stop hiding myself, so it's too bad if you're ashamed of being seen with me now."

They instantly start talking over each other and Jake's arms fold around me from the backseat.

"You're so beautiful, baby," Jake says when Connal falls silent. "And look, we told you, some girls go there and party with multiple guys over a weekend. We want to make sure no one gets the wrong idea about you."

"I will stay with one of you, Riley, or Bree at all times," I promise. "I've taken care of myself for a long time now, so you have to have a little faith in me also.

They both seem to exhale at the same time.

Knowing the fight has gone out of them, I throw them a bone.

"Is there anyone I should absolutely avoid?"

They go on to describe a couple men. Then sharing a look, add in 'any woman we don't introduce to you.'

"You know, I'll probably run into your conquests sooner rather than later." I laugh, more at Jake's continued attempts to cop-a-feel than at their attempt to put me in a bubble.

CONNAL

As the mood in the truck starts to lighten up, I bring up my next point.

"Baby girl, we talked about being discreet for starters. If that's what you still want, and if we want to be sure no one thinks you're fair game, I'm going to suggest that Jake be the one by your side tonight," I tell Charlie, having already discussed it with Jake. "Me being your boss and all...well, I thought that'd make sense. Of course, those we're closest to already know."

"I don't mind people knowing, not after meeting Riley and everyone now. But I agree with your points, especially since I don't know what I'm walking into. I'll follow your lead," she agrees, taking my hand and kissing it. And just like that, her trust, so freely given to us, enforces to me that she's the one for us.

Pulling into the lot at the clubhouse, Flint and Bree are near the door. He nods at us and we fall in behind them. Seconds after brothers turn to acknowledge Flint and Bree's entrance, silence falls until Diamond is heard calling out.

"Holy shit! Are those real?"

And everyone who's caught a glimpse of Charlie either chuckles or starts to cat-call and moving toward us until Vice and Royce push through.

"See, I told you she had..." Vice's eyes go from Charlie's boobs to my face behind her, then over to Jake's stern glare. "Uh, hi Charlie. Come on, Gunner and Riley are at a table past the bar. Uh, hey, Bree, didn't see you there."

"Shiiiit, Charlie! I thought Vice was fucking with me." Royce's eyes are trained on her tits and he seems to have momentarily overcome his fear of Charlie. I move to remind him and he instantly backs off.

Meanwhile, Diamond leaves Frank's side and moves into Charlie's path.

"Hiya, hun. Thank fuck I'm off the market or I'd be jealous as shit of you." She studiously ignores Jake while Charlie looks between Jake and Bree for direction. Jake just maneuvers around Diamond without a word. "Don't be like that, Jakey," Diamond purrs, so I lean over to make myself clear.

"Back the fuck up."

"I'm with Frank now, you can't..." she blurts out.

"Then back the fuck up to Frank," I growl, splitting off to the bar before joining them.

I get to the table with shots and a fresh pitcher and glasses in time to hear the latest on Diamond from Bree.

"So, her real name is Lucy. She thought her nickname was cute because of *Lucy in the Sky with Diamonds*." Bree nods her head over towards Diamond, who's licking her wounds at Frank's side. "She wants everyone to call her Lucy now. She's been showing up at the Ol' Ladies homes or businesses trying to get in good with them after all this time."

"Jesus, tell me she didn't show her face to Anne?" Gunner asks, choking on the sip he just took. Riley's sitting on his lap and grabs his glass before she's wearing his beer. At confused looks from the rest of us, he continues. "She was determined to get Hawk when she first rolled in here. She told Anne he knocked her up and just to let him go 'cause he was ready to upgrade."

"The fuck you say!" Vice nearly shouts. "When the hell did that happen?"

"Ahhh," Flint speaks up, looking to Charlie and Riley. "You were a guest of the State of Colorado at the time. That little misunderstanding that eventually got tossed out?"

"Huh," Vice chuckles to himself. "Surprised Diamond wasn't found in a ditch."

"I have a feeling that if Anne wants to do you in, no one will ever find a trace," Riley speaks up. I'd say that Riley and Anne respect each other, but sure as shit won't be braiding each other's hair. "That or she's biding her time."

The table as a whole takes a glance over to Diamond. Apparently, she's annoyed at the looks and comments Charlie's tits are still generating, cause she's stripped off the top she had on over a camisole and is letting Frank motorboat her.

Jasper comes out signaling for Vice and Gunner, so I head up to get us more drinks. Bree is right behind me. We get separated by all the brothers who have something to say or ask about Charlie and next thing I know, I turn to see the three ladies throwing back more shots.

Fuck.

CHAPTER THIRTEEN

CONNAL

THEY DO A COUPLE MORE SHOTS OVER THE next few hours, mixed with beer. Jake and I keep an eye on Charlie, with him walking as an escort when she needs the bathroom or when Riley and Bree introduce her around, mainly to other girlfriends or Ol' Ladies. It's when they get up to dance that we get twitchy.

"Let it happen, brother," Gunner speaks up, watching as Riley and Charlie run up to the dance floor, excited about some song. "Flint's on the other side of them talking to Roy, plus you and Jake are spread out within fifteen feet of her."

I'm apparently not the only one who keeps a close eye on his woman's surroundings.

Jake must think that's too far a distance as he gets up to stand on the edge of the dance floor. Shade turns from one of the honey holes and starts to make a move in the direction his eyes are pointing. Right at Charlie's chest.

Jake doesn't even have a chance to intercede. Riley's on it. Staring him down and pointing in the other direction. His eyes flip up to see Gunner watching and Shade quickly turns back to available women.

The next song is slower, so Jake simply slides in and wraps himself around her. Gunner lets out a growl but moves to the dance floor, pulling Riley into his arms. I'm left holding my dick, wanting a chance to grind against our girl.

JAKE

"You feel so good, baby," I growl into her ear. Letting her see me peek down her top and flashing her my dimples.

"Do I, 'Jakey'?" Charlie responds, mocking Diamond's misuse of my name.

"I'll get you for that later, Charlie," I promise her. "Trust me when I say it's been a long time since we laid a finger on her?"

"I trust you, Jake. And Connal." She grins up at me, shooting Connal a glance. "Are you alright to drive home tonight?"

"Yeah, just had a few beers," I respond, lifting an eyebrow in question.

"Connal's feeling left out…" She peers up at me.

"Wanna sit in the back seat with him on the way home?" I grin down at her, getting a quick nod in return, pleased beyond words that she's taking this seriously. "That's our good girl, watching out for both her men."

The next song is even slower and ends with me pressed against Charlie in the back corner. As it's wrapping up, Connal is beside us.

"I need you, baby girl," he whispers, before walking towards the back stairs. Waiting a moment, I kiss her thoroughly. Leaning back I wait for her acceptance. She eagerly smiles and turns, following Connal's lead with me close on her heels.

Hearing Connal in the bathroom off our old rooms, I rip off my boots and head to the bed as she gives me a smile and heads into the bathroom to join him.

"Hey! Are we at that point, baby girl?" He laughs at her.

"I missed you too." I hear before silence reigns. A couple minutes go by before Connal is striding towards the bed. Charlie's naked from the waist up and her legs are around his hips, her arms holding tight to his shoulders. His hands are holding her boobs together while he licks her large nipples. When his legs hit the bed, he tosses her down next to me.

Laughing, she rolls over onto me while he pulls his boots off. Once that's done and seeing that I'm occupied with her tits, he starts wrestling her boots and jeans off her. Charlie's very persistent when she wants something, so by the time he has her undressed and is getting her up on her knees, she's already sucking my dick.

The first swipe of Connal's tongue through her wet folds has her squealing and opening her mouth wider, almost gagging on my cock. I nearly shoot off right then. My eyes are closed, just enjoying the feel of her hot, wet mouth when she suddenly pulls back from me.

"Connal!" she squeals.

Shit. I look down her body to see his index finger buried in her asshole. She's looking over her shoulder at him, getting a wink in return before he shoves his face back down into her pussy.

She shifts herself, adjusting to the intrusion. After what seems forever, she shyly smiles back up at me before retaking my cock in her mouth.

Reaching my hand down, I roll her nipples in between my fingers hoping to do my small part in getting her to come for us. Her moans vibrate along my dick, making my balls tighten up. Looking at her face, I'm distracted when she starts wiggling her bum. Connal is actively finger fucking her rosebud while his face is still buried in her pussy.

"Harder!" I cry out, not at either of them in particular. Just the scene in front of me makes me want more of everything.

As my release approaches, I shift my hands up to caress her hair. "Almost," I start groaning, trying to give her some warning. Then she reaches for my balls and I'm shattered, spraying my cum down her throat uncontrollably.

Swallowing every bit of it, she lifts her head looking at me dead on, letting me see every emotion as her own orgasm overtakes her. Her reactions are so innocent and natural each time we're with her, they nearly undo me.

"Don't stop, Connal," I demand. "Goddamn, her face is unreal. Keep going."

"I can't." She looks at me pleadingly, panting heavily. "Please?! No more."

Cupping her face, enjoying the long, low moan that passes her lips without thought, I stare at her, silently encouraging her to accept it. To take it all from him. Dropping her head, she places kisses and soft bites all around my stomach, until her shudders cease and Connal draws back.

He looks up at me, his freshly shaven face coated with her juice. He smiles down on her, removing his finger from her ass and turning her into his arms.

CHARLIE

Holy shit.

Just Hole-ly Shit.

"I just needed you, baby girl," Connal murmurs, kissing my temple. "I hated not touching you out there."

"I need a moment, Connal," I whisper. "That was, both of you, it's just so intense. I want to…"

"Shush," Connal cuts in. "Don't need anything else, Charles."

"The things you do to my dick, to me, baby," Jake whispers from behind me. "Seeing the look on your face when you came for him. Ain't never known anything like that before."

Looking between them, my heart explodes. I've never felt anything like this. I feel the need radiating from both of them and all I want is to be theirs. To be wrapped in their world is unlike anything I ever imagined.

"I want this. Connal, Jake?" I roll to my back and reach to hold them to me. "I want us, but there is so much, well, so many things to consider."

"What do you need, baby girl?" Connal kisses the corner of my eye as tears start to well up. "Tell us and we'll work it out."

"Can I do more? What do you want from me? You both just give and give." I get scared, wondering how to find a way to balance our relationship.

"We want you, Charlie Scott," Jake says definitively. "I want a family. You, Connal, me, and any children that come along. I want to pick you up from work, with cute little grease streaks on you, take you home and clean you up before we all get sweaty making you come over and over again. Then someday, we'll go out back and push our kids on that swing you love."

My tears are freely flowing. I lost everyone who would have loved me. My mother was an only child and, while my Grandpa had met my father, he really only knew that my father had been estranged from his family for a couple years, no other details.

So when I was born, Grandpa was the only other family member around and he died when I was thirteen. To be loved by these larger than life men, and as many children as we can manage, sounds like heaven to me.

I try to speak but when I open my mouth, only a sob comes out.

"Ya gotta do better than that, baby girl." Connal kisses my cheek, smiling at me. "Jake's never spoken as much as he has since he met you. You run out on us, and he'll become a full-on mute."

"Everything," I croak out. "The three of us together. That's all I want. But how, I mean, when we have children, and, both your families? What do we do? If one of you walk away? I've lost everyone. So... Yeah, I'm pretty fucking scared. How do you both see this going?"

I lay there bordering on terrified, waiting for their response. They raise their heads up, exchanging a nod and I try not to be annoyed at their silent communication. Then I grin to myself, looking forward to the day I understand everything they've learned to exchange with a glance.

"We'll make you our Ol' Lady," Connal starts. "Claim you in front of the MC. It might draw a little fire right now, but Jasper will back it."

"Fire?" I ask, not understanding.

"Frank tried claiming Diamond. He was given a trial period." Connal looks at Jake.

"She's never one we thought would be around long term," Jake adds. "We all like Betsy and would never object to her, but Frank's not over a Girlie that was kicked out and he's claiming Diamond as a failsafe. That's recent, but we'll claim you and not give two shits about his hard feelings."

"There's something else." I swat Connal's hand away from my nipple. Can't concentrate with that distraction. He laughs and then Jake swoops over to lick the nipple closest to him.

"Stop!" I yell. They laugh but then snuggle in closer to *the girls*.

"What's that, baby?" Jake asks, as both he and Connal place light kisses around my breasts.

"Yeah, that. Babies?"

CONNAL

"We want them with you," I tell her. "You good with that?"

"Um, when?" she asks.

"Would love to feel a woman bareback," Jake tells her. "Would love to feel you raw."

Her hips arch up, into us, at the thought.

"Fuck," I mumble. "It's getting late. Don't want to be here all night. Let's finish this at home."

Rousing them, we pull on our clothes and Jake heads out to pull the truck around back. I pull Charlie to me, kissing her, trying to show how much I want her.

"Whole package, baby girl," I whisper into her ear. "You and me, we'll work side by side. You, Jake, and me, we'll love all together. Your children will have two fathers. You'll have two men who'll only just be with you. Just don't give up on us. Please?"

"Let's talk in the truck? With Jake," she clarifies, stretching up to kiss my chin.

I nod and we head downstairs. The party is in full swing by the sounds of things so we slip out the back, passing one of the prospects on the way out. I shrug off the startled look on his face when he sees me with Charlie.

Charlie insists on riding in the back with me, so I hold her close. She's quiet again, but when I open my mouth to speak I see Jake quickly shake his head at me. A few minutes later, I realize he was right. Sometimes people just need to think things through silently.

"I won't choose between you," Charlie says firmly. "Some decisions I want you two to make. I will sure as hell speak up if I disagree, but I don't want to be in a position of choosing between you."

"What decisions, Charlie?" Jake asks. Charlie's face flairs red, so I kiss her forehead to encourage her on.

"My virginity," she says quietly. "I want both of you, but you two decide who my first is."

"Hell, baby..." Jake exhales. "That's a bit intense for rock-paper-scissors."

I snort at the same time Charlie bursts out laughing and leans forward pretending to strangle Jake. "Better be *best of three* if that's how you decide it!" she says. Pulling her back against my chest, I bring up something I've been obsessing over.

"Unless I'm mistaken, you have more than one virgin hole down here?" I slide my fingers along the center seam of her jeans as I say this. "Here and here?" Her mouth drops open but no sound comes out.

"How'd you like my finger in there earlier? All lubed up with your juices?" I ask. "You came so hard, got my face all wet."

"Connal!" She turns into my chest; my hand gets squeezed between her thighs.

"Everything at your pace, baby," Jake reminds her, pulling in behind Rusty's. Waiting for him to get out, I slide her into his arms when he opens the back door. "Let us talk it through, then we talk to you? That what you want?"

"Yes," I can see her nod her head as he carries her in. "I can walk, you know?"

"But I like you in my arms," Jakes murmurs back. "How about you, Connal?"

"Fuck yeah," I growl, eager to get into that bed with her. "Get her clothes off. I'll be there in a minute." I veer off into the bathroom as he continues with her.

A couple minutes later, I walk in, finding a very naked Charlie straddling Jake's lap; he's pushing her breasts together, feasting on her tits.

"Lay on your back, baby girl," I growl. "Something I've been dying to do."

Seeing the bottle of lube in my hand, Jake swears then backs away. I slide my boxers down before stretching out next to her. Kissing her, I move to the shell of her ear.

"Let me fuck you here?" I ask, drawing an imaginary line between her breasts. She gasps then smiles up at me.

"Show me what to do?" she asks, blushing wildly.

"Here, a little of this first," I rub some lube in the valley of her tits. "Now hold them together around me?"

Straddling her rib cage, I slide my dick into the deep valley as she pushes her breasts tightly together.

"Aw Fuck, baby girl!" flies from my mouth during my first thrust between her boobs. She smiles up at me, before turning to Jake. He's sitting in a chair off to the side, stroking himself over his jeans.

"Lick his head, Charlie," he murmurs, giving the direction I've been unable to get past my lips. Charlie's eyes quickly widen. Not needing any more hints, her mouth and tongue are ready and eager for each of my forward thrusts.

Watching my cock disappear between her milky globes, watching her pinch her nipples, feeling her hot, wet mouth on the tip of my cock is too much. It's doesn't take long before my balls tighten and I'm yelling out a warning that my release is near. Charlie moves her hands from her breasts to my hips and sucks my cock in further, nearly to her throat, just as I come.

Holding the headboard for balance, I reach down, stroking her silken hair as she eagerly swallows every drop. Her eyes occasionally shifting from mine to Jake's, she finally draws back from my dick with a little pop.

"God Connal! The look on your face," she whispers. "I've never seen anything like it. You too, Jake. You both looked...I don't know. Feral? Maybe."

I'm silent as I stretch out beside her, Jake slides in on Charlie's other side, allowing my brain time to process a response. Watching him nibble her shoulder and neck, I've never felt so many emotions for any woman before. Possessiveness, admiration, respect, tenderness, but most of all, I think, love. I can't help thinking it's way too soon to confess that, saying it now would put a burden on Charlie and Jake that they might not be ready to bear.

As the moment stretches on, I realize that even Jake is waiting for my response. That for once, I'm the one who can't form the words to express myself.

CHAPTER FOURTEEN

JAKE

LYING SNUGGLED UP AGAINST CHARLIE, I know the struggle Connal is waging inside himself. She's so fucking right for us. It's terrifying that we may be this close to our perfect relationship and screw it up.

My thoughts are interrupted by Charlie's huge yawn. It serves to shake Connal and me from our thoughts, chuckling, we refocus on her.

"I'd say more like 'possessive as fuck' right now, baby girl," Connal finally grunts. "That sound about right to you, Jake?"

"Do I really get to keep you both?" she asks, before pecking me on the lips. I grab her chin before she turns to Connal.

"Just so long as you mean it," I say firmly. "No games, Charlie."

"No! No games, Jake," she says. Wide-eyed, her sincerity shines through. "I want this."

Connal presses his lips against her temple and pulls the cover up around her. "Get some rest now."

I kiss her again before I peel away. Heading out to the main room, I grab a beer and start pacing. Fifteen minutes go by and Connal has come out and is grabbing two beers from the fridge.

"What the fuck was that, Jake?" he growls, handing me the spare beer.

I shrug. I have no answer.

"Sit down," Connal points to the other chair.

"Is she alright?" I ask him.

"She was worried about you, that she had upset you. Wanted to come apologize to you. I soothed her until she fell asleep." Now I really feel like shit.

"I don't know. Got worried she might be like the others," I sigh. I've been surrounded by gold diggers or woman just looking for an easy ride my whole life. Deep down I know she's not like that. I just got skittish.

"She's not." He confirms what I'm thinking.

"I know."

"You should be her first," he says, throwing me off.

"What? After what I just did? No, you…"

"I'll lose control. I'll be too rough with her," he interrupts me. "You're tender with her in a way I've never seen before, Jake. She deserves that."

I take a moment, humbled by his words.

"Do you love her?" Connal asks next. Looking him straight on, I hold his gaze and nod unable to find my voice. "So do I, brother," he whispers.

"When she's ready for her ass, Connal, that's you," I say.

"We'll claim her before we get to that." I'm nodding along with him when he drops the next bomb on me. "When you think it's time, you'll be the one to marry her, Jake."

I shoot up, unable to process what he's already decided on.

"No. I said, if she couldn't take us both I'd be the one to leave." I'm fighting to keep my voice low. "We do this together, all of it or we don't do it."

"Jake, sit down and listen," Connal says quietly, waiting until I snag two more beers and sit back across from him. "There's every chance we'll get her pregnant. Look how she's been. Once she has a baby by one of us, she's going to want to give a baby to the other one. And what we do, brother?

"There's always the chance something could happen to one or both of us. Shit goes south and what would she be left with? If she's your wife then she and any children'll inherit, won't they?" he finishes.

The realization hits that if the *worst case* does happen, she'd be worse off than when she got to town. I can prevent that by marrying her. We sit in silence while I check off all the boxes of what I would need to do.

"It'll have to be one hell of a prenup and will," I finally sigh.

"You don't still think..." he starts, glaring at me.

"No, to protect her from the wolves, not to be protected from her," I assure Connal. "A child of hers that looks like you? They'd try to go after the money if I wasn't around. What resources would she have to fight my family without losing most of it?"

"Fuck, Jake. I never considered that." He looks dazed.

"Never underestimate the blinding need of the truly rich to keep every dime within the family, brother." I chuckle. "There's an estate attorney I know of in Boise. We got kicked out of a prep school together a lifetime ago. I'll go see him next week, get started on the paperwork."

CHARLIE

I wake the next morning in Jake's embrace. Connal is in the shower. It's my Saturday off and I'm happy for the opportunity to make things right with Jake. As the water shuts off, Connal soon pops his head back in to peek at us.

I start to shift towards him but he holds his hand up, silently asking me to stay put. He quietly walks towards me and leans in to kiss me.

"Miss you already, baby girl," he whispers, before grabbing a pile of clothes and heading out.

I doze on and off, really just waiting for Jake to wake up. Before long, I startle awake from some half dream.

"Okay?" Comes Jake's sleep mumbled voice.

"Sorry," I turn into him. "About last night…"

"I'm sorry about that. Just a couple demons I had to fight, baby," he apologizes, kissing me soundly.

"This is new…"

"Huh?" he grunts.

"In bed with just one of you," I smile at him. "What are the rules?"

"No rules usually, but today I'd say no 'firsts' for you. There'll be times when I'm on a job and you'll be with Connal." He pauses. "We just all need to be upfront about everything. No sneaking off."

"Did you two talk about the other thing?" I wonder out loud.

"Yeah. How do you feel about me being your first?" he asks shyly, smoothing his hand through my hair. I smile and nod, getting a huge grin from him in return. "No rush, Charlie."

"But Connal will be with us, right?" I ask, strangely relieved when he nods again. Then I laugh to myself. "Never imagined my first time quite that way, Jake."

"Are you sure you're alright with that?" he asks, looking concerned.

Rolling on top of him, I pretend to pin him down.

"Absolutely," I assure him, before wiggling my core over the massive boner he's hiding in his boxers. I lean in, scattering kisses from his neck to his well-defined pecs. Slowly sliding down in between his legs, I look up at him with large eyes.

"Now, since you said we shouldn't do anything we haven't done before, maybe you'll bear with me while I practice giving a better blowjob?" I keep a straight face while raising an eyebrow up at him.

"If you must." He sighs imperiously, grinning down at me while he crosses his arms behind his head.

Laughing, I wrestle his boxers down and start

exploring his cock and balls with my tongue, trying to keep my hands on the bed for support. As his breathing gets more and more ragged, I pull back from his thick, spit-wetted cock, making him cry out in need.

Lifting up, I press his cock in between my tits. Jake lets out a loud groan and quickly starts thrusting his hips up and down. Eagerly catching his head in my mouth, I'm filled with satisfaction between the look on his face and later the feel of his balls tightening, knowing he's going to come.

I lean back, taking his cock in my hand and finish him off with my hand; spraying his seed all over my chest.

"FUCK!" he pants. "Jesus Christ, Charlie. Fuck." He's collapsed against the pillows when I raise myself onto my knees. I swipe a finger through a string of his cum, sucking it clean as I back off the bed.

"Come shower with me?" I ask, making a beeline for the bathroom. A throaty chuckle follows me. Jake enters the bathroom just as I've gotten the water to the right temperature. Luckily, he grabbed extra washcloths.

Jake's arms quickly surround me, pushing me up against the back wall of the shower. He has no issue with the fact that he's now smeared his seed over his chest as well, but the shower quickly rinses that away.

"You're so fucking sexy, baby," he murmurs in between kisses. "Just keeps getting better, every day we wake up together."

I'm so overwhelmed. I can't hold back the tears that flow from my eyes.

"No, no, baby. No tears now." He holds me tight, and pulling me down onto the bench. Reaching over he grabs the shampoo bottle and starts massaging it through my hair. "You've got us now, Charlie. You've *got* us."

He finishes his gentle ministrations then takes a moment to run shampoo through his own hair. Toweling ourselves off, he reminds me of a delivery at the new house. Heading that way, we stop off at Gunner's workshop. I know he and Connal had mentioned the bed platform they had ordered from him but seeing it is another thing. Gunner is truly gifted; the guys had picked the design of the bed out already but Gunner goes through shades of stain for me to decide on the finish.

As they start to talk about people they know, I wander through the shop. There are pieces that I absolutely fall in love with, but I feel so beholden to Jake and Connal already. I would never say anything for fear of them doing more than they have.

Turning back to them, I see Jake pass Gunner an envelope then they do the *man slug* thing and part ways laughing. I throw a little wave to Gunner and cross to meet Jake at the door.

"What was that?" I ask him.

"He works his ass off on his business," he says, taking my hand. "Gotta pay the man. He fucking wanted to give it to us at cost."

Jake's been hard at work on the house. An en suite bathroom has been outlined against the outer wall of what will be the master bedroom and the framework for the closet is set inside the existing walls of the house. He's made the choice of putting wood floors throughout and started pulling out the old carpeting. He sits me down to select paint colors for each room. Narrowing down options is as far as I get. Before long it's time that the garage will be closing so we arrange to meet Connal at Ray's for an early dinner.

Getting to the diner, Connal is already in a booth and I slide in next to him. Eager for his kiss.

Marge gives us quite the look as she comes over to take our order.

"How was your day?" Connal asks as she wanders away.

"Well, mine was fucking amazing," Jake cuts in loudly, quickly lowering his voice. "Woke up to our girl, all warm in my arms. Then she licked The Beast awake before she finished me with her Bounty."

First, my jaw drops open then I burst out laughing so hard I'm snorting. Connal wraps an arm around my shoulder, nuzzling my neck.

"The Beast?" I get out between giggles. "My Bounty?"

"Shiiit," Connal chuckles. "Don't know about The Beast, but *Bounty* is the perfect fucking nickname for your, um, hmmm." His eyes are fixed on the points he's trying to describe.

"What do you call your package?" I turn on him.

Now it's Jake's turn to crack up.

"What?" I turn, now I have to know. Connal shrugs but Jake is smirking. "Please? I promise not to laugh."

"Boss," Jake snorts out, not letting him off the hook. "He calls it The Boss."

I keep a straight face for zero point five seconds. Until Jake's eyes meet mine and we bust up, our heads thrown back howling.

"Come on," Connal inserts. "Don't we remember The Beast? How is that any better?"

"Naw," I gasp out. "Y'all both named your dicks when you were like ten, right?"

CONNAL

Sitting around eating and laughing with Charlie and Jake takes away all the stress of the day. I lean back taking this in and think how a few months ago I'd have been rushing to get cleaned up and party with my brothers and nameless women at the clubhouse. Now all I know is that Jake is as eager as I am to get Charlie back to the apartment and explore her body. Make her fucking come all night.

I don't realize that I've completely zoned out until Charlie squeezes my thigh.

"You're alright with it, Connal?" she asks once I look into her eyes and I have no idea what she's talking about. Catching that, she specifies. "With Jake being my first?"

"I won't be far behind him, baby girl. You alright with that?" I draw my finger down her nose and tap her lips. She nips it, giving me a wicked grin.

"Let's get out of here," Jake growls and I can see the desperate need in his eyes.

Tossing some cash on the table, we head out running into one of the town sluts, Janine, and some of her friends in the parking lot.

"Who's that Connal? Jake?" Janine calls. "New toy?" she adds to overly loud laughter from her friends.

Jake growls and I start to open my mouth when Charlie slips her hand into mine.

"Seriously, guys, if you slept with that, I want you on a full course of antibiotics, in addition to condoms, before you touch me." Charlie laughs, pulling on her helmet without looking back.

Janine's cry of fury rings out but is quickly eclipsed by even louder laughter from her so-called friends.

Charlie snuggles behind me on my bike and I can see Jake's wide grin in my mirror as we pull out of the lot. At a light on Main St., Jake pulls up next to us. "I never touched her," he calls over.

"Neither did I," I call back before the light changes.

"Is she what they call a honey hole?" Charlie asks when we get to the apartment.

"She tried pretty fucking hard to be," I say. "But she got banned for both disrespecting Ol' Ladies and pissing off the Girlies. Betsy, she's kinda the lead Girlie. You'd like her. Actually, most the Ol' Ladies do. Not what you'd expect from a club girl, not like Diamond.

"Well, Janine, I don't know what exactly she did, but she messed with Betsy and Betsy went from sweet-as-pie to I'm-gonna-fuck-you-up in the blink of an eye. Dragged her outta the clubhouse by her extensions and spit on her. She banned Janine and Prez backed her up."

"I don't think I've met Betsy?" Charlie asks. I just

shrug and say she's been away a little while. Then it hits me, she hasn't been around much at all since meeting Russian at the cabin a couple weeks back.

Letting it drop, Charlie looks tense in the apartment, so I grab the whiskey bottle and a few glasses, indicating the couch. She sits in the center and looks surprised but pleased when Jake drops to the floor in front of her, leaning against her leg. I cozy in next to her, pouring a full glass for each of us.

"I don't really know a lot about you two. I know we've talked about trying this, but can you tell me more about where you're both from, your families?" She is looking into her glass, her groan startles me till I see Jake has removed her shoes and started rubbing her feet. "I'll answer anything you want me to also."

"Stop making that noise and I'll tell you everything." I grin at her.

I tell her about my Mormon mother running away to marry my nominally religious father. He worked two jobs and she tried to keep up with what soon became four children. I was the youngest and they were tired. They weren't bad parents, they just never loved anything as much as they loved each other. My siblings and I aren't close but we email with news and call at Christmas.

Jake skims over part of his story. I know he's got to get to the fact that he's seriously rich with her sometime, but understand that in his head it just isn't any part of who he is. He tells her how he's from Massachusetts, the middle of seven kids. His father and mother expected and planned socially mobile positions or marriages for each of their children.

He walked into a recruiting office on his way home from his high school graduation and went his own way. His grandfather, a Vet himself, loved that Jake thumbed his nose at them and they talk weekly. That's where I jump in, teasing him for being his favorite.

"My brother's getting married next month." He surprises us with this news. "I haven't been home in a while and gramps is really after me to be there."

"You should!" Charlie encourages him.

"Be my date?" he asks quietly, after a moment. Charlie's jaw drops open, she looks between us both.

"I can come with, skip the family parties…" I add, trying to help her make up her mind.

"Um, I don't know?" she says quietly. "I've never been anywhere, and never to a family thing or a wedding…I wouldn't know how to be…"

"You'll be with me. Nothing to worry about," he says, kissing the inside of her knee.

"Jake," I say, glaring at him. Knowing his family's scrutiny would be hard on Charlie, especially considering her background.

"We'll get some fancy clothes, baby. Let me show you off?" He shrugs at me. "I'll coach you on them on the flight East."

"You should go, Jake," she states firmly. "Can I think about it?"

CHAPTER FIFTEEN

JAKE

I KNOW SHE'S NOT TURNING ME DOWN, SHE'S just unsure of walking into the unknown. I respect the fuck outta her for not just agreeing to go to a big party, but thinking about what it would entail especially cause this ain't going to be a bash at a VFW hall. This'll be a few-thousand-dollar-a-head shit show of over-extravagance.

"Y'know what I really want to know right now?" I ask, looking at Connal.

"Huh?"

"How many times can we make Charlie come tonight?" I answer, grinning widely as our girl nearly chokes on her whiskey.

"I'm thinking at least twice each. You up for that, old man?" Connal laughs and shoots his shit eating grin my way.

Reaching up, I start wrangling her jeans off of her and he takes the glass from her hand.

"Shimmy on out of these now," I instruct her. By the time her pants are down, Connal has removed her top and bra. I lean my face into her puss, getting fucking hard as hell at the smell of her. I dive straight in, flicking her clit with the tip of my tongue.

She arches her hips up towards my face, her groans swallowed by Connal. He's got his hands full, kissing her and her *bounty*, as I'll now only think of her tits. I sink my finger into her core, swirling it in her juices before shifting it back to her asshole. It's my first attempt back there and so goddamn tight I can barely get the tip of my finger in. Gradually twirling it around the edges she loosens up and I slip in, knuckle by knuckle.

Looking up at Connal, I tell him to rub her clit for me. As soon as he takes over working her sensitive nub, I slide a finger into her tight, wet core. Gradually I'm able to add a second finger into her center while I continue to slide the index finger of my other hand in and out of her tight ass.

"Connal, let me!" Charlie isn't happy unless she's occupied. "Please?"

At this, he starts rubbing her clit faster, determined that we'll get her off before letting her take care of us.

Her body succumbs to our attention and her screams reach a high pitch as shudders overtake her, her pussy and asshole convulsing tightly around my fingers. We quickly move to the bed, the three of us naked, the night speeds by in a series of short naps interspersed with orgasms. Charlie is always our focus but our woman gives as good as she gets.

———

Waking up sometime the next morning, I blindly reach over for Charlie, snapping my hand back when my fuzzy brain realizes that her chest isn't hairy.

"Sorry, brother," I grumble, sitting up with a rapidly deflating cock.

"How many times do I gotta tell you, I'm not bending over 'cause you got cute dimples?" Connal cracks. "Hey, I smell bacon." Sitting up suddenly, he grabs his shorts off the floor and hits the john.

Charlie grins at me over her shoulder as I head out to the great room. "Good, I've been making pancakes, almost done with all the batter."

"Don't like not waking up next to you, baby," I slide my arms around her body, cupping her breasts through the black nightie she has on. She starts to say something before I kiss her temple. "But I really appreciate breakfast."

"Where's the bacon, baby girl?" Connal asks coming into the room. "I may need that more than coffee right now." He reaches for the spatula, handing it to me before pulling her into his arms for a kiss.

"You have to protect me, Charles," he whispers loudly. "Jake tried to cop-a-feel while I was sleeping just now."

"Jacob! We had a deal. I'm the only one you're

supposed to molest!" she says in mock fury before Connal starts laughing.

"He's not a Jacob, *Charles*," Connal corrects her, as Charlie grabs the spatula back from me to flip the cakes. "May I introduce you to Jarrett Willis Forsythe?"

Instead of mocking *Jarrett*, she goes straight for the kill.

"Willis?! My God! Dick would have almost been kinder! Certainly not as high-brow sounding as Willis!" Connal and I lose it; she isn't wrong. I hate both my names equally, Jake suits me fine. "Oh shit! Do you have a sister named Muffy? Please tell me now!" Connal and she are both holding the counter for support but I stop laughing.

"That's my brother's fiancé's name," I reply, grinning at them. "I do have a sister, Kathleen, who goes by Kitty. And I've always called Tabitha, Tabby, but I'm the only one who does."

"Hell," she throws her arms around me. "Now I've *got* to go to the wedding!" I pinch her ass and bury my head into her neck, giving in to the laughter that floats around the kitchen. She pulls back and motions us towards the table, reaching into the oven she pulls out the tray of pancakes she had been keeping warm.

"Um, I know I smelled bacon, Charles?" Connal asks again.

"It's in the pancakes—which I also cooked in the bacon grease," she replies, quietly adding. "My Grandpa taught me this way. Breakfast food was really the only thing he cooked."

Mine are already covered in syrup so I dive right in.

"Fucking A," I growl, before diving back in. That's enough to encourage Connal along and in the next twenty minutes, we've devoured the entire pan of cakes. "Fucking A."

"I'm glad you like it. Pancakes, ramen, and frozen pizza are about the extent of my cooking skills." She laughs at our enthusiasm.

When I finally look up, she's leaning back grinning at us and I just reach over and pull her onto my lap, sliding my hand up her nightie like the fucking Neanderthal I am.

"We're claiming you when I get back, baby," I tell her.

"Get back?" She looks confused and pushes away from my chest.

"Gotta be in Boise for a day or two," I tell her.

"Club business?"

"Nope, personal," I answer, trying to pull her closer again but not wanting to discuss the visit to the lawyer I need to make.

"You didn't tell me," she murmurs. Connal puts his fork down and I freeze, not understanding the hurt we hear in her voice. "Did you know?" she asks Connal, who shrugs in response before looking at me. I can see he's as confused as I am about why she's turning red.

Sliding off my lap even as I try to hold her, she walks back to the bedroom telling us to handle the clean-up.

"What just happened?" I ask Connal.

"No idea, brother." We stare at each other a moment. "Go back there and ask her."

I stare at him a moment longer trying to figure out what I'm in for, then I stand to follow her. As I get to the hallway, she's coming out of the bedroom fully dressed and her eyes are puffy. I reach out to her but she ducks around my arm and walks straight out the door without a word.

"Seriously, brother, what the fuck just happened?" Connal asks me. I stand, staring at the door for a moment.

"Wait—where are the truck keys?" I ask and we both kick it into gear to get dressed and after her. The keys are still on the dresser and I'm a little relieved seeing her knapsack in the corner. She showed us the contents a couple days back and I know she would never leave that behind, her family pictures and documents are in there.

"She may just need a little time, Jake," Connal reasons.

CHARLIE

I head out and in the direction of the overlook Jake had taken me to. Bree had told me about her regular walks up there when she lived at the bar, so I know it's doable and the walk will help me sort things out.

Ever since I started working here, I'm pretty much always with one of them. Now we're living at the bar and I have no transportation without them. Being included in texts between Riley, Bree, and Emma make me feel like a part of something bigger. But at the end of the day, and in such a short period of time, my life has begun to revolve around them. Just them.

I've been on my own since my mom died. Grandpa did the best he could, but he expected me to look after myself. If I wanted more from him, I made my way out to his garage to watch and learn. He taught me a lot, in his own way, not just about cars but about life. The unedited version of an old guy who didn't remember he had to filter it down for a seven-year old.

When he died, I was alone for two days before anyone thought to come look for me. Then I was in the system and no one actually gave a damn. Mack was the first person since Grandpa's death that showed me kindness without expecting anything.

Yesterday, Jake and I had talked about going to get paint samples and other final items for us to be able to move into the house. He made other plans though and never thought to tell me. I get that they have their own lives, but realized I don't. Without them, right now, I don't.

That hit me hard and makes me feel so trapped and sick inside. Realizing that they can so easily make plans like no one else factors into them.

By the time I sort this out in my head, and try to figure out a way forward, I've been sitting on the stone wall of the overlook staring out without seeing anything. The sound of motorcycles snaps me out of my funk. As they come to a stop behind me, I stay still waiting. In another moment, Jake is on one side of me with Connal on the other.

CHAPTER SIXTEEN

CHARLIE

Jake reaches out, putting his hand on mine.

"I'm sorry," he starts. "We talked about starting the painting. I had reached out to a friend of mine and didn't think he'd fit me in so fast. I…"

"Shut up," I say. Not knowing how to explain how I feel, I just sit there trying not to cry.

"The garage has that loaner car," Connal starts after a while. I almost grin, knowing how hard long silences are for him. "Barely ever gets used but it works. I want you to take it."

"You shut it, too," I respond, but reach one hand out for his, drawing it onto my lap, next to the hand that Jake is holding. Just sitting beside them, I stare out over the town.

"Do you want space, Charlie?" Jake finally asks, sounding pained.

"Yes. No. NO," I gasp and Connal leans over to kiss my head as Jake breathes a sigh of relief.

"I'm not good at telling people how I feel, what I want to do, or what I'm thinking, Charlie," Jake says, squeezing my hand so tightly. "I feel so much though, I just was kind of taught early not to air my emotions. It embarrassed my family when I did. Then I pretty much stopped talking unless I had to. There were always so many people around that I could go days without talking and as long as people weren't interrupted, they were happy.

"Connal is closer to me than anyone. He's had a while, under pretty fucking bad circumstances, to get used to me. He's truly my brother. You? You're the love of my life, Charlie. Even if he gets mad at me saying it, the love of Connal's life also. I know and feel this so strongly," he says and I can't stop the tears from rolling down my cheeks as I study our hands. "I feel so connected to you but I have to get used to talking to you, to discussing plans and shit. I need you to be patient, just for a little bit?"

I stand and draw Connal into the space I was sitting before I straddle Jake's lap. Burying my face into his neck and drawing Connal in towards the other side of my head. I'm helpless to do anything but sob. I just sit this way for long moments. Connal rubs my back while Jake holds the back of my head tenderly.

"He's right, baby girl." Connal directs my face to look at him. "I do love you," he says, before pulling me in for a deep kiss.

Pulling back from him, I lay a kiss on Jake. When I

lean back, I get a look behind him. A family had pulled in and the parents are staring at us in disgust. Catching my eyes, the mother pulls her children back towards the car. Their oldest son is looking at us with his mouth gaping open, the father tugging heavily to get him back into the car. He looks back over to us again and yells "BIKER TRASH."

And at that moment I know, that's how most the world will see me for every single minute I am with Connal and Jake. My arms tighten around them, stopping them from moving after the man.

Grabbing both their chins, I redirect them to look at me. "I don't care what anyone thinks. I love you both. I know we just met but I need you to believe that I love you both and will proudly be yours," I gush in between tears. "We'll love and argue and have as many children as you want, but this is forever, it has to be forever."

"Forever, Charlie, that's what I want with you," Connal says.

"Fuck yeah, baby, for-fucking-ever," Jake elegantly pledges. "Tell me though," he asks after a moment. "What set you off back there, Charlie?"

I let out a sigh.

"My world kinda revolves around you both. That's new for me. And your worlds are separate. I know our relationship is new and moving so damn fast." I let out a breath. "I, I don't know. I'm not used to feeling dependent on anyone else for my happiness, for my daily plans. But even to get back and forth to work right now, I need to have a ride. I don't know how to explain it right."

"Take the extra car, baby girl," Connal says, pulling me over to his lap. "Make plans with Riley, or any other friends. The three of us, we'll just work on talking. Just know, my...our focus is on being with you. I think you feel that also."

"I love you both," I whisper again, giving them my agreement that way.

CONNAL

Charlie walking out was exactly what we all needed. We have been in this sweet little bubble of happiness with a side of walking on eggshells, and this jolted us out of it.

"Baby girl?" I start, not knowing about the next topic I want to ask about. "Tell us about these scars of yours?"

She stiffens in my arms.

"It's my fault mom died," she whispers and Jake and I instinctively lean in to hold her tighter.

"I had a tantrum about a movie I wanted to see," she finally says. "Money was always tight and Mom was tired from working two jobs but eventually agreed to take me. Our car was hit by a deer on the way to the theater. Mom lost control and we flew off the side of the road. I woke up a couple days later, but mom had died at the scene. After he told me, Grandpa held me and let me cry, then he said, 'That's enough now.'

And that was it. We never spoke about it again. We never spoke about her again. The scars are my reminder," she finishes, holding back more tears and from the sound of it years of guilt.

Jake lets out a breath. There's no denying Charlie's had her share of troubles. "Come back home with us, baby?"

Charlie nods into my chest. Standing, I toss her over my shoulder and am quickly rewarded by her laughter. Setting her on her feet near Jake's bike, he produces her helmet from his saddlebags, and she mounts behind him. We spend the next few hours making up, properly, until Jake pulls himself away to get on the road.

After seeing him off, I take her out for a ride that I wrap up by swinging by the clubhouse. Seems Gunner and Riley had the same idea, so I park next to his bike and quickly seek them out inside.

Betsy and Russian are back and looking mighty close. After a few minutes of catching up, Riley pulls Charlie over to meet Betsy. Halfway through their discussion, Jasper walks in and Russian jumps to his feet.

"Prez, brothers," his deep voice rumbles. "I'm claiming Betsy as my Ol' Lady. We all good?"

"What the fuck?" Vice roars. Pushing one of the new Girlies off his lap and suddenly sounding territorial. "Betsy?"

She moves away from Riley and Charlie, wrapping her arm around Russian's waist. "We good, Jasper?" she asks, ignoring Vice's outburst. Vice stops midstride, realizing his zipper is still down he starts shoving his dick back in even as he glares between Russian and Jasper.

"I got no problem with that, anyone else speak now." Jasper looks around the room. Silence prevails for a moment and all eyes are darting between Vice and Russian.

"What the FUCK, is right?!" Diamond hollers. "You won't accept Frank's claim on me but *Betsy* gets a pass? That bitch has fucked as many of you as I have!"

"Anyone who's authorized to vote, speak now. Otherwise, shut the fuck up," Jasper rephrases his previous statement and Diamond flies across the room towards him.

"Frank ain't here, he wouldn't stand for this bull-shit!" she roars, only stopping when Vice grabs her around her waist before she can reach Jasper.

"You keep this up and you'll lose clubhouse privi-leges before he gets back, Diamond," Vice tells her. Jasper is pretending to ignore her but there wouldn't have been any help for her if she had struck him. "Where is the old coot, anyway?"

"He had a friend who needed some help. He's gone for a few days," she replies, getting a snort from Shade. "What's your problem? You're not really backing this bullshit, are you? I've always been real good to you." She turns on him next.

"Heard Frank's been getting texts from Deb, maybe that's the friend he's helping?" Shade replies loudly from the corner. He ignores Diamond as she starts cursing him out. "Russian, man, you take good care of Betsy. Betsy, you let me know if he ain't. I'll get him sorted." He grins and nods at her. Shade's considered a borderline psychopath by most of us, so that statement gets a tight smile and nod from Betsy, with Russian pulling her in tighter to his side. Betsy, like Russian, is not one to crave any spotlight so this scene has got her ducking her head into his chest.

"Alright now. Congrats, Betsy. Russian." Jas nods at them, before crossing to the hallway leading back to his office. "Shade, let's have a chat."

Riley and Charlie, still standing near the new couple, are quick to hug Betsy. Vice crosses over to Russian, his eyes on Betsy with every footstep closer.

Extending his hand to Russian, Vice leans in to say something, getting a near growl from Russian before he taps him on the shoulder and follows Jasper and Shade down the hall. Betsy never looks at him.

Crossing back to me, Charlie sits in the remaining chair between Gunner and me, knowing that Riley will just sit in his lap when she wanders back.

"Um, what the hell just happened?" she asks quietly, getting a grunt of amusement from Gunner and a sigh from me.

"Deb was a Girlie, she was kicked out for embezzlement. Frank always had a thing for her. She, uh, had an unreturned thing for Gunner here," I start.

"Because I'm hot," Gunner cuts in, smirking at us.

"Stop listening to Riley, Gunner, you look like an ogre," I laugh before continuing. "Frank tried to claim Diamond here. Now let's just say Diamond's skanky, even by MC standards. Jasper gave them a trial period, but wouldn't agree to it flat out. But, Betsy here, well she more or less keeps the clubhouse running and coordinates things with Jasper and Emma in addition to, y'know, other Girlie *activities*. She had a thing for Vice for years, but to be honest, Russian has been after her for a while."

"Diamond's pissed at the world. Vice is pissed at himself for not stepping it up with Betsy. Betsy and Russian look happy," Gunner sums up the situation when I pause. "Riley, we gotta go."

"What's up?" she asks him, crossing back over to us.

"Grocery store," he mumbles.

"It's already closed, I'll go tomorrow," she tries to get him to sit back down.

"Sweetheart, can't you just take a hint?" He growls before swinging her up in his arms, nuzzling her neck as he walks to the door. "Remember what I did after I claimed you?" I guess we're all cavemen cause I feel the overwhelming need to get Charlie outta here now also.

Russian crosses over to us as I start to stand.

"Congrats, brother," I slap him on the shoulder. "Surprised that didn't happen sooner."

"Needed to make sure she was over Vice first. Wanted to be sure I wasn't the fall back." He shrugs.

"You'll be better for her, not that you need my opinion," I say, getting a nod from him.

"You and Jake going next?" he asks, flicking his eyes quickly to Charlie and back to mine. I shrug, reaching down for Charlie's hand, eager to get her home.

"Let me know, I'll be here. Diamond'll really lose her shit then," he calls after me.

CHAPTER SEVENTEEN

JAKE

MONDAY GOES SLOW AS HELL. SPENDING MOST of the day going over trusts, titles, and accounts in my name and sewing everything up so Charlie will be protected is a fucking nightmare.

Then I went and mentioned that any child she bore by Connal would be done with my knowledge and agreement and I wanted those kids to inherit equally, naturally that created another dozen or so clauses.

"You sure about this, Jake?" William asks for the fifth time. "They could just be conning you. There's a lot of money at play here." I don't even answer him anymore, just stare him down until he gets back to it.

Everything's ready when I get to the office the following morning, signing the will and a few other documents to leave on record. I take off with the prenup, eager to get back to Rowansville.

I head straight to the garage. Charlie rolls out

from under a car when she hears the bike pull up, a smile lighting up her grease streaked face as I walk towards her. Helping her up, I quickly have her legs wrapped around my waist and am kissing her for all I'm worth.

"Hey, hey, none of that," Connal growls, entering the garage. "I don't get to touch her here, neither do you."

Charlie laughs as she breaks our kiss and slides back down to the ground. Leaning over to my ear, she loudly whispers, "He's been getting grouchier every day, at least until we get home."

I nuzzle her neck before letting her go. "What's been happening, brother?"

"Russian claimed Betsy on Sunday night," he starts.

"No shit?!" I grin at the thought.

"Diamond lost it," Charlie cuts in. "Then Vice was quiet and pouting last night at Riley's dinner, so no one talked about it." She eagerly catches me up on the news.

"Men don't pout, baby," I correct her, getting a snort from her.

"That's what I said," Connal jumps in. "You almost done there, Charlie?"

"Yep, I was just cleaning it up," she tells him.

"Get the paperwork done so we can head out early. I'll let Royce close up today," Connal says. "I need some of those kisses too."

"Actually, I thought we could have sex tonight," Charlie drops that bombshell on us nonchalantly, before turning back to her lane.

The two of us freeze, staring at each other, unsure if we heard right.

"Get home, get cleaned up!" Connal says, coming to first, then running towards his office. "I'll stall her a little."

I immediately take off, forgetting to say goodbye to Charlie. I stop off for flowers, candles, champagne, and condoms.

Shit, my basket is like an advertisement for 'I'm getting laid after the Prom.' But what the fuck? It's her first time. This has to be done right.

I've just finished my shower and tugging on shorts when I hear Connal's bike pull in. He's chasing her up the stairs when I open the door.

"Save me!" she cries dramatically, laughing and hiding behind me.

"You—Shower. Now." I direct Connal, keeping her behind me. He chuckles and follows my direction, throwing a big wink to Charlie.

"You sure about this, baby?" I whisper, turning to pull her into my arms.

"Yes, Jake. Completely." she hugs me to her.

"Good, now why don't you go help him with his back?" I smile down at her. Leaning forward, she flicks my nipple with her tongue and starts to strip as she backs away from me. Fuck.

Getting into gear, I move to light the candles in the bedroom and spread the rose petals from the bathroom to the bed. Connal will probably take my MC cut from me over this but Charlie missed out on a lot of things. I'm giving her this.

Yep, there's a bark of laughter from him when the bathroom door opens. Charlie tells him to shut it and enters the bedroom first. They both have towels wrapped around them, and she drops hers as she steps into my arms. I can't help but give Connal the finger behind her back.

"Come here, baby," I whisper, pulling her down onto the bed. Connal moves the other side of her, sitting against the headboard; he cups the back of her head. "You know we love you?"

She nods, biting my shoulder and reaching a hand up to hold Connal's.

"Do you want me to wear a condom?" I ask, glad we were able to show her our blood tests earlier this week.

"No, Jake. If you two don't want to, just with me, I'm good with that," she says. I start kissing her, grinding into her, a frenzy has kicked in and neither of us is interested in slowing down now. Moving a hand down to her pussy, I start massaging her clit, determined to make her come before I enter her.

"Only with you now, baby girl," Connal grunts. "We'll go bare and see what happens, ok?"

Connal and I shift, each suckling a breast. As she gets closer to her orgasm, I slide my finger into her leaving my thumb to rub her sensitive nub. Hitting that sweet bundle of nerves inside her tunnel, she screams loudly, arching her hips and begging for more. I add a second finger, working to stretch her tight pussy; trying to prepare her body for the girth of my dick.

"Please, Jake!" She finally pleads. "Don't make me wait any more."

Connal leans up to kiss her before shifting back, I move on top of her; holding her tight, wet entrance open with one hand as I start to nudge into her with the head of my cock. Tired of my slow movements, she cups my face and arches her hips up to meet me, nearly impaling herself on my rock-hard dick.

Crying out when I draw back, she merely whimpers when I push all the way back in through her wet velvet folds, this time breaking through her barrier.

"Fuck!" She pants. "You're so goddamn big."

"I'm sorry, don't move, I'm sorry," I repeat over and over. Hoping her discomfort will quickly ease, I kiss her and notice that Connal has his fists balled up, watching helplessly. "You better now, baby?" I ask, caressing her face.

"I'm sorry, Jake." She painfully smiles up at me. "Maybe you should start moving?"

"Yeah?" I ask gritting my teeth together I get a frustrated noise from her, she moves her hips herself. "Oh, God. Baby, you're so tight."

The friction sets me off. I try to hold back but the primitive part of my mind takes over and I start thrusting in and out of her. Before I know it, her legs are around my hips and she's arching up to meet my movements.

"Connal, she's amazing!" I call out. "Never felt like this. Shit. You're squeezing me so tight, baby." At my words, Connal groans beside us, stroking his shaft in concert with our motion.

"Jake, there! Faster, oh God, please!" she calls out and I feel her sheath shudder around my dick. My balls tighten up impossibly hard and I'm gone. Shooting off my cum into her womb, I yell out.

Coming inside a woman for the first time in my life and knowing she's mine. Ours. I lean down, unable to kiss her gently, I consume her, squeezing her tightly in my arms.

CHARLIE

Holy. Shit. As I start to drift back into myself and my vision sharpens again I reach a hand out to Connal, my other arm still secured around Jake.

Tears are rolling down my cheeks and I'm just utterly sated.

"Jake," Connal says quietly. "You're smothering her."

Jake grunts, then rolls off of me and Connal slides up alongside me. For once he doesn't seek to fill the silence, just lets us catch our breath. Finally, I pull him down for a kiss. It's filled with the tenderness I usually find in Jake's kisses. Connal's aggressiveness seemingly replaced by calm.

"Baby girl," he says against my lips. "I could watch you all day long."

"Just watch?" I grin up at him.

"Smart ass." He lightly flicks my nipple.

"Baby, you gotta go to the bathroom now," Jake says. "After we come in you, I don't know. It's a health thing…"

"It reduces the chance of a UTI," Connal says,

getting a look from both of us. "What? I always paid attention in Sex Ed class!"

I grab a nightie as I head to the bathroom, following their instructions. Jake has my discarded towel around his waist and enters the bathroom when I exit, dropping a kiss on my forehead.

"Fancy!" I call out, loud enough for him to hear when I see Connal setting up a few glasses and a bottle of champagne next to the bed.

"You have one Mr. Jarrett Forsythe to thank for thinking of this. For all of this." Connal motions around us at the candles and flowers.

Grabbing me from behind, Jake lifts me up bridal style.

"Wanted to make it nice for our woman!" he grunts.

"It was beautiful, Jake," I say, cupping his cheek. "Thank you."

"Hush now," he says, shyly. "Here, let's trade." Jake transfers me to Connal's arms, taking the bottle from him. He deftly twists the bottle, removing the cork with a soft pop and pours glasses for each of us.

"Here's to us, finding each other, to knowing, acknowledging, and freely living the way we want." He says, and we all clink glasses. The champagne is my first and it tastes amazing. I look around Connal at the orange label on the bottle and try to remember the name for future celebrations.

Connal leans into me. "Seriously, baby girl, you've made him verbose."

"How the fuck do you even know that word?" Jake laughs.

"Saw it on the Word of the Day calendar in Jas' office," Connal shrugs, getting Jake laughing harder, nearly snorting champagne through his nose. Connal and I exchange a glance and wait for him to catch his breath.

"That thing's been there for like three fucking years!" He finally gasps.

"Finally came in handy then." Connal laughs along. We all do, we laugh and talk and snuggle. I hold my men close. Not worrying about how this came to be, but how easy it is and how happy I am.

"Connal?"

"Yeah, baby girl?" He looks at me, finishing his drink.

"Lie down with me?" I hand Jake my glass.

"Charles, I don't want you to be sore." He steps back. "Maybe tomorrow?"

"Now, Connal," I reach for his arm. "Please?"

Looking at Jake over my shoulder, he stands stiffly. I put Connal's glass down, and pull my nightie off. "I want you now. Both of you, always, Connal. That's my promise." I shift down to the bed. Sitting beside me, Jake strokes my ankle.

"Give our Ol' Lady what she wants, brother," he orders Connal, nodding at me. "Look how sexy our girl is?" He draws a finger across the soul of my foot, pulling a surprised giggle from me.

"Where else are you ticklish, baby girl?" Connal growls. Leaning toward me, he pounces at the last moment and I shriek in surprise as he pulls me on top of him. "You set the pace, little one. Don't want to hurt you."

As he pulls my legs apart, I quickly slide up, giving his mouth access to the *bounty* he seems to enjoy so much. Jake stays beside us, pulling my head over to give him a kiss. I moan into his mouth as Connal alternates sucking and nipping my breasts.

"Slide on down him now, baby," Jake whispers, our lips barely touching. "Let him feel how tight that sweet pussy is. Let him feel you then fill you up."

I nod, smiling down at Connal, his eyes pleading with me. He moves one hand to line his cock up with my core, and the other on my hip. A low groan escapes his lips and both hands clench my hips as I steadfastly edge all the way down his shaft. My insides tender from having Jake's cock in me less than an hour ago, I sit up tall once I've taken him all in me. Holding him there I swivel my hips, enjoying the feel of having Connal in me and the power I feel from the frustrated groan that falls from his lips.

"Goddamn it, baby girl." He tries to grind further into me, holding my hips tight enough to leave marks. "Do that again. Oh shit!"

I obey, enjoying the look of sheer need on Connal's face. In another moment, leaning down and bracing myself on his wide shoulders, I start rocking up and down, catching the rhythm we need.

CHAPTER EIGHTEEN

CONNAL

"SORRY. SORRY. SORRY." I CAN'T STOP, I JUST need her harder but I can feel how tight she is; not just from the intrusion of my dick but from Jake's earlier pounding. "So fucking tight, Jake. That's it, Charles, ride my dick just like that."

Her pussy fits my cock like a glove, I have no idea what I'm saying. I just need more of her sweet, wet friction.

"Help me, Connal," she moans and I finally start moving my own hips, having held back to keep from hurting her. Her plea sends me past the point of thinking and I start thrusting up into her. Her ragged breathing accelerates, then Jake leans over and sucks one of her nipples into his mouth.

Just like that she comes. Fucking loud as hell, slapping my chest with one hand, screaming for more. I shoot rope after rope of cum up into her, I've got no control left at this point and just pull her into my body, rolling us over, needing to keep my dick in place even as it softens.

"You ever feel anything so good?" Jake asks quietly. Pulling back, I shake my head at him, looking back down to Charlie, I kiss her gently.

"Never," I whisper.

"Aren't you glad you didn't wait until tomorrow?" She shoots me her cockiest grin, getting a chuckle from Jake and me.

"Smart ass." I kiss her nose before rolling off of her, Jake tosses me a towel. "Hit the bathroom, love."

As she waddles off, trying not to get my mess all down her thighs, I look at Jake again, trying to sort out my thoughts.

"Let's get to the clubhouse," he says, voicing my unspoken thoughts. "Let's just go claim her. You get cleaned up, I'll text Flint, Jas, and Gunner, make sure they get there."

I feel the same driving need to do this, so I get moving without a word. When Charlie exits the bathroom, I tell her to get dressed, then jump in for a quick shower.

"What's going on?" I hear her ask Jake before the water drowns out anything else. Toweling myself off a couple minutes later, she's already dressed when she barges in for her makeup bag. "A little heads up next time, Connal!" she exclaims.

Coming up behind her and wrapping my arms around her, "You don't need any of that, beautiful. But we need you. Need to make this official. Need you to understand we mean it." Nuzzling my head into her neck, I start with the topic she won't like.

"I can see straight down your *bounty* to your belly button, Charles," I say firmly, looking down her shirt. "Ouch!"

Luckily her boots weren't on when she stomped my foot. Then, she leans towards the mirror to apply her mascara and with her ass snug against my dick, I forget everything. Holding her hips again, I fantasize about when she'll let us in the back door. When she'll take us both.

"You feel ok?" I ask.

Straightening up, she slides my hands from her hips, slowly up to her tits, cupping them with my hands.

"I swear I can still feel you in me," she purrs, leaning against me. "Go get dressed now, Connal."

I nod and without thinking, I go and get dressed; no longer worrying about her cleavage anymore.

Jake has her pressed against the front door when I join them, kissing and wrapped around each other. I know we've made the right choice. Jake turns to look at me over his shoulder, giving me a nod. When he pulls away from her, I lift her over my shoulder and head out to the parking lot. Ignoring her laugh and slaps to my ass. Putting her down, I catch the helmet Jake throws my way for her and we're off.

Full house at the clubhouse, between bikes and volume. Should be an interesting reaction to our news. As we enter, I see the mid-week ruckus is due to a group from a Colorado MC that has stopped in. Greetings are barely out of their mouths before they notice the *bounty* and nearly start towards Charlie en mass.

"BACK THE FUCK OFF!" Jake bellows, pulling himself up to full height. I'm right beside him, with Wrench and Russian immediately filing in behind Charlie. Looking around the room, Jas waves his hand so I can see him in the crowd.

"Prez!" I call. "Jake and I are claiming Charlie."

In a second, the noise level has gone from deafening —full of catcalls, music, and drunken boasts—to dead fucking silence. The vice president of the other MC looks around.

"Wait, I want a go at the one with the tits, though," the guy says, looking at Charlie. I step forward to hit him but Charlie has grabbed my arm.

"Jake and Connal are taking Charlie as their Ol' Lady. Any objections *Northern Grizzlies?*" Jas calls, specifying who has a right to answer.

"I fucking object," Frank calls. "I been around longer than those shit stains combined and you won't agree to me taking Diamond but now Ol' Ladies need multiple brothers fucking them? Which one of you boys can't get it up for a girl?" Frank slurs out to continued silence from our MC and laughs from the guests.

"Flint? What do you think?" Jas asks, knowing he needs to justify his reasoning.

"Ain't the norm, so we vote. Northern Grizzlies only," Flint calls from near the bar.

"Against, let's hear a nay," Jas says. Frank and his buddy are the only two nays out of nearly thirty brothers, Royce manages to keep his mouth shut. "Settled then. Welcome, Charlie. Frank, you want your own vote now?"

"Fuck off. The lot of you," he says, much more subdued. Pulling Diamond after him, he heads towards the stairs.

"Wait. Is the one with the tits an Ol' Lady now?" asks the very slow VP from the other MC. That time I do hit him.

JAKE

"We got you something, Charles," Connal says, once the fight dies down and we've all had a shot or two to relax everyone. We located her in the corner with Emma and Bree. Bree's watching over a very pregnant Emma like a mother hen. He unrolls Charlie's *Property of* cut, one with both our names marking her.

Charlie immediately slides it on before thoroughly kissing us both. That's when she notices our hands, still bloody from that little disagreement.

"Don't you worry about this," I tell her, holding her close. Feeling a touch on my back, I quickly turn to see Betsy with Russian close behind her.

"I'm sorry!" Betsy starts, knowing I'm still riled up from the fight. "I just wanted to congratulate Charlie."

We step away from the women to catch up with Russian.

"Still living here," he grunts. "Wanted to talk to Bree about renting that apartment of hers when you three move out. Betsy's still gonna work here, so it'll be close for her, but we can have some privacy too."

"Yeah?" I ask, a little surprised by that. But Betsy has kept this place running for a couple years and I'm sure Russian doesn't like being a few doors down from Vice right now. "We should be out in a couple weeks."

"Fuck. I even missed a fight?" Gunner growls from behind us. "I had a delivery a few hours from here. Sorry I wasn't back in time." He claps the two of us on our backs. "Riley has a test tomorrow, but I don't think she goes more than a few hours without texting Charlie anyways."

"Wasn't much of one," Connal contributes. "Not taking any shit over her physical attributes, is all."

"Uh huh. Gotta cut that shit out so no one will do it," Gunner says, trying really hard not to smirk, right up until he and Russian make eye contact. Russian's been quick to *handle* anyone who forgets Betsy's new status.

"So, we'll be neighbors later this year." Gunner changes the topic, looking back at us. "Gonna build a house on the land next to my workshop. Vice and you'll be working on that project before long."

"Perfect timing," I laugh, looking at Russian before making eyes at Betsy then over to Emma's heavily extended stomach.

"There'll be an empty two bedroom on the market next year, y'know, in case you need a second bedroom for any reason, Russian?" Connal picks up on what I was thinking.

"Da fuck do I know about kids?" Russian asks, getting Betsy's attention.

Looking over and seeing Betsy sitting between Emma and Charlie, I see her with new eyes. Over the years, she had become almost invisible to me. Now, her makeup is more subtle and her skirt a little longer, but more than anything I can see how happy she is. She eventually excuses herself and slides back over to Russian, leaning up to whisper in his ear. They hurry away, Betsy throwing a wave over her shoulder.

"Thank God, Riley wants to finish her degree before starting a family," Gunner contributes, before catching the look Connal and I exchange. "Going right for it, huh?" He quickly guesses.

"Guys?" Charlie tentatively slides up to us. "I'm sorry, but with work tomorrow…"

"Shit, Connal," Gunner chuckles. "Tell me you took your Ol' Lady off probation at the garage already?"

"As a matter of fact, Gunner, he hasn't!" Charlie sasses back.

"Cool it. Next she'll want a raise!" Connal hugs her to him as we say our goodbyes.

Feeling her snuggled up to my back on the ride home, I'm torn about telling her about the money.

Screw it. When we get back upstairs, I grab a few beers and motion Connal and Charlie over to the couch.

"Baby, there's something I want to talk to you about." I pause, taking a pull from my beer. "Connal knows this, Jasper and Flint, maybe Wrench, but I don't want it talked about."

"Are you alright?" she asks, leaning into me, looking instantly concerned.

"Yeah, it's just that I've got money," I say, trying to assure her I'm healthy. Connal laughs and she looks at me like she just noticed I have two heads.

CHAPTER NINETEEN

JAKE

"Money?" She looks confused.

"Serious money," Connal contributes. "His great-grandfather invented something and the family has been printing cash ever since."

"I don't have any," Charlie says in a small voice, gripping my hand.

"Connal and I talked about that. We want to make sure you'll be protected Charlie," I say, setting my beer aside, I pull her onto my lap. "You know our plan is to be all together, to have kids?"

She nods, looking worried and a little sad. Connal's leg is bouncing and I know he can't contain himself.

"So, we want you to marry Jake!" he explodes and instantly realizes he screwed that up a bit.

"Marry Jake?" Charlie says, pulling away from me. "No. The three of us. I'm your Ol' Lady, not a wife.

That excludes Connal," she says angrily and I smile at her.

"Listen, baby," I start. "Charlie, we love each other. We both love you and Connal is a brother to me. If you…when you have our children, if anything were to happen to me, or to us, I need to know that you're secure. That money will never be an issue. This is how we do that.

"Jasper has a license, he can marry us quietly. I had a lawyer draw up some papers these past couple days. Connal is listed in there. Any child you have with him during my lifetime will also be considered my heir. But if we aren't married, my family may very well come after the money."

"I can't really process this now, Jake. I'm sorry. Can I just go to bed and we'll talk tomorrow night?" Charlie looks blindsided.

"Tell us you love us, baby girl," Connal insists, leaning over for a kiss.

"I do. I love you both." She kisses him, then me before hightailing it to the bedroom.

"Well, I fucked that up," Connal admits, grabbing a couple more beers.

Charlie

Every time I think we're close to even footing, one of those two make an announcement that throws me off. 'Serious money'. I can't even comprehend that.

My mom never said much about my father that I remember, just that I looked like him. We lived in a one bedroom apartment and saw her dad on weekends and holidays until she died and I was with him until his death.

Taking this job, meeting my loves, I just feel like I'm falling ever faster down a rabbit hole. And I always despised Alice in Wonderland.

I finally lie still and I can hear the quiet rumble of Connal's and Jake's voices in the other room. I know they're trying to give me my space, but I miss the feel of them next to me in bed.

———

"Baby girl?" Connal whispers. "Time to get moving."

I groan and snuggle back against him. His warm chuckle tells me he's as disappointed to leave bed as I am. Shooting my head up, I realize Jake's not with us.

"He left earlier," Connal murmurs.

"What time did you come to bed?" I ask.

"Late." He sighs. "Too much beer and we're worried we're pushing you too much."

"Connal, if I'm his wife...I, I mean the three of us? What happens?"

"You'll be my wife also. In my mind and heart, baby girl." He kisses my forehead. "Not legally, but that's how I'll live, that's how I'll treat you and any children you have. I know it's not conventional, but we want you protected and this is the only way we can see that happening."

"I don't ever want to put a wedge between either of you. I can't imagine one of you without the other." I look him in the eye, trying to ignore the growing heat in my body. "I will walk away before that, Connal. Shush. Don't say anything else, just know that I won't be a thorn between you."

"Come on," he grunts, lightly slapping my ass. "Work."

Rolling out of bed, I put on one of my tighter sports bras, then a tank top with a loose fitting shirt. Riding into work and looking at the docket for the day, I know I can't do lots of late nights drinking then dealing with smells around the garage. Royce rolls in some time later and pats me on the back. Seemingly making his peace with me being in the garage and my new status in the MC.

Things go well until he shoots out from under a car on his creeper. I was walking by but looking at a text from Riley, so didn't notice him and land my knees into his chest.

"FUCK!" He screams when he can once again suck in oxygen.

"Charles?!" Connal yells.

"Sorry. I didn't see him," I say while trying to get my phone from where it landed and off of Royce without any further damage.

"Office," Connal says.

Following him back, I just apologize when I walk in.

"Sit." He looks at me with his *boss* face. "Charles, don't get upset with me, but really?"

"I don't mean to!"

"Ok, but no one gets hit by lightning this much." Connal is using the sweetest tone with me even though I know he's frustrated. I don't mean for these accidents to keep happening. "I need you to be really careful."

"I'll try really hard. Promise."

"Not mad at me?" he asks, raising his eyebrow.

"Of course not, I understand." I smile at him. "When I'm here, I'm your employee. I want constructive criticism from you. And I want to take on more, little by little. I'm not asking for a huge project but to learn more."

"Absolutely, and you've earned that. You catch a lot of things when you're doing general maintenance and you are solid with customers. You were right last night. We'll consider your probation period over and I'll up your hourly a bit. I just need you to work on not maiming Royce."

"Thank you!" I'm really stoked about this. "Um, what time do you need me here till tonight?"

"Unless we get a rush, we'll say five, alright?" Connal raises an eyebrow as he asks.

"Sure, Jake wanted to pick me up and I'd like to talk to him a bit, then the three of us?" He gives me a nod then he finally looks down at my chest. I wink at him before leaving the office.

Jumping on Amazon, I buy a small whiteboard. I figure starting a "Days Without an Accident" board might make Royce despise me less. Or at least give him an outlet to make fun of me.

When Jake rides up later, I mount behind him without a word and he takes us straight to the overlook.

"So…"

"Wait," I cut in. "Marriage kind of threw me for a loop. Connal and I talked a little this morning."

"You wait, baby. I missed not getting snuggles from you, Charlie. Let me have those first?"

"Big, bad, tattooed Biker needs snuggles?" I grin up at him, as he holds me tight.

"Well, fuck, baby. Don't go writing me a social media profile or anything..." he says before nipping my earlobe.

He sighs, pulling me close to his body. "I left work early. I wanted to get something that shows you how I see us." With my back to his chest, sitting on the half wall like we have several times before, I look up at him.

Jake pulls a box from his pocket and holding it in front of me, opens it. There are three silver rings—two large ones with the third, feminine ring in between them. Each with the infinity symbol on them.

"These are for us. You and I will be on paper, but the three of us? We'll be committed." My eyes well up in tears and he reaches into the box, placing the smallest ring on my left ring finger. It's a little big but I love it and curl my fingers into a fist.

"Will you marry me, Charlie?" he asks. "Will you spend your life with Connal and me? Be the mother of our children? Love us no matter what anyone thinks?"

I can't speak. I can't stop crying. I start to wish that...

"Will you, baby girl?" Connal's voice comes from behind Jake.

CONNAL

"Yes!" Charlie sobs. "All of it. Always."

I reach out and wipe the tears from her cheek. "Take our woman home, Jake."

This weekend is Bree and Flint's wedding. I figure we can announce our news afterward. I just hope Charlie's not planning on a long engagement or a big wedding. I have something in mind, and we'll see what she thinks after she sees our other surprise.

After Jake rides past Rusty's, I can see her tugging on his cut, unsure of where we're headed at first, she keeps looking around. I breeze past them to make sure the house looks good. Some of the furniture is in, at least in the parts that had wood flooring hidden under the awful eighties carpeting. Most of all, our bed is here and set up. Jake and I are ready to surprise her with that.

"No peeking!" I hear as he guides her through the home. "We got something to show you."

"I believe I've already seen *them*, Jake! Boss and Beast?" Our little smart ass sasses back. I step forward and grab her, turning to toss her on the bed. Grinning as her scream turns to laughter. She tugs off the bandana Jake tied around her face and takes in the bed, the size of the bed.

"It's huge!"

"Hush, Charlie, you'll make Connal jealous," Jake says, dodging my attempt to smack him and crawling across the space to her. "Look, there's a light, cup holder, and nook built into the center of the headboard for you. We know you like to have water near the bed at night, now you don't have to squirm all around us."

"Connal! Join us. Jake, this is so great!" She eagerly checks the details.

"Like it, baby girl?" I ask, tugging her boots off before working on mine.

As I reach over to work her jeans off of her next, she starts kissing me while Jake starts to unbutton his shirt, as soon as that's off he tugs her shirt over her head. He and I unzip our jeans and groan as she shifts between us. I cup her pussy; pleased to find it wet already. I dip my thumb into her core while massaging her clit with my fingers, working it faster and faster.

Knowing what I need tonight, it's almost like she's on the same page. Without any direction, she rolls onto her stomach, hitching her knees up under her, and spreads herself open for me. After first sliding a couple fingers into her wet tunnel, I start to rub her juices from her center to her clit and back to her asshole.

With a glance back to me, she starts licking Jake's already hard cock, jutting her ass back in rhythm with my fingers, making me groan as her rosebud is spread open and on full display for me.

"Connal, please!" I can barely make out her moan, her mouth stuffed with Jake's cock. Lining my seeping dick up with her slit, I spread her open before wiping some of her juices over my length for lube.

Just as she's turning to growl at me a second time, I ram it into her soaked pussy in one thrust; she throws her head back in a scream, coming on my first thrust. Her wet pussy squeezing my cock for all it's worth. I manage to keep leisurely working it into her, wanting to hold my orgasm off as long as possible.

"Yes!" she cries. "So good." She swivels her hips around before turning back to eagerly work her mouth up and down the thick dick in front of her.

"Easy there, baby," Jake moans when she gags after taking him too deeply.

"I want more of it," she pouts. I'm so fucking turned on watching her work to deep throat Jake that I just start pounding into her. Her pussy contracts around me each time I move to withdraw, like its begging for me to stay.

"Coming. Can't wait. So fucking tight," I yell while gripping her hips and pulling her body back, flush with mine. She has no choice but to release Jake's dick but he follows her forward to suck on her beaded nipples. As I start to come, I reach around, grabbing her throat and holding her tight to me until I've completely emptied myself into her womb.

I've barely finished before Jake pulls her onto her back and enters her in a single thrust. Reaching down he massages her clit while slowly pumping into her. She seems dazed at the switch but soon starts chanting 'More' and 'Harder'. I'm exhausted and can't do anything but kneel beside them, watching.

"Can you take more, baby?" he teases her. She wraps her arms around him, grabbing his ass cheeks for leverage, she starts meeting his thrusts.

They come together moments later.

I wait until they collapse before going to look for a towel, getting back just as she starts to notice the sticky mess Jake and I left with her. Spreading her milky white thighs apart, I gently rub the towel against her slit in time to catch a creampie as it slips out. Thinking of our seed mingled in her body sets me off, my cock perks his head up, poking against her leg.

"I can't, Connal," she moans, reaching up to caress my face. "Not down there."

"Quiet," I whisper and give her a wink. "Don't worry about me. I'll just hump your leg for a couple minutes."

"Asshole," Jake and Charlie laugh out at the same time. Scooping Charlie into his arms, Jake carries her towards the old bathroom on the other side of the house.

"Come on. Let's bathe our woman before we head to the apartment."

"Wait!" she calls, looking at me over his shoulder. "Aren't we staying here?"

"Not yet," I say, following them. "They've got to get the master bathroom and kitchen done. We'll worry about the rest later."

Any further complaints are forgotten as we take turns fingering her to orgasms in the small tub; all under the guise of soaping her up and rinsing her off. Her *bounty* takes an especially long time to clean.

At least to our standards.

CHAPTER TWENTY

JAKE

CHARLIE'S PUSSY IS TOO SWOLLEN TO consider entering her again anytime soon. By the end of her bath, our attentions caused her clit to become even more engorged. Our woman is dead on her feet by the time we get her tucked into our bed back at the apartment. Connal falls asleep almost as quickly, leaving me to watch her sleep.

———

Getting up earlier for work than Connal and Charlie sucks ass. I want so badly to lick and kiss her, but know that she needs her sleep. Instead, I focus on her left hand as it rests on my arm, loving the look of her engagement/wedding band on her small hand. More than anything, I love the fact that I'm marrying a woman who burst into tears over a simple silver ring. A woman, intelligent and loving enough not to buy into the diamond myth.

Watching her sleep between us, my eyes shift over to Connal. He's watching me. Smirking at me, actually.

"She said if she ever thought she was coming between you and me, she'd leave. Sound familiar?" he whispers.

"Want to make this official soon, Connal. Flint's wedding this weekend, maybe the week after for us?"

"I was thinking Jas could marry you two, during a Monday night dinner? Nearest and dearest, unless you want something bigger?" he suggests.

"She may want Mack here? He was good to her," I say. "I'll keep my family out of it for obvious reasons. You want anyone else? Other than our group?"

"I don't mean to exclude the MC, but Charlie's private. We'll ask her but I don't expect she'll want a big fuss." Connal pauses. "I'm going to give her some time off. Suggest she goes dress shopping for Bree's wedding and her own?"

"Sounds good. But just for Bree's wedding. I want to take her to Boise. She'll need some outfits and dresses for all the parties around my brother's wedding," I groan, knowing what I have to do. "Plus, I'll need a suit and a goddamn tux."

Connal chuckles, right up until the next part.

"So, the three of us will stay in my gramp's guest house. There'll be a party there the day before the wedding then a brunch the day after. You'll need clothes for both events. When I told him you were coming, he insisted; didn't want you lurking around scaring people."

"Fuck. A suit?" he whispers back, looking disgusted.

"When are you wearing a suit?" Charlie murmurs, waking up slowly and arching her back so her tits rub against me and her ass bumps Connal.

"For my brother's wedding, we'll go shopping this weekend, alright?" I ask them both before leaning over to soundly kiss her, sucking on her bottom lip before rolling out of bed.

"I'm going to be late." I've been splitting my time between the spa job and working on our new house. Vice has promised to get a crew over to our place next week to help me, so that'll speed that up.

On the way to work, I call Nordstrom in Boise and arrange for a personal shopper for Charlie. I specify events and price range, knowing I don't want that done in front of her. Once the woman assures me that Charlie won't see any price tags, I get on with the day.

"Hey," I pick up Connal's call that afternoon.

"Yeah, Riley just picked Charlie up to go shopping, she'll bring her to the clubhouse when they finish."

"Ok, I'll swap out my bike for the truck and get out to the house for a bit. Meet at the clubhouse when you close up?" His grunt seems to be agreement.

CHARLIE

While I feel like I'm taking advantage of the time off, I know it won't be an ongoing thing.

"Riley, I really need your help," I say, getting into her truck.

"Shopping? Wait, holy shit! You have a ring!" she screeches.

"Oh, yeah. Jake and I are going to get married, but it's still the three of us," I say, still giddy about the three rings. "But that's not…"

"You. Are. Engaged!" she screams again. "I know you aren't a girly-girl but back the hell up and tell me everything!"

I laugh at her enthusiasm and give in, because really, Riley won't focus on anything else until that's covered. As she drives us to the next town over, I tell her all the details except the mind-blowing sex that I can still feel in my tender pussy.

"And he got matching rings for Connal and himself?" She sighs. "That's so thoughtful. I'll have to let Gunner know not to propose for a week or two. We should celebrate this after Bree's wedding."

"Wait—your turn! Gunner's proposing?!" I yell back at her.

"I'm not supposed to know, but I think I have him figured out…" One side of her mouth curves up into a knowing smile.

"Ok, so what I need help with is Jake's brother's wedding. We're flying east in a few weeks and, well, can you keep the next part a secret?"

"The part where Jake's filthy rich?" She rolls her eyes at the shocked look on my face. "Yep, I know the signs; been around those types my whole life, then I ran searches on some of the guys when I was bored one day."

"His brother is marrying a woman named Muffy, for fuck's sake! Riley, I have no idea how to act with people like that. I don't want to embarrass him. Can you show me what to do when faced with a formal place setting? I started googling stuff but just got more confused," I admit while pleading for help.

"Ok, next week let's carve out some time. OH! Actually, can I enlist my Gram to help? You can come to dinner with me on Friday and then we can practice with her again next week. She's wonderful and knows more about etiquette than I ever will." She pauses. "Has he mentioned clothes that you'll need?"

"We're going shopping on Sunday. He and Connal will need suits also," I say, getting a raised eyebrow from her. "We're staying in his grandfather's guest house…"

"Charlie, don't get nervous on me, but don't be surprised when the guest house is bigger than the house Jake just bought." I sigh, I had guessed as much. "Take his advice on clothing. He'll know what is expected, alright? And I'm sure he'll pay for it all," she continues.

"There'll be some parties at that house, so his grandfather told him that Connal should plan on attending those but I guess not the wedding."

"No, the wedding list was probably a nightmare to negotiate and no one will want to revisit it." She shrugs like this is normal.

"For our wedding, I just want our dinner group and

Mack. Is that weird?" I ask quietly. "I mean, Betsy is nice but I've only talked to her a couple times at the clubhouse."

"I think that's perfect." She squeezes my hand, pulling into a parking space outside the department store. "It'll be even more perfect if Jasper marries you at one of our dinner parties... The three of you can request any dishes you want."

I burst into tears.

"Charlie!" She pulls me into a hug and waits out the storm.

"That sounds perfect to me, too," I finally say. "Maybe they'll want some others there though, I'll ask tonight."

I end up with a simple black dress that hits above my knees for Bree's wedding. Riley then steers us towards the bridal department, where we take turns trying options on.

Getting back to the clubhouse, I feel like a huge weight has been lifted off of me. Riley called her Gram to ask for her help, so I'll also get a crash course in table manners.

"Leave your bags, we'll sort it out later," she says heading towards the double doors. I grin to myself at her confidence. This will be my first time walking in there without Jake and Connal flanking me, but like Riley, I feel shielded by the Property cut I'm wearing. Although, the cuts certainly drew lots of stares and glares at the mall.

"Riley?" I call before she reaches the doors. "Thank you. I really appreciate everything."

Entering, she grabs my hand. "Bree's like a mom to me, Emma's more like an aunt. You? You're my first real friend my own age, and I know we're going to be best friends. I knew it when we met. Just like I knew Gunner was going to be mine. I hope that's not too freaky a thing to say."

"I'd like that Riley, really." I shyly smile back, squeezing her hand.

"Are you two gonna kiss? Cause that would be great spank material," Royce slurs out from the bar.

"Shut it, Royce!" we simultaneously yell back, then laugh at each other.

"FUC...!" Royce's scream is cut off.

Our heads spin back to him, Gunner has his hand wrapped around Royce's throat and has lifted him to his eye level, more than a foot off the floor.

"Did I just hear you say something to my Ol' Lady, maggot?" he growls.

Royce slaps at Gunner's wrist, trying to suck in oxygen.

"I was kidding. I'm sorry," Royce croaks out when he's able to breathe. Gunner shakes him, still holding him off the ground.

"And Connal and Jake's Ol' Lady? Any shit you want to spew there?" Gunner continues, not caring that Royce is nearly purple.

"Sorry. Riley, Charlie, I'm sorry, alright?" Royce gasps out. "Gunner... Brother?"

Riley has crossed to Gunner and reaches for his free arm, looking up at him with absolute love. Her touch has a visible effect on him, and I can see his body relax but he doesn't lighten the glare he's giving Royce as he releases him.

The scary-as-shit, *there really are monsters under the bed* face doesn't fade until Gunner looks at Riley. Reaching a hand behind her neck, he leans down so his forehead is resting against hers. Royce has, wisely, crossed to the far corner of the room.

"We had fun today, Gunner," Riley starts like Gunner didn't nearly strangle a man in front of us. "Let's have a drink with them before we go home?" He nods, as he lightly rubs his scarred cheek against her smooth one.

"Anything you want, sweetheart," he says, standing back to full height and smiling down at her with absolute devotion.

Next, he looks at me, tilting his head to where Jake and Connal are standing near a table, waiting to see if they'd be needed. Soon, sitting around with drinks in front of us, Riley tells Gunner about our engagement from her customary seat in his lap. He grunts, so I jump in.

"We weren't going to say anything until after Bree's wedding, just one thing at a time, you know?" I say, trying to help Riley give him the message about waiting a couple weeks to propose to her. I decide she's right about that being on Gunner's mind because he does not look happy even as she winks at me.

"Connal, Jake? When, who, and what are you thinking for our wedding?" I ask, turning to them.

"Soon. Us. Small," Jake replies, in typical *Jake speak*.

"I'd like Mack to be included. And Riley suggested if

we want it small, that we could do it at a Monday dinner? Would that be alright?"

"Oh—will you make your red velvet cake, Riley?" Connal sighs and I swear I hear Gunner growl.

"Soon?" Riley asks, elbowing Gunner. "This weekend is all about Bree and Flint but how about a week from Monday? Just tell me what you want me to cook, and yes, I can bake that cake. Or cupcakes?"

"Riley, I cannot have my guys drooling around you like this!" I exclaim in mock outrage. "You must teach me to cook. Otherwise, you can't be my Maid of Honor."

"Yes!" Gunner pipes up, tightening his arms around Riley. "Perfect. Riley'll teach you to cook then maybe she'll stop giving away her treats." This gets everyone laughing. Everyone, except the behemoth who is extremely territorial about all things Riley. I really don't think he's kidding, even if she's laughing at his statement.

"Charles set the toaster on fire last week," Connal pitches in, getting a smirk from Gunner.

"Her pancakes and frozen pizzas are really good," Jake, kind of, comes to my defense. "She adds stuff."

"Enough," I beg, laughing at myself. "Riley, can we wait until we get into the new place? Then I would love any direction you can give me, but I know you're busy with school."

"Oh!" Riley jumps in. "With you so close to Emma and Jas, we can do some dinners over there when you move. I can come over early and we can work on them together! Now, can we back up to where you asked me to be your Maid of Honor!?!"

"Will you?" I openly smile at her.

"Yes! Oh, my God! So excited!" She pauses for a minute. "Wait, can I go shopping with you all on Sunday? I can help you decide on your dress. Gunner, can we all go to Boise together? Make a day of it?"

He nuzzles into her hair, slightly nodding as he settles his face into the crook of her neck. I think that's his agreement, I can't imagine him ever saying no to something she was excited about.

"Give me my goddamn phone back, you bitch!" Frank's roar is suddenly heard from the hallway, causing the room to go dead silent. Diamond comes darting out ahead of him.

"I know you're still fucking her!" She screeches for all to hear. Quickly looking around, Diamond runs toward Vice, who is sitting in a dark corner. "Here! There's a 'no contact' on Deb, but he is, look in here and take this asshole's cut."

Frank grabs Diamond's wrist as she's tossing the phone to Vice. There's an obscenely loud snap before she cries out, falling to her knees. Vice's face is frozen. What I hadn't seen at first was that he's getting a blowjob, but he grabs for the phone, only slowing its descent as it hits the booth beside him.

Every other Northern Grizzlie in the room shoots forward at the sound of Diamond's arm breaking.

Gunner is arguably the slowest, and only because he gently sets Riley in the seat that Jake vacates, before moving in. Frank is literally tackled and Diamond is lifted out of the fray. An older man I haven't met is soon shouting orders for Diamond's care.

"What..." I don't even know how to phrase my question to Riley.

"Roy is great. He'll take care of Diamond. Frank, I don't know what they'll do. Deb stole from them, they let her walk. But she was supposed to go away and not speak to or about any Northern Grizzlie again. If he's still involved with her..." She bites off the end of her sentence, looking at me earnestly. "These aren't men you cross. You don't break your vows around here, Charlie."

"But isn't Frank..."

"Son of a bitch!" Frank screams, so I break off my question. My head snaps from Riley back over to the men, it's immediately clear that Gunner just broke Frank's arm in an act of instant retaliation for Diamond's arm.

Turning back to Riley, she is looking at her lap, her face pale. "Gunner's the Sergeant at Arms, Charlie."

"Frank, you're confined to your room until Jasper calls church. Prospects alternate guard duty," Vice commands, still trying to get his penis back in his pants. Jesus Christ, but that thing always seems to be swinging around out here.

CHAPTER TWENTY-ONE

EILEEN RILEY

I HAVE TO SAY THAT I WAS MORE THAN MILDLY interested in my granddaughter's latest request. Etiquette and basic deportment lessons for her new friend. Wanting to know more about this creature before she arrived on my doorstep, I had Rogers look into her.

Her background was about what I had expected, based on Riley's request. Her career choice baffled me, but the little fact that Riley excluded nearly knocked me over. That this friend of hers is apparently in a ménage relationship. Now I simply have to meet this Charlie.

"Good Lord, child!" I unexpectedly blurt out when Riley leads her into my parlor.

I'd like to think that not a lot surprises me, but the beauty with an ample bosom that trails behind Riley is not at all what I expected. She is dressed plainly, black pants and a wine-colored scalloped top, her hair is neatly braided, and at most, she has lip gloss on.

Riley greets me warmly and introduces Charlie. I'm taken aback by her already. Most strangers enter this house and gawk at the details. Her eyes haven't left my face, and the intelligence I see within them is undeniable. This I can work with, I decide immediately. She'll have nothing to feel self-conscious about at that wedding she's attending.

"It's nice to meet you, Mrs. Riley," she starts softly. "I appreciate you taking the time."

"First of all, call me 'gram'. You are correct though, anyone you are introduced to from close to my generation should be addressed as Mr., Mrs., Dr., what have you, until they give you permission otherwise." I nod. "Now, please sit down and tell me what you know about this event you are attending. And will both young men be attending with you or just your fiancé?"

Charlie nearly jumps up from the chair she had perched on, throwing a startled glance at Riley, who looks equally shocked.

"Riley, close your mouth, dear. You'll need to help me set examples for Charlie while she's here." I pause, looking to the young lady in question. "Well?"

"Connal will travel with us and attend a couple of the parties, but not the wedding." She continues straightening her spine with the steel I knew I had spotted in her. She will not cower from my judgment. "Jake and I will be married a week from Monday, they wanted me to be..."

"Protected from a family that will be outraged their

son didn't marry an heiress? Yes, dear, you have a much better chance coming out of this unscathed as his wife than merely a girlfriend." I nod firmly.

"Mrs. Riley?" She looks at me. "I'm not a gold digger, I didn't know about the money. I'm not with Jake and Connal for any other reason than I love them dearly and can imagine what you think of me for that alone. I don't, I mean, I'm not a slut, even if you must think…"

"Enough," I say, slapping my hand down on the arm of my chair. "Riley wouldn't have brought you here if you were either of those things. Furthermore, unless you are hurting someone, you owe no one an explanation nor an apology for how you choose to live your life. You're certain about your choice?" Charlie nods immediately. "Then keep your head held high, especially when you're in a room full of society people. Do not flinch."

I move us to the dining room where Rogers has laid out every piece of silverware that Charlie might encounter. Her eyes grow large, but she manages to keep up with the instructions I give along with hints to help her remember everything.

"Now, I'm aware of Bree's wedding tomorrow, but tell me about your matrimonial plans. A week from Monday, you said?" I ask over dessert.

"Yes, Riley has us over for dinner on Mondays. Jake and I got a license and Jasper will marry us. Mack, he was friends with my grandfather and knows Connal through the MC, he's going to come and give me away."

"In Riley's living room?" My word. They are trying to give me a heart attack.

"Yes." She smiles at me, her eyes alight with excitement.

"No." I place my spoon down on the saucer and look at them. "You'll be married here. Riley's apartment is fine to have a weekly dinner in, but, well, never mind. The living room will be prepared. You can get dressed upstairs and I'll have someone come to take care of your hair. What kind of flowers do you favor?"

The child bursts into tears. Riley only hesitates a moment before going to her and wrapping her in a hug.

"Why would you? You don't know me..." she gasps out at last. "Thank you, but I don't want to inconvenience you."

"Charlie." I reach out to take her hand. "You'll be married here. If my Riley was alone in the world, all I could hope for would be for others to extend kindness to her. I won't do any less than that for a friend of hers.

"Now, Riley, I'll want a list of those attending and what ingredients will be needed for the dinner. I will leave that to you but we'll have servers and a proper bar." I pause. "Charlie, you aren't exactly conventional so I hope you'll take my next suggestion in the way it's meant. Women always want to wear a white dress. It's foolish and your skin tone is much to pale. If you must, I'd say a champagne or silver color, but with your eyes, think about blue."

Riley draws back from her, looking like she's going to tell me to mind my beeswax, but Charlie stops her. Actually, her laugh stops us both.

"Oh, Mrs. Riley, look at my hands! They're always slightly tinged with oil no matter what I do, so white would be silly. I've always wanted a fancy blue dress. I'm so happy you said that!" Getting up, she throws her arms around me. "I was so scared when I walked in here. And when I realized you knew about, well, about my men, I nearly peed myself.

Before you told me I could call you 'gram'? May I? Riley, would that bother you?" she adds, looking back to my granddaughter.

"Charlie, I told you we'd be best friends. Now you'll be my sister instead!" Riley squeezes her shoulder and Charlie looks back to me.

"Settled," I say, refusing to cry. "However, in the future, please do not discuss 'pee' in the dining room. Now, it's late for me and I'm sure you have a party to get to, so let this old lady get some rest. Email Rogers the details." I dismiss them, before enduring another round of hugs and kisses.

CONNAL

The clubhouse is full and the party is raging. I look around knowing half the group won't make it to the wedding at this rate. Flint refuses to be separated from Bree tonight. They're hand in hand making their way around to talk to everyone. Flint's got quite a following with other MCs, so there are reps from all the friendly regional groups in the house tonight.

Really, I'm just twitchy waiting on Charlie to get here, nervous about how tonight might have gone with Riley's grandmother. I only met her briefly when Riley had been taken and she seems pretty heavily starched.

Suddenly the conversation near the door cuts off and Gunner is pushing me. He's a bit taller than I am, allowing him to see our women enter immediately. Jake was near the bar listening to an animated Wrench but turned without a word when he saw her enter. I don't slow my stride even after I see Jake kiss her. Riley is stuck behind her with her eyes locked on Gunner. He shoves a guy without a cut aside to get to her. I move through his path quicker than I could have created one, and I soon have my lips latched onto Charlie's neck as Jake devours her mouth.

She turns to me, one arm still around Jake, laughing into my mouth but submitting to my need.

"Mrs. Riley," she gasps, coming up for air. "She's hosting our wedding. She was wonderful. She said she's my *gram* now also."

Charlie is vibrating, not just with her desire for us, but over Riley's grandmother's reception of her. As Jake pulls her close, I look over and mouth 'Thank you' to Riley, who is tightly held to Gunner's side.

"Still in ten days, though?" I hear Jake ask her and realize I missed something.

"Yes! The wedding will be in her living room, and she's getting flowers and someone to do my hair." Charlie gushes.

"No make-up, Charlie…" I start.

"Just a touch," Riley cuts in. "She doesn't need much."

"She's perfect without it," Jake says, nuzzling into her neck.

"Jake, get drinks. Let's move. They're being eyed here." Gunner growls. "Too many I don't know."

"Shots and beer!" Riley calls out before Gunner maneuvers us past the bar.

Moving back, we stand to the side near Betsy, Russian, Amy, and Wrench, and I see Gunner's point. Even with all the honey holes and random chicks who came in for the pre-celebration, Riley and Charlie stand out. By the morning, any woman who isn't a steady girlfriend or Ol' Lady will be tossed out first thing. Charlie only has the slightest hint of cleavage, but the contrast of her cut on top of her shirt accentuates her *bounty*.

Russian has his hands full. Even with Betsy wearing his Property cut, too many outsiders recognize her face and move towards her before noticing his claim. Without being obvious, Gunner and I block her from the crowd, warning them off. Emma makes an appearance but is obviously exhausted from her pregnancy. The women, including Bree, go to spend time with her in Jasper's quiet, smoke-free office.

"Betsy looks mighty fine in your cut, Russian," Flint says. "Should have happened a long time ago."

"Well, we all got shit to get over, don't we?" he responds, shrugging. "Water under the bridge."

"Hear there's another wedding right after ours?" Flint adds next. Everyone's head turns to Gunner who's lighting up, what's become for him, a rare cigarette.

"Don't look at me, can't get a fucking chance to get

to it with all this other shit going on." Gunner exhales, tilting his head towards Jake.

"Wait?" Wrench asks. He looks at me, unsure of saying anything that'd be taken wrong. "She'll be your wife but still…"

"We want her protected, especially if she gets pregnant. Jake marrying her seemed like the right call." I explain, shrugging. After a slight pause, we both get pats on the back.

"So many children around here, gonna need to open a nursery," Flint laughs.

"Truth," Russian says, a wide grin crossing his face.

"Fuck! Really, Russian?" Wrench asks. "That's great!"

"It's early. I wasn't supposed to say anything," he responds, accepting all of our slugs to his arm.

"Oh God," Wrench looks panicked. "Amy's with them, I gotta go get her or she's gonna want another child!" He pushes me aside and plows past the crowd to get to Jasper's office, obviously terrified of adding to their brood.

JAKE

Russian and I share an amused look, watching Wrench run off.

"We'll be out of the apartment next Monday, if you and Betsy are still thinking of moving there," I tell him.

"Yeah, we worked it out with Bree. That'll give us time to figure out something more permanent." He slaps me on the back. "I've got a run coming up but the prospects are lined up to clean it and move our things over there. That kid, Madda? He's got his shit together but I want to get him working out. He'd get his ass kicked in a fight right now..." Russian starts but trails off suddenly.

All of our Ol' Ladies have emerged en masse from the hallway. They look like they've been crying so as a group, we surge forward to meet them. Wrench follows them, shaking his head, with an arm around Amy.

"Baby?" I ask, pulling Charlie into us. Her answer is cut off by Riley's response to Gunner's own inquiry.

"I don't want to wait. I thought I did but I want to get married. No babies, yet, just us...you can ask me any time. It's stupid of me to worry about it happening on top of everyone else's news," Riley babbles, barely noticing Gunner pulling a ring from his pocket.

"You're mine, Riley. I've known it since I first saw you. Let's make it forever?" His gravelly voice stops all noise around us as he drops to one knee in front of her.

Sighs burst forth from all the women, a loud sob escaping Riley as she wraps herself around Gunner and plants her head into his neck. Unwinding her arm to slide an antique looking ring onto her ring finger, he then easily stands and walks toward the door with her still attached to him. "Taking that as a 'Yes', sweetheart."

"Looks like we may end up with a double wedding," Connal interjects, our heads tilted down toward Charlie's.

"Oh! That would be great," she sighs.

"Guess Riley won't be baking that wedding cake for

us though." She stomps Connal's foot at his comment. "Ouch! Charlie! I was kidding, kind of..."

"Come on, I want you both so badly," Charlie murmurs, tugging us forward. With no complaints from us, we say our goodbyes.

CHAPTER TWENTY-TWO

JAKE

THE WEDDING THE NEXT DAY IS LARGE AND fun. Bree's nephew walks her up the aisle to Flint, with Riley as the Maid of Honor and Flint's son standing up for him. There's a sharp contrast between their blood relatives and the MC brethren, but with so many families present, the reception doesn't get out of control and fun is had by all.

Connal and I both notice that Charlie is a bit off so we leave as evening falls.

"I'm sorry, guys." She sighs against my chest in the backseat of the SUV. "I don't know why I'm so tired."

"Shhh," I whisper. "We'll get you to bed, big day of shopping tomorrow." I remind her, getting a groan from Connal. He's made his preference for avoiding all of my family's parties known but will attend to be close to Charlie.

———

Luckily, Charlie seems perky the next morning. At least that's my impression when I wake up to her alternating her mouth between my cock and Connal's.

"Jesus Fuck, Charlie," he moans. "I love feeling your sweet little mouth sucking my dick so hard!"

"Move closer," she breathes out, shifting from Connal's cock back to mine. "Make it easy for a girl, will ya?" He immediately moves closer to me. I'm too busy enjoying the feel of her tongue wrapped around the tip of my dick to register her comment.

When she shifts back off of me to give him more loving, I sit up, getting into position behind her. I pull her hips up and quickly sink my middle finger into her pussy. It's dripping wet as luck would have it.

"Gonna be a rough ride, baby," I moan, slamming my cock into her before she understands my warning. "Need your sweet pussy so bad. Went to bed starving for you."

She arches her head back as she screams for me when I hit her cervix and immediately withdraw. Her hips move to meet my next thrust. I smile, reaching down to push her head back onto Connal's dick. From the noises he's making, he's close, and I know I can't hold out long this morning. I reach around her hip, locating her clit, pinching and rubbing that sensitive bundle as I shift to hit her G-spot with each thrust of my cock.

Connal falls silent as she swallows his load. Her

moaning getting louder as I start to spray my release into her, has her looking back at me.

"Don't you dare stop, I NEED it!" Charlie yells at me, so I continue to pound into her as I come, ignoring the slurping sounds of our mingled juices. Connal reaches for her nipples, a sure-fire way to send her over the edge.

"Fuck." Charlie sighs as she collapses, her shuddering tunnel massaging the last of my seed out of my dick.

None of us move for long moments after Charlie's release, we're all lying at a weird angle to the other and perfectly happy. Shifting my head, I bite her ass cheek before kissing it. Looking at the red marks left by my teeth, I start to consider a more permanent mark, one for my body to symbolize our love. Not a lot of real estate left, but I'll work on something.

"So, breakfast?" Connal asks.

"I'll text Riley then jump in the shower. Ray's before we hit the road?" Charlie asks sliding off the bed, Connal quickly follows her. Our new shower will have space for all of us; this one not so much. So I just lay back and wait for them to clean up.

FLINT

I never thought I'd marry again. Waking up the next morning, seeing Bree sacked out next to me, her wedding dress over a chair across the room, my heart just expands. I thread my fingers through hers, "Ouch!"

"Dammit, Ragnar!" I yell at the dog that just

jumped up to wake Bree like he always does. She giggles, snuggling closer to me but giving her baby belly rubs. Fucking dog. I mean I think he's great, but...

"Let me go feed him and let him out, then I'll come back for some more 'hide the bone' with you!" she says, wiggling her ass against my morning wood. I growl into her neck.

"I'll go. Me and him gotta come to an understanding about these early ass mornings." I say, rolling off the bed to find some pants. "Come on, Ragnar!"

A new wife and dog at my age, I think shaking my head. Nothing could make me any fucking happier.

CHARLIE

"Congrats you two!" Margie is hovering over Riley as I slide into the booth across from her. "Let me see the ring!"

God only knows how Margie found out about Riley's engagement already, but she takes time to ooh and aah over her ring. It really is something with three small sapphires embedded in a silver band.

"About time, Gunner," Margie winks at the table. "Lotta weddings happening nowadays."

"Yes!" Riley says. "Jake and Charlie are getting married next week."

"Oh? Jake and Charlie are, huh?" Marge replies, giving a hard look to Connal, who's sitting with his arm wrapped around me while Jake has pulled a chair up to the head of the booth.

"Riley," I start as soon as the waitress moves on. "I'm open to a double wedding, if...I mean, we're getting married at your Gram's and all..."

"No, Charlie," Riley smiles at me. "You get your day, and Gunner and I will get married next month when you're back from the East Coast."

"I got some Corps buddies I'm inviting, and my half-sisters," Gunner contributes. "Besides, Mrs. R will murder us if she doesn't have time to prepare. We talked to her this morning and she said your wedding will be a great practice run."

Moving on from the wedding topic, we eat and talk, all eager to get on the road. Rolling into Boise around lunchtime, we go directly to meet with the personal shopper Jake set up for me.

"Gonna leave you to it, baby." He nuzzles my neck before he, Connal, and Gunner go to look at suits. "She's got my card number; don't you worry about anything."

"Riley?!" Comes a high-pitched voice as we're about to enter the dressing room.

"Crap," she mumbles. "Hi, Mother."

My head spins around, and indeed, I'm looking at a younger version of Riley's grandmother. She's got some inches on her daughter and complete *resting bitch face*. I'm saddened by the mask that comes over Riley's face, one I've seen many times on the foster kids I was raised around.

"Take that vest off immediately," she demands, her eyes flick to me, quickly taking my measure and dismissing me before she glances around us. "What if someone sees you?"

"Then they'll know I'm an Ol' Lady," Riley calmly replies. "I was going to call you tomorrow. Gunner and I are engaged, the wedding will be at Gram's house next month. Would you like to come?"

"That's Mom's ring!" Mrs. Maddock nearly snarls, noticing Riley's left ring finger.

"Yes, she gave it to Gunnar when he asked for permission to marry me. This is my friend Charlie, Mother." Riley completely ignores her mother's ire. "She's getting married next week…"

"To another gangbanger by the looks of her!" her mom hisses, without looking at me again.

"Hey!" I start before Riley catches my eye and shakes her head. I turn, not caring if her mother sees the two names on my cut and move towards the dressing room where the personal shopper is standing frozen, having a near panic attack after hearing the exchange.

"Back off." Riley glares at her mother. "Actually, why don't you walk away like you've been doing my whole life?" She turns away from her to follow me into the large room.

"What?" Her mother sees which dressing room we have and turns on the saleslady. "Excuse me, you must be new here. My selections are always brought to me in that room."

The personal shopper is nearly trembling as Riley walks into my dressing room closing the door on her mother's words.

"Ms. Scott's fiancé requested it previously. No one

knew you'd be here, Mrs. Maddock. It's all set up for Ms. Scott." She babbles as I embrace Riley, trying to comfort her yet not saying a word that could be overheard outside the room.

"Get started, Charlie. I'm ok, just didn't expect to see her." Riley squeezes me tightly before releasing me.

The next hour is spent laughing at the hideous and deciding between all the outfits Jake thinks I'll need for the wedding, plus a dress for my own day. Finally, I collapse knowing I've now spent more on clothes and shoes in this one day than I have my entire life, but mostly relieved it won't be a common occurrence.

Finishing up, we text the guys to come help with all the bags. Throwing my arms around Jake, I beg him for one promise.

"Please don't ever make me shop again?!"

"Deal, baby." He kisses me. "Well, maybe for lingerie every so often?"

"Yes!" Connal agrees. "Gonna need a lot of that!"

"Only 'cause you two keep tearing mine off!" I exclaim to their delight, blushing when I realize how loud my voice was.

CHAPTER TWENTY-THREE

CONNAL

Besides the hiccup of Riley running into her mother, the day and following week fly by. Charlie works hard beside Royce and me at the garage. Royce is only, accidentally, wounded twice that week.

Jake, Charlie, and I are all sleep deprived at this point. We can't keep our hands off of her and she eagerly reaches for us whenever she wakes up. Waking up early to start licking Charlie or waking from her tongue wrapped around our cocks has become our life.

Monday morning, Jake wakes up first and goes to town on our girl. I wake to her grabbing my arm, her moans and pleas for release make me instantly hard. Seeing his mouth has her pussy monopolized, I move up and nudge my cock into her mouth.

Opening eagerly, she takes as much of me in as she can. Moistening my dick, she grips the base with her small hand while swirling her tongue around the helmet, flicking the ridges. As Jake brings her to orgasm, her moans vibrate around my cock, driving me insane while I try to hold my release back.

Jake leans up, eager to slide his dick into her core while she's coming. I suddenly feel her knees in the small of my back as he spreads her wide open for him. Thrusting hard, it doesn't take him long to come. Having her sweet pussy contract all over our cocks does that to us every time.

As soon as Jake pulls out and rolls over to her side, I move back and keeping her legs up like Jake had them, I line my cock up to her wet slit. Charlie moans as I slowly slide into her, inch by inch. Her orgasm had started to subside but my dick seems to start it off again. I massage her clit, just like her tight sheath is massaging my length and she wraps her legs around my waist.

"Connal, come in me. Now, please, it's too much, I can't…" she moans for me. I languorously stroke into her, not giving in to her pleas or the need I see on her face. Slowly enjoying her wet heat, I eventually feel my balls tighten and long streams of my jizz shoot into her.

Jake lies at her side, his arm wrapped around her, watching with half-closed eyes, still breathing heavily as our girl takes this second load of hot cum into her womb.

I finally draw back. Fucking love that she comes so hard for us. I cover her body with my own and she clings to me.

"Hey, baby," Jake's voice breaks through my haze. "What is it?"

I hadn't realized she was crying and feel like an ass. Looking down at her, she shakes her head and draws him towards us. I shift so we're shoulder to shoulder looking down at her.

"Shit, baby girl!" I whimper, terrified I did something she didn't like. "Please tell me I didn't hurt you."

"I'm happy," she finally croaks out with a shaky breath. "I'm sorry."

Exhaling in relief, I lean down to start spreading kisses along the closest side of her face to me.

"Scared us, Charlie," Jake whispers, caressing her cheek. "We don't mean to get carried away like this, and not ask..."

"It's so fucking hot." She grins up at him while placing a kiss on my forehead. "I mean, I'm a bit of a mess down there now, but I like having both of you without a break. Both of your cum in me." She looks away almost shyly and stops talking.

"I love you so much, dirty girl," I chuckle, and she shoves at my chest. "Hate seeing your tears though."

"Tonight will be both of you, won't it?" she asks, blushing heavily. "How, um, I don't know what you'll want me to do?"

"We wanted to both be in you tonight...after the wedding, in our new home," Jake starts. "Think you're up for us at the same time, baby?"

Her cheeks flame even brighter as she nods in agreement.

"Maybe I should have that plug you got me in during the wedding, so I'll be ready?" she whispers while focusing on running her fingers through my chest hair.

We both groan and collapse. Charlie so fucking gets us.

"Now how the holy fuck am I supposed to sit through the dinner with that image in my head?" I finally ask, getting her giggles in reply.

"That's easy." She and Jake exchange big grins. "Riley's red velvet cake!"

"Good point," I concede, laughing with them. "But don't think we aren't dragging you out of there as soon as we can."

I head out to check things at the garage, leaving Charlie to relax before Riley picks her up for girl stuff before the wedding.

JAKE

After Connal heads out, I sit down with Charlie to go over the prenup and my will. I try to explain the funds that I have and other accounts that will be transferred to me when I turn forty, but she's not interested and starts pacing around the room like every word I say is painful.

"Tell me what you want me to sign, Jake." She finally takes the pen, her eyes welling with tears. "This is stupid, I don't want your money. I'll sign off on whatever you want me to."

"Stop and listen to me, Charlie. Some of these items, the attorney forced on me and I want you to be aware of them." I hold her wrist, gaining her attention. She finally settles down and I explain how cheating is only defined as someone other than Connal. That would be grounds for divorce with no alimony, just a pre-set amount for child support, based on joint custody.

"You and Connal are it for me, Jake." Charlie looks defensively up at me. "I'm scared of you two walking away from me."

"Not happening. Staying right where I belong." I hold her chin and try to reassure her. "Besides, if you'll listen to me, if you'll look at this it says if I cheat on you, you get everything. All the money I'm entitled to from my family."

"But without you? Or without Connal? Why would I care?" The tears that she was holding back flood over her lids.

At that, she yanks the pen back from me and signs at all the sticky notes that were left as markers.

"Jake, about children." She climbs onto my lap, kissing me lightly. "I want to give at least one to each of you, so…"

"So, after we know who fathered our first child and you're ready to carry another one, either Connal or I will be the star of the show until we got you knocked up." I give her my most lecherous grin.

She narrows her eyes and tries to keep a serious tone and straight face. "Well, that, but without making me sound like a broodmare."

"And our third child?" I ask, getting a groan from her.

"Let's see how we do with two? But I think random, like our first, would make sense?" Charlie has been lightly kissing my neck and I groan, noticing the time. "See you tonight?" she asks, as I begrudgingly move her from my lap.

"Wouldn't miss it," I grin.

Walking out, I make the call I've been putting off.

"Hey, Gramps," I start as soon as he answers.

"Jarrett, how are you?" he instantly replies.

"Good. Really good. I sent the RSVP back last week and called Blaine but I haven't heard back," I start.

"Yes, apparently, you bringing a date has upset Muffy. It seems she promised her bridesmaids, you and your trust fund would be available," he responds dryly.

"Well, that's why I'm calling you actually. Charlie and I are getting married tonight." My statement is met with silence.

"She's pregnant?" he asks, after a moment.

"Not that I know of, but I'm trying awfully hard," I respond in a rigid voice. "She signed a prenup this morning, didn't even care to listen to me explain about the Trusts. I made a will to include her also."

"Does she work?" he asks but quickly adds. "Don't get angry, could you at least tell me about her?"

"Yes, she's a mechanic. She works in Connal's garage. She's beautiful, Gramps." I pause. "She's had a hard go. Her father died before she was born, her mom died before she was eight, then her grandfather took her in but he had a heart attack when she was thirteen. It was foster care until she turned eighteen. Her grandfather was a mechanic and showed her the ropes. She went through training after high school then ended up here."

"Her name is Charlie?"

"Charles Scott, actually. Her mom named her after her father." This statement is once again met with silence, so I continue. "She's only twenty, so I'm robbing the cradle a bit, but she's sweet and proud and funny. She's an awful cook, but great at her job and works hard."

"I'm not accustomed to you talking so much, Jarre...Jake," he replies, remembering to use my nickname this time. "Charles Scott, hmmm."

"Connal says she's made me verbose. And, it'll be Charles Forsythe soon enough," I laugh. "Ah, there's a well-to-do woman in town, a friend's grandmother. She's been showing Charlie how to navigate Blaine's wedding... Charlie was worried about embarrassing me. Not that that matters to me."

"No, I don't think you'd care if her manners shocked everyone. Will you send me pictures from tonight?" he asks next. "You know I just want the best for you."

That resolved, I hang up.

———

Before I know it, I'm standing between Jasper and Connal in Mrs. Riley's living room and the soon-to-be Mrs. Forsythe is walking towards me as Mack glares at Connal and me from her side. He had already cornered me to threaten my balls if I hurt her. It wasn't easy keeping a straight face as I nodded in reply.

Our baby has a trick up her sleeve. It's revealed as soon as Jasper starts the ceremony.

"Today, Charles, Jake, and Connal stand before us, committing themselves to each other. While I can only legally bind two of them, there's no doubt from those in this room that these three are committed to each other. Charlie, please start with the vows you wrote."

"I, Charles Scott take you, Jarrett Forsythe to be my husband and you, Connal McKay to be my husband in my heart. I will bind my life to yours, build our dreams together, and support you both through times of trouble. I promise to give you respect, love, and loyalty through all the trials and triumphs of our lives together. This commitment is made in love, kept in faith, lived in hope, and made new every day of our lives." Our beautiful wife is beaming at us as she recites her vows, and I see Connal wiping his eye at being included.

"Now I need you two to recite after me," Jasper says before feeding us standard vows, witnessing as we both bind ourselves to her.

Mrs. Riley looks like she'll faint when we take turns kissing the bride. And Mack is still glowering at us.

CHAPTER TWENTY-FOUR

CHARLIE

TONIGHT HAS BEEN A WHIRLWIND. FROM walking down the aisle all the way through dessert, I could not stop smiling. Riding to our new home, holding onto Jake as we ride across town as Connal keeps pace next to us on his bike, I still can't believe the turn my life has taken.

Arriving at our new home, Connal helps me off the bike as I'm clumsy in my dress. He waits for Jake to sweep me up in his arms before unlocking the door. Walking straight to the bedroom before setting me down, he eagerly unzips my dress.

"Did we tell you how beautiful you look?" Connal checks again.

"Once or twice." I smile and lean up to kiss him.

"You really didn't mind us in our cuts?" Jake murmurs against my neck.

"And start the rest of our marriage by making you

both miserable?" I click my tongue at them. "Now, I have something I want to go slip into."

"No," Jake growls, pulling my back flush against his chest.

"Ain't fucking waiting another minute, baby girl." Connal steps towards me, reaching forward to slip my nipples out of the cups of my bra.

"Show us another time," Jake whispers as his tongue outlines the shell of my ear. He presses his thick cock into my back as Connal kneels to start licking my nipples. "All I want is your tight, wet pussy wrapped around my dick, riding me hard, WIFE."

Pulling me onto the bed, Jake leans over me and we start kissing like teenagers. Alternating between pecks and long intense kisses, only parting when we need air. He drops kisses around my face and neck, making me giggle. Connal goes looking for lube, nudging my legs apart upon his return.

"You smell so fucking good," he groans before he starts to lick my clit. Fingering my pussy, he sucks my nub into his mouth while spreading my juices around with his fingers. "This all for us, baby girl?"

"Mmmm" Is all I'm able to get out.

"Here, Charlie," Jake reaches down to stretch my knee up, giving Connal better access to the plug that has been in my asshole since before the ceremony. After a few teasing taps to the base, Connal finally tugs it from my rosebud.

Without a chance to feel empty, he starts thrusting his finger in and out of my rosebud. "Please!" Is the only word I'm able to form as his mouth and the plug work to get me off. Jake holds me tight, caressing my breasts and plying me with his gentle kisses, pushing me over the edge.

My orgasm has barely subsided when I push Jake back, lining his throbbing length up to my gushing slit, I slide down onto him.

"Now!" I cry, looking back to Connal. "Both of you."

Connal pours lube into his hand then strokes his cock, Jake pulls me down flat onto his chest. Spreading his legs wider apart, I keep each of my legs on the outside of his to give Connal space to move into position.

"Just relax, baby, we'll make it good for you," my husband says, kissing my forehead then nods at Connal over my shoulder. Connal grips each cheek, opening me and I instantly feel his velvety head pushing at my entrance, nudging gently into me as I force myself to push out. He pushes in, inch by inch, finally slamming in the final inches.

"Oh FUCK!" I moan. My body feels so full and I'm about to ask them to give me a moment when Jake sneezes, his dick shifting inside me.

"Sorry!" he calls out.

"Oh God! More, I thought I wanted you still, but I need more movement. Now. I need..." I babble on like I'm possessed.

Connal chuckles warmly and starts to slowly withdraw. Jake's mouth finds mine and all thoughts fly out of my head as they fall into a rhythm. A perfect rhythm. Their hands caressing my body, their grunts and moans

music to my soul. I give myself fully over to the pleasure of feeling them move within me, of them moving
me to bring us all to our pleasure.

Only a thin membrane separates their cocks, and
the intensity of feeling them thrusting into my body
builds quickly and harder than anything I've ever felt.
My next orgasm hits and it doesn't seem to end, my
contractions pull Connal and Jake to their finishes, and
while, on some level, I register the feeling of cum
shooting up into me, I simply wilt onto Jake's chest.

CONNAL

In my whole fucking existence, I've never felt the like.
I've never felt so connected, so needy, so fucking good.
Our tough, innocent woman has completed me. I want
to beat my chest like a Neanderthal at the look on her
face as she rests on Jake's chest. I slowly withdraw and
moving down, I gently kiss her sweet ass, while all I
really want to do is bite into it.

Moving to the new bathroom, I come back with
washcloths and a towel. Giving Charlie a few minutes,
Jake gradually lifts her up and moves her to the toilet.
Coming to the door to give her privacy, he gives me a
look. I know he felt everything I did. Before either of us
can think of how to express ourselves, Charlie's arm is
sliding around his waist.

"I want more, but I don't think I can right now."
She smiles softly at us. Jake swings her up into his
arms.

"Good thing we have the rest of our lives then,

Wife." He laughs and deposits her into the center of the bed.

I roll over to her as she snuggles under the covers, giggling at Jake's antics.

"I'm not your 'baby' anymore?" She watches him crawl across the bed towards us.

"You'll always be our 'baby', Charles," I say while teasing her nipples. Jake reaches down to pull the covers over her. "Now, rest up, we all have tomorrow off, and I'm sure Jake would love to feel your tight ass around his cock."

"I love you," she says, pulling us both close, all of about three seconds before she starts her delicate snores.

"Goddamn, Connal," Jake whispers. "If she left us tomorrow, I'd never have sex again. Nothing could ever top that. She was so…"

"I hear ya. She's…fuck, I don't know how to say it either. She's everything, just everything." I sigh. Charlie snorts in her sleep and rolls into me, Jake moves over to spoon her.

"You're right, we probably didn't need a bed this big," he says before drifting off.

———

The next morning is a shit show. We're woken up by sirens.

Sheriff Michaels is on the front porch, hat in hand, explaining about a search warrant to check all the deliveries that had been made for the home remodel in the past three weeks. The build-out supplies are being checked—and by that, I mean ransacked—by the State Police.

Before I can pull out my phone, Michaels lets me know that Jasper and Gunner's places—both across the road from us—are being searched as well.

The MC's lawyer is running ragged. Jake is livid, so he calls the lawyer who handled his will and prenup. After five minutes of growling at the poor guy, he calls his grandfather on the East Coast. I know they're rich but don't understand how he could help.

Twenty minutes after that call, the State Police are apologizing to Gunner, Jasper, and us. There's a hard stop from searching any of our properties. Jasper was hit the hardest, especially since he has upset twins to deal with, besides Emma being pregnant.

"Fucking Maddocks won't back off," Gunner fumes, lighting up a smoke on Jasper's front porch. "Shit, they're hitting all of us, over and over again. And god-fucking-damn these things taste like crap now." He scowls at his cigarette before stomping it under his heel.

"Look, Jake...I'm sorry you had to make the call you did. I know...well...I'm sure it sucked, and I owe you," Gunner starts. "It's just the foundation for the house is supposed to get laid today and I want everything perfect for my sweetheart. Those fuckers won't stop though."

"Gunner. Jasper," Jake starts. "You all are family to Connal, Charlie, and me. I fucking hated calling my gramps, but he's got the DC connections that the

Maddocks can only dream about. They can't rile up Jasper's family at that hour, your workshop, or our wife. They need to slow their roll. Just keep my call *in the circle*, ok?"

"Thing is, Jake." I look up at him. "Now the Maddocks are going to wonder who, in their backyard, has more power than they do."

Jake's eyes harden like I've never seen, not even in battle. "No one threatens my—our, family or home."

CHAPTER TWENTY-FIVE

A couple weeks later

CONNAL

"I'M SO EXCITED," CHARLIE SQUEALS FOR THE ninth time. We're heading to Jake's brother's wedding and while I know she's nervous about meeting his people, she's never flown before and is bouncing.

Unknown to us, Jake bought First Class seats for us so we have plenty of room as the seat next to me is empty. Halfway through the flight, Charlie moves to sit next to me, throwing the flight attendants into a panic as we start kissing as passionately as she was with Jake. His blasé manner helps to calm their nerves.

Disembarking and claiming our luggage, we're immediately met by his grandfather's driver, putting us on our best behavior for the ride to his hometown.

"Gotta let me hold onto this for a bit, baby," Jake says as he pulls Charlie's Property cut off, getting a pout in return. He usually folds every time her bottom lip extends, so he quickly compromises with her. "Wear it to bed for us?"

"Of course," Charlie says, satisfied but is quickly distracted by the surrounding area. "Should I change? Are jeans really ok to meet your gramps in? Fuck. I know he's not royalty, Jake, I'm sorr…"

"Shush." Jake cups her cheek. "Charlie, he's gonna love you. Like we do. Now, the rest of the family might be, well, with the wedding and them not knowing I got married. Just know I love you, right?"

Jake no sooner finishes that statement than the limo stops and the door is being opened by an older man. I've met him before and immediately greet him.

"Mr. Forsythe, nice to see you," I say, as I exit the car first.

"Connal, yes. Where is she?" He practically pushes me aside, quickly seeing Charlie behind me. "Oh, Jake. She's everything you said."

"Nice to meet you, Mr. Forsythe," she replies as he helps her out of the car.

"How are you a mechanic and not a model?" Forsythe asks her, making her blush and laugh. "Call me gramps, please? Like Jarrett does. Oh, wait, Jake. Like Jake does."

"I can't believe your home, it's so beautiful," she says ignoring his question. He gushes over her, almost oblivious to Jake and I, as he escorts us all through the main entrance and out to the pool where he shows us to the guest house.

"The fridge in here has been stocked. If there's

anything else you would like simply dial one on the house phone in the kitchen. Mrs. Donna is my house-keeper and will help you while staying out of your hair. Speaking of hair, there's a stylist coming two hours before the party tonight and the wedding tomorrow..." Jake's grandfather rattles on.

Without thinking, Charlie reaches for my hand as I walk beside her. I quickly sidestep her, making sure Mr. F. didn't see it. Jake steps up and wraps her arm through his.

"Now I'll leave you to get settled. Oh, I haven't told anyone your news, thought it would be more fun to watch it spread tonight, Jake." He rubs his hands together in mischievous glee and finally stops talking.

The three of us groan at the same time.

"Please tell me Mom is still taking her Prozac?" Jake mutters. Mr. F. is smiling as he leaves us to ourselves.

"So, no one lives in this house? It just sits here?" Charlie asks, her eyebrows drawn together.

"Yup," Jake says walking towards her and reaching for the hem of her shirt. Quickly catching on, I kneel down and take off her shoes. "Later, baby," Jake says, kissing her as she starts to ask another question. "I'll answer one question for each orgasm you have."

"Gotta catch me first!" Charlie squeals before darting away from us. We pull our shirts off, letting our wife get a head start.

"Ready or not, here we come," I call out to her and fist bumping Jake, we take off in pursuit. The little minx throws us diversions, turning on a shower in one bathroom and closing the door to the master but Jake finally finds her behind the guest room door, her giggles giving her away.

The next hour finds Jake and me loving or just snuggling our wife, finally settling down for a nap before she has to be ready for the hair and make-up stylist who's coming to take care of her.

———

"Just remember," I say, waking her gently. "No googly eyes for me tonight, baby girl."

"Just remember," she returns, after snorting. "Any woman touches you too much and I'm smashing her hand with my wrench."

"Now, why is that such a fucking turn on?" I ask, picturing it. "Let me be the one to eat your pussy tonight?"

"Maybe," she teases, sucking my bottom lip in. Then we both jump as we hear the doorbell. I quickly slip out of the master bedroom, into my own room, as Jake goes to answer the door.

JAKE

The stylist has left and Connal is sipping a whiskey while we wait for Charlie to emerge from the bedroom. I can't stop pacing; my heart and mind are racing at the thought of introducing *a wife* to my family tonight. My youngest sister, Tabby, will be my strongest ally. She always has been, no matter the time between visits.

I spin, hearing Connal's gasp. FUCK.

"Goddamn, Charlie!" he finally gets out, but I'm still struck mute. She's in a purple cocktail dress and black stilettos, her hair is pinned up on one side, and her eyes have been seriously made-up. She's gonna have every woman at the party ready to claw her eyes out. No joke.

"It's not too much?" she asks, indicating her eye makeup.

"Marry me?" I ask, smiling at her.

"OH SHIT!" She spins back toward the bedroom. "I forgot my ring!" she calls out.

Connal and I laugh. He'd come out of his room without his ring earlier and I sent him back for it. Don't give a fuck if catches anyone's attention.

"Ok, I'm really ready this time." Charlie comes back out and we all make our way to the terrace to join gramps. My parents have already arrived, so holding Charlie's hand I move forward to introduce them. As soon as they spot us, my father's jaw drops but mother's face settles into a frown. Here we go...

"Father, Mother?" I tilt my head in greeting, I wrap an arm around Charlie. "I'd like you to meet my wife, Charlie. Charlie, this is Rick and Elsbeth."

"Wife? Surely you haven't married this girl!" My mother hisses causing Charlie to stiffen. Her face falls from a shy smile to an expressionless mask, as she sucks in a breath.

"Els," my father says, taking her wrist. "Tonight will be pleasant." Gramps comes up to us at this moment.

"Charlie, you are a vision!" Gramps announces, moving to warmly kiss her on her cheek.

"You knew?" Mom turns on him, shifting her simmering wrath onto a new target.

"Charlie?" My father starts, trying to calm the hostile atmosphere. "We look forward to getting to know you. I hope you can forgive our surprise at Jarrett announcing this now?"

"Nice to meet you...both," Charlie replies, reaching her hand out to shake his offered hand. "We had a bit of a whirlwind romance, most days I'm surprised myself," she says, getting a chuckle from my father and grandfather.

"I don't suppose you work, do you, Charlie?" My mother pounces, as though she's ever worked.

"Yes, I'm a mechanic. I work for Connal." She smiles, almost innocently, indicating Connal, who's standing off to our side with his fists clenched. "What do you do, Elsbeth?"

"A mechanic?" Mom hisses again. Dad chokes on his drink and gramps' laugh seems to echo through the night.

"Yes, ma'am." Charlie widens her eyes and looks earnestly at my mother. "I was recently certified and met Jake the day I started working for Connal."

"What an interesting profession, Charlie," my father starts, somehow making 'profession' sound dubious. "Are your parents in Rowansville?"

"No, they died a long time ago. My grandfather was a mechanic. He took care of me for a bit but he died a while back also."

My gramps cuts in, signaling to the tray of champagne flutes that a server has arrived with. "Well, I for one am happy to welcome you to the family, Charlie."

"Welcome who to the family?" A high-pitched voice cuts in. Turning around, I see my brother ushering in a woman I can only guess is his fiancé. I go to shake his hand and am surprised when he embraces me.

"Good to see you, Jarrett," he says. "It's been too long."

I nod, stepping back I extend my hand to the tall brunette by his side. "Muffy?"

"Yes! And Guest of Honor tonight, of course!" Fuck me, she's obnoxious.

"This is my wife, Charlie," I say, reaching back for her, ignoring the shocked look on their faces. "Charlie, this is Blaine and Muffy. Blaine, you've met Connal before. Muffy, Connal and I served together."

"Wife?" Muffy looks miffed. I can't hide my grin.

"Congrats! That's great news, Jarrett!" my brother quickly cuts in.

"Well, that remains to be seen," my mother says before warmly hugging Muffy. "Muffy is an attorney, in family law," she throws over her shoulder to Charlie and me, as she draws Muffy towards the bar, whispering furiously.

"Look at me, baby," I murmur, ignoring Blaine and looking down to Charlie. "Look in my eyes and see how much I love you." Our eyes lock and she leans towards me for a kiss.

"I'm alright, Jake. I'm just sheathing my claws since they're your family," she whispers and winks at me before turning back to make small talk with Blaine.

CHAPTER TWENTY-SIX

CHARLIE

"Yeah, but there might suddenly be a whole crazy series of 'accidents', Jake," Connal says from behind me. "I mean, there is a pool right here…"

"Ha! Well, it would serve them right!" Jake laughs into my ear.

"Accidents?" Jake's father asks.

"Yeah, this other guy who works for me offended Charlie on her first day. Ever since then he's…" Connal is just warming up and Jake is chuckling.

"Please! You know nothing happened on purpose, Connal!" I butt in laughing.

"Now you have to tell us," Blaine jumps in, barely concealing the laughter in his voice.

"Hi, everyone!" A woman who can only be Jake's sister, announces her entrance and that of several other people, saving me as our small group shifts to greet everyone.

His sister, Tabby, is the closest to Jake in coloring but is just about my height with curves she knows how to accentuate. My eyes flick between her and the rest of their siblings; the other five could easily be clones—all tall, blond, and thin. It doesn't take me long to realize that Tabby and Jake have similar personalities, other than the fact she barely stops talking.

"Jake, you really did it!" She laughs gleefully after hearing the news, turning to confide in me. "I always thought I could keep saying 'Well, Jake's not married' to mom's inquiries about my status."

Moving over to stand between us, she quickly starts chattering away. A few moments later, I'm stunned to find out she's an OB/GYN. My jaw drops and Jake starts laughing.

"She's the smartest of all of us, but you'd never guess it," Jake quietly says as I reassess Tabby. "She decided she was going to be a doctor when she was five and never wavered."

"Some would say Jake's the smartest," she quickly replies, lifting her chin and looking around us. "He got away from this nonsense."

"You're done with school and your residency now. What's stopping you?" He raises an eyebrow at her.

"Charlie!" Mr. Forsythe calls out to me and waves. I consider tugging Jake along but decide to excuse myself and join him alone. Jake and Tabby circle the crowd and stay close to us as Mr. Forsythe introduces me to all his guests, proudly informing one and all that the Forsythe's are now celebrating two marriages in the family.

Muffy's glare intensifies after repeatedly hearing the news, which subtracts from the attention she seems to crave.

Connal stays close to us as the night progresses, his patience is wearing thin as he is constantly asked what type of bike a beginner should purchase. I can see the thought rolling through his mind—could there be a more annoying question?

Later when returning from the bathroom, I find Jake and Connal surrounded by a flock of women. I cringe noticing that they are polished in ways I will never be, no matter how much time I spend with Mrs. Riley. After a moment of studying them, I know exactly why Jake left this life and why he married me.

I never set out to be a non-conformist. Looking at the carbon copies standing around my men, I see how miserable they are, but also, how unwilling these people are to search for anything outside their realm. Suddenly it hits me for the first time, the life I've had, the pain I've lived through, it made me stronger, and now happier than any of these women will ever allow themselves to be.

"Oh, be a dear and go get me another wine," Muffy orders when she sees me returning to Jake. I raise my eyebrow at her, brushing past her and the willowy blond beside her.

Jake flashes both dimples at me and starts to turn on her, closing his mouth when I shake my head. I've decided ignoring Muffy's existence is the best tactic, and it has the added bonus of infuriating her. As I'm reaching out for Jake, another towering blond puts her hand on his shoulder.

"Blaine told Muffy that most of your body is tattooed, I can't imagine…" Nameless blond number two sighs.

"Coming to rescue me, Charlie?" Jake speaks up, shrugging her hand off. "You know I have no tolerance for this shit, right?"

"I was only gone a few minutes!" I smile up at him, ignoring everyone around us and their gasps at his words. I slide my hands up through his hair and pull him down for a kiss.

Jake doubles down. His hands pull my hips into his body and his tongue plunges into my mouth, roughly at first, until my moans sooth him. With swift and sure movements of his tongue, he perfectly relays what he's thinking of doing to me when we're back in bed.

Opening my eyes when he pulls back, I'm surprised the women haven't fled. They're openly gawking at us. Leaning up to his ear I loudly whisper, "Guess what I want you to do tonight?"

The blond who asked about his ink is close enough to hear me and she finally turns to walk away, the others quickly filing into her wake.

"This is my wedding and I'm sure it's a foreign concept to you, but try to control yourselves so you don't embarrass this family anymore," Muffy huffs out.

"Oh, you'll soon understand how newlyweds are, Buffy!" I turn to smile at her as Jake leans down to nibble at my ear.

"Keep those fucking twats away from me if you

don't want to be embarrassed," Jake follows up with a threat of his own. Muffy actually stomps her foot before making a beeline for Blaine.

"When the fuck can we get outta here, brother?" Connal growls as he nears us, pulling at his tie and unbuttoning the top button of his shirt.

"Now," Jake says. "Head in and we'll go say good-night to a few people. Hey, make sure no one from the party wandered into the guesthouse, alright?"

Jake leads me over to say goodnight to his siblings and grandfather. He throws a wave in the general direction of his parents. Our eagerness to be alone is written all over our faces.

"Charlie!" His sister, Tabby, calls out as we move towards the guesthouse. She steps forward to hug me.

"It'll get easier, alright?" she says, giving me a tight squeeze. "I haven't ever seen him so happy, and he deserves it. I'm thrilled you found each other." She kisses me on my cheek before stepping back.

"Thank you, Tabby," I respond in kind. "I hope we get a chance to talk more this weekend."

"What did she say?" Jake asks as we maneuver around the pool.

"That I make you happy," I say softly, smiling up at him.

"If she only knew how much," he replies before sweeping me into his arms bridal style.

CONNAL

Fucking had to hang back all night. Watching the useless party attendees make snide remarks about the gold digger that Jake married. *Our* wife handled it all with grace, ignoring all the looks, eye rolls, and comments. The few times I was ready to step forward and handle things my way, Jake's gramp was there with a hand on my arm, steering me away.

"Now, now, son. Wouldn't do for them to think you have feelings for her," Mr. Forsythe murmured more than once. "Let them have their day, it will all sort out," he added, turning away before I could question that statement.

Finally! I hear them come into the guesthouse and, already naked, I meet them in the hall between the bedrooms. Jake sets her down and I immediately sink to my knees. Lifting her hem and finding her smoothly shaved pussy uncovered, I groan and sink my tongue into her pink folds. Desperate for a taste of her.

Without a word, Jake unzips her dress and pulls it over her head, tossing it aside he immediately reaches for the clasp of her bra releasing her *bounty*.

I shift one hand to her juicy ass, in between the crack and swipe it down to catch the moisture from her core then start thrusting it into her tightest hole. Her panting tells me how much she loves it, but her next action surprises me. She tenses and relaxes her ass muscles in a rapid pattern, using my now still finger to find her pleasure in her own way.

"Come for me," I whisper. "Ride my finger, baby

girl." I lean forward again, furiously flicking her clit with my tongue.

Jake is holding the back of her neck, keeping their eyes locked as she lightly bounces on my finger. Undressing one-handed, his other arm supports most of her weight. He gently pecks her lips until her panting becomes more frantic.

"Connal! Please!" Charlie begs for release. Our girl hasn't figured out that she never needs to beg us for anything, especially not to come. I go all in, delivering what she needs. Jake and I support her weight as her knees buckle.

"Come on, baby." Jake gives her a moment before picking her up again. "That was just the warm-up."

Depositing her on the bed, he pulls her over his chest, letting her slide down on his dick. I lean back, watching her ride him as I stroke my own cock. Charlie arches back, their fingers intertwined; our girl has gained confidence in her movements and I love watching her come into her own. Tightening my grip on my dick, I almost shoot off when she looks over at me, reaching a hand out to me.

Standing, I lean into her, cupping her cheek and kissing her lightly. Pulling back, I watch what Jake got to see earlier. Charlie's face, as she comes. It's simply spectacular. Jake and I exchange a quick look as I grab one of her firm ass cheeks in my hand. She rides him harder, his end is close as he's bucking into her faster and faster.

Their cries reach a peak together and Charlie falls forward, her hands supporting her weight on Jake's shoulders. I lightly caress her back, knowing she's done in. Plucking her from Jake, I carry her to the bathroom.

"Connal…"

"Shhh." I gently remove the pins from her hair. "Let's go curl up together?" She smiles gratefully, and after she cleans up I carry her back to bed.

CHAPTER TWENTY-SEVEN

JAKE

CONNAL HAD BARELY SLIPPED FROM THE BED the next morning before my gramps, his housekeeper, and the stylist come walking into the guesthouse. Fucking staying in a hotel the next time I come back this way.

"One of the groom's men is ill, Blaine needs you to stand in," gramps leads with, holding some kind of scarf in his hand. "You have a tux, don't you? Just put this on."

"No."

"Jake?" Charlie reaches her hand around my bicep. "Just for the pictures? For Blaine's wedding?"

"Was this planned?" I look him dead in the eye. He blinks and sighs.

"Yes, actually," gramps says. "Blaine never thought you'd come, but when you finally committed he made room for you to be in the wedding party. That turned into a bigger battle after your comments to Muffy last night, so decide quickly but it's up to you to tell Blaine no. If that's your decision."

As much as it pisses me off to be played, I'm pleased by gramps leveling with me. I just wish Blaine felt comfortable enough to have asked me last night. Holding Charlie close to me, I look back to him.

"I won't wear that thing," I start in. "And I want you to escort Charlie."

"I knew you wouldn't, it's ridiculous in this day and age. But—Muffy." Gramps snorts and tosses it over his shoulder. His housekeeper catches it with a little grin on her face. "I have other duties, but I'll ride to the church with Charlie and Tabby. They'll get to the reception together."

"Tabby's not in the fucking wedding?" I growl. "She lives here, she spends time with them."

"Not on purpose, she doesn't. Not for a long time," gramps informs me. "She turned down the *honor*. Your mother was furious."

I smile, pleased that Tabby has made her own small stand.

"Car will pick you up in twenty minutes, Jarrett. Charlie, it's time for your hair and make-up, if you could show Elise what you're wearing today?" gramps continues.

"Jake?" Charlie looks nervously to me. I open my mouth, but then Connal walks out. Having just showered, he is just wrapped in a towel and the stylist nearly, or maybe does, wet herself.

Charlie sees red.

"What's going on?" Connal asks.

"Brother, mind escorting my favorite women to the wedding ceremony?" I ask, trying, and probably failing to make things easier. Everyone in the room freezes.

"Huh?" Connal grunts.

"What?" gramps asks.

"Hi! I'm Elise, and single." The stylist walks towards Connal on her five-inch heels.

"Not interested." Connal shuts her down.

"Mr. Forsythe, I can handle my hair and make-up. Elise, you can just head out now." Charlie turns on the stylist. Connal smirks at me before he heads back down the hallway. Charlie glares at Elise then heads back to the main bedroom.

"Jarrett, we need to discuss something..."

"Not now, Gramps. Got to get ready to be a fucking groomsman," I say, following my partners down the hallway and leaving the three intruders behind us.

"Charlie?" I call out before locating her in the bathroom. "Are you alright with this?"

"I liked Tabby." Her eyes flip to me in the mirror as she continues applying makeup. "We'll be together at the reception, so it's not a huge deal."

"Do you know how much I love you?" I ask from the doorway, not wanting to touch her when she has a pencil so close to her eyeball.

"That's a relief!" she says turning to me. "Jake? Your family? I mean...I understand why you left."

I pull her into my arms, resting my chin on the top of her head, content to just stay frozen here.

"Come on, you need to get ready." She gently nudges me as she kisses my chest. I just hold her tighter until she starts giggling. "I'm serious, Jake." When I still don't move, Charlie starts tickling me, and damn, that gets me moving.

"I didn't know you were so ticklish, Jake!" She laughs, chasing after me.

"Stop, seriously! I'll get dressed." I dart to the shower, holding the glass door closed so she can't torture me. Backing off to the mirror, she mumbles something about 'later' before finishing her makeup.

CHARLIE

Jake gets ready and nearly runs to meet the car coming for him. A moment later he runs back in to kiss me and tell me I look beautiful, before darting out again.

"You do," Connal states, watching me from the doorway. He's dressed to escort Tabby and me to the church, neither man would agree to let me go without one of them being with me. He's in the same suit with a different tie on today.

"Men have it so easy," I sigh, thinking of the money Jake spent on my clothes for the weekend.

"Cause we can pee standing up?" he quips, crossing to me to help with the clasp of the necklace I'm fighting to get on.

Laughing I turn in his arms, staying there until we hear a knock on the front door. Grabbing my shoes and a clutch, I head out to see Tabby waiting in the doorway.

"Gramps left already but we have a car and driver here for us," she informs me, tearing her eyes away from Connal as I get closer. "WOW! You look amazing, Charlie."

"So do you, Tabby," I greet her warmly, even if she was checking Connal out. "I love that color on you."

"God, wait until you see the bridesmaid dresses! They're a horrible color and not made for my figure at all. Glad I dodged that bullet, even if mom nearly had a stroke over it." She laughs, indicating her full hips and thighs as we follow her out to the driveway. The driveway that covers more land than any home I ever lived in.

Tabby is great fun, even if she is a chatterbox. I can see Connal rolling his eyes in frustration though. Getting to the church, we all slide into a pew and she continues to tell us about everyone who walks by. The ceremony seemingly goes off without a problem, though I see Muffy's eyes bug-out once she notices that Jake isn't wearing the assigned neck-scarf thingy.

Connal rides to the reception with us, escorting us inside prior to getting a ride back home with the driver. Tabby completely takes me under her wing until we get to Jake in the receiving line. He immediately peels out of it once he sees me, coming to wrap me in his arms.

"Come on, let's get drinks." He nuzzles into my neck.

"We'll need them," Tabby agrees and I follow, moving away when I see a table that has place cards with seating assignments.

"Unbelievable!" I whisper to myself, taking our three cards I cross to catch up with Jake and Tabby.

"Jake, you're seated with the wedding party," I announce, showing him that Tabby and I are seated at the same table but he's at table number two.

"Think I give two fucks about where she wants me to sit?" He shrugs, handing me a glass of champagne. "Someone will move. I'll sit with you two."

"Wow." Tabby looks to me, wide-eyed. "He just spoke two full sentences. I call him and he just grunts into the phone until I get frustrated and hang up."

Laughing, I smile up at Jake. He quickly guides me to a quiet corner while Tabby wanders off to talk to other guests.

"Tabby checked Connal out," I fill him in when we find a table to stand at in the corner. "I decided she could live, though."

"Fuck." Jake smirks. "It's like there's a goddamn sign on my back for these other women and it sure as shit isn't: *Married*."

I smile back and he leans in to kiss me. From time to time various guests approach us, but as he leaves me to answer most questions, they all walk away soon enough.

"Have you seen my gramps?" he asks, right after they dim the lights to get us into the ballroom.

"Holy shit, Jake!" I had meant to mention that Mr. Forsythe left right after the ceremony but once I see the room I freeze up.

"Come on." He quickly takes my hand and leads me

in search of the table I'm assigned to. He sits down in the seat between Tabby and me, tossing the other name card away.

"Muffy will have a stroke," I mock whisper to him, getting a kiss in return.

CHAPTER TWENTY-EIGHT

CHARLIE

THE DINNER GOES WELL, EVEN AFTER JAKE sends a cousin to his assigned seat and eventually we notice his grandfather entering with an older couple. He quickly has them seated and takes his own place, right in time for the cake to be cut.

When the dancing starts with various groups being called on, Jake escorts me to the floor instead of the bridesmaid he was partnered with. She eventually finds someone to escort her but burns me with her eyes.

I have never danced with a man before, but hold tight to Jake. Secure in his arms, I feel like a princess and all my nervous energy melts away. At the end of the song, his grandfather signals to us to join him.

Approaching him and the older couple he arrived with, my heart starts to pound and I'm not sure why. The look of expectation on their faces, then the satisfied look on Mr. Forsythe's face as he looks at Jake and

I, must also trip Jake's instincts because he removes his arm from around me.

Taking my hand in his, he walks a little in front of me and I try to keep from dragging my feet.

"I'd like to introduce you to my grandson, Jarrett Forsythe," Mr. F. starts as we near. "But here is the young lady I've told you of. His new wife, Charles Scott Forsythe—Charlie."

The older couple is looking at me with such expectation, though they both have gray hair they seem extraordinarily pale and the woman has tears in her eyes.

"Jake, Charlie," he continues and I'm clutching at Jake's arm. "This is Charles and Mona Scott."

The world spins and I understand the panic I felt when I saw them. I look like her. I have her face and her, well, dammit... Mona Scott has some big jugs. Jake ushers me to the nearest chair and although Mona steps forward as if to comfort me, I turn away from her, clinging to Jake.

"Do you really think this is the best place..." Jake begins until he sees a waiter and orders water for me.

"Please, we just want to find out..." Mona starts before her husband grasps her arm.

"We've had the news for three days. Give the girl a moment, Mo," he says, although he is looking at me every bit as hopefully as she is.

Pulling two chairs around, he motions to her to sit before taking the seat beside her.

"Baby?" Jake looks to me. "We can put this off..." He and I maintain eye contact, and in an action I've seen between him and Connal dozens of times, he blinks. He perfectly understands that I need a moment. I may still get up and flee, but I need to focus. Jake leans his forehead down and presses it against mine, giving me the time I need.

Long moments tick by as a thousand questions fly through my head. Eventually, I deeply exhale and pull away from Jake, nodding at him.

"Gramps." Jake looks at him, eyes narrowed. "Explain."

Clearing his throat, the man who is most likely my grandfather says, "If I may?"

Awaiting my nod, he continues.

"I was the CFO for one of his companies for most of my career. Mona and I are not tech savvy and we eventually lost touch after I retired and we had moved away. Until your grandfather finally tracked me down a few days ago, well... I need to start with our son, I suppose." He looks to his wife, then back to me.

"We, well we always pushed him in the direction we wanted him to aspire to. He wanted to ski, we wanted him to play an instrument. Well, that was many years ago, but the examples go on like that. His first year at college was a disaster. We forced him to come home, I got him an internship and he'd go to school locally or be cut off. He tried it for a week and looking back, I just didn't know another way. We fought terribly and said we'd cut him off if he didn't comply.

"He left. He left his phone, he'd withdrawn a large sum but just walked away." His breath is shaky and Mona is silently crying. "A month later, he sent a long email to us, detailing grievances. I was too hurt to reply. After a year, we started to, almost, demand he call us. He finally replied, told us to *chill*, that he was working as a ski instructor. Nearly another year goes by and he sent word he was in love and thinking about getting married. We responded, asking him to tell us where he was, if we could visit him but we never heard from him again. Eventually, we hired a private investigator."

"Two months later, we found out he had died." Mona takes over when Charles becomes overwhelmed. "We simply never knew he had married, or..." She tentatively reaches out to lightly touch my hair, smiling kindly. "Well, we don't need a blood test with you, do we? You, my son, and I are nearly—wait, do you have a small red mark just above your hairline on your neck?"

JAKE

"She does," I answer for her. I often kiss it when I see it. "It's the size of a nickel."

Charlie has yet to say anything, and I don't think she will. I look back to her and she nods at me, still looking like a deer in headlights. I open my mouth to excuse us when Tabby's voice comes from behind me.

"Here, I bribed the bartender. Don't know what's happening over here but from the look on Charlie's face, I thought shots for all of you would do." She's at my side before she notices the tears streaming down the Scotts' faces. Barely pausing, she shrugs and offers them the pickings from the tray first.

Charlie reaches past me, mumbling '*God, yes*' before snatching one, holding it up and shooting it. This gets a bark of laughter from her grandfather before he does the same. I smile at Tabs, suddenly thankful for her interruption.

Mona delicately sips hers. I take mine and place it in Charlie's hand before Tabby downs her own shot.

"We haven't met. I'm Jake's sister, Tabitha." She finally thinks to introduce herself.

"Tabby, a word?" Gramps calls from behind the Scotts.

"Charlie?" Charles gently probes her once Tabby has walked away. "This is sudden for all of us. But when offered, we couldn't pass the chance to come here, to see if it was possible that we have a granddaughter. We aren't asking for anything but the chance to know you and to say, that if we *had* known about you…" His voice chokes off again.

"We would have done anything to be a part of your life," Mona finishes, taking another delicate sip of her shot. Evidently, Gramps has filled them in on her past.

Charlie looks between them and then hands her second shot to her grandfather. He grins, readily accepting and downing it.

"Maybe we could talk tomorrow?" Charlie finally offers and relief flashes across their faces. I get the name of the hotel they're staying at and give them my number. As we all stand together, they quickly move to embrace Charlie while she still clings to my hand.

When they release her, she nods, not making eye contact with any of us. I tell them I'll call the next day, then lift her into my arms and carry her out into the night. Luckily, Gramps' driver recognizes me and calls out as he breaks away from a pack of other drivers.

I follow him to the car, apologizing that he'll have to make a couple trips.

CHAPTER TWENTY-NINE

CONNAL

GETTING BACK FROM THE CEREMONY, I GRAB A bottle of tequila from the guest house and wander out to the pool. The rest of the evening I enjoy on a float, sipping tequila fancier than anything I could ever afford.

Fucking don't mind visiting this but couldn't imagine living it. More than ever, the differences between how Jake and I were raised are clear as day. Thing is, we're just the same.

We can't tolerate routine. We need to be out, riding, enjoying life. But now, we both need Charlie also. Need to make her family, make sure she's safe and secure. But the thing is her spirit matches ours. She likes to fix things, fiddle with machinery like I do. Jake likes to build, and perfect his craftsmanship in the bathrooms and kitchens he works on.

As I walk into the guest house, I hear my phone

buzz. Crossing and looking at it, I'm filled with dread. Jake sent me our code for *shit hitting the fan*.

I quickly dress and wait for them, feeling somewhat relieved when I see him crossing the terrace to the guest house. When Charlie sees me, she smiles and reaches a hand out. I quickly take her from his arms.

"I can walk," she says, giving me a quick kiss.

"How many times we gotta tell you, we like you in our arms?" I smirk back at her.

"I think I met my grandparents tonight, Connal," she announces and I almost drop her, whipping my head around to Jake.

"Fucking gramps. I told him her name and background the day we got married and something must've clicked," he says, looking pained. "He brought them in for the wedding."

"Is that why he was gushing over her last night?" I ask, pissed off. Charlie tenses in my arms then holds me tight even as I try to set her down in the master bedroom.

"Jake? He was so nice to me. I mean last night? Your parents were…" Charlie pauses, and I'm sure is trying to figure everything out.

"Come here." he pulls her into his arms, and I push up against her back. "Love you, baby."

"He was only nice because…fuck, Jake. I liked him. And I thought he didn't judge…but he knew and…tonight"

"Stop it!" I bark at her, grabbing her chin so she has to make eye contact with me. "This isn't our life, baby girl. Remember that. Jake loves *you*. I love *you*. We fly home Monday and if he was being fake as shit with you cause of that, then fuck him."

"I didn't know, Charlie, and Connal's right. I don't give a shit about anything else than us being us," Jake softly vows. "You two, you're my family."

Charlie takes a deep breath before leaning back to kiss me. When I release her, she meets Jake's mouth.

"Tabby can be our family, too. I liked her." She smiles at us. "Connal, can you unzip me?"

Charlie's request and look in her eyes leave no doubt as to what she wants to do to erase this day.

JAKE

Connal and I take Charlie in turns, never speaking of it but we're both aware of how fragile she is right now. We devote ourselves to worshipping her body, licking her pussy lovingly. Kissing her like grammar school kids. Making love like it's our honeymoon.

She reaches for us constantly and we give her everything until she's sated.

Waiting until her typical light snoring has kicked in, I tell Connal what happened in barely a whisper.

"Last night, he said something about everything sorting out. He fucking knew she had grandparents and played up to her last night. Knowing that your parents wouldn't mind her background as much, once they found out," Connal responds, trying not to raise his voice.

"I know. And agree his lead up was bullshit, but dragging her away from them tonight until she was ready, wasn't right. Tomorrow, we see what she wants and go from there," I insist.

"Both of you," Charlie whispers. "If they want to be a part of my life, they may figure that out. You okay with that, Jake?"

"Not changing my mind. The three of us." I kiss her thoroughly, so she knows I'm all in.

"Connal, come with us to see them tomorrow?" she asks quietly.

"Not leaving you again during this trip," he vows. "Get some sleep now, we'll watch over you."

———

I get up early and ring the housekeeper for a breakfast tray, staying in the front room until it's delivered so I won't disturb Connal and Charlie with my pacing.

One way or another, last night was going to be interesting but what my Gramps pulled was shitty, and we will have it out before the three of us return home. I'm lost in thought and barely notice my phone vibrating.

"What the hell happened last night?" Tabby asks without preamble.

"Gramps figured out who Charlie's grandparents were, that they had no idea she existed and fucking sprung them on us," I growl.

"Oh, shit," she replies, nearly speechless. "Is she alright?"

"TBD," I reply, getting a giggle from her.

"Sorry, that's the Jake I know. Still not used to you

using full sentences," Tabs explains. "Look, I have a shift in an hour and some patients who are overdue. Will you call me when you get home?"

"I'll text."

"Whatever. I have an opportunity I wanted to talk to you about, so call." She sounds like she's brushing her teeth and talking at the same time. Who does that? "Love you, big brother."

"Me too," I say before disconnecting.

Looking through the window, I see someone rolling a cart this way so I quickly step forward to get that and take breakfast back to Charlie and Connal.

CONNAL

"I could get used to this," I grin at Jake, lifting my head to watch him roll a cart, overloaded with food, into the room.

Rolling over, I cuddle into Charlie. Cupping one of her breasts in my hand, I lightly kiss her neck until she wiggles back into me, smiling, but refusing to open her eyes.

"Jake, she needs bacon!" I loudly whisper, getting her to giggle for my efforts. Jake crawls onto the bed from his side, hanging a piece over her head. Barely opening her eyes, she lunges for the bacon, snapping half of it off.

"Shit, it's dangerous here!" He laughs, having dropped the other half.

"No kidding?" Charlie mumbles around her bacon, finally opening her eyes.

"How you feeling, baby girl?" I ask.

"Hungry now, then we'll talk," she responds as Jake backs off to dish up food for us. More importantly, coffee for me. "We're still leaving tomorrow, right?"

"God, yes," he says before thinking. "Unless you want more time with the Scotts? But eat first."

CHAPTER THIRTY

CHARLIE

"Jake?" I ask as we're finishing breakfast. "I know you didn't get much time with your family. Maybe we could go to that brunch before w…"

"I'm good. I got time with Dad yesterday when they were taking pictures." His words bring relief. I can't imagine seeing his family right now.

"What do you want to do?" Connal asks.

"Jake, if you could call them? I don't know how far away they are. Maybe figure out a time we can go and see them?" I ask him as I dig through my suitcase.

Grabbing fresh clothes, I head off for a long shower. Both Connal and Jake are acting like I'm made of glass right now, but really, I'm just sad.

Sad for the heartache that couple endured.

Sad for my mother, working so damn hard to provide for me, not knowing there would have been some help.

Anger wells in me but I push that away. It serves no purpose right now. I can't say what my father would have wanted, all I can do is hear them out and move forward based on how they treat not only me but Jake and Connal, as well.

I snort to myself. How does that conversation go? *'Nice to meet you, I have two husbands. Please don't judge.'* That sounds better in my head than, *'I was a virgin, and, well, it was an accident.'*

Regardless, I'm not giving either of them up. If the Scotts want to be in my life, they will have to accept me, as is.

Dragging myself out of the shower, I braid my hair and put on my armor. Jeans. I'm sure we're going somewhere fancy, but the beautiful clothes aren't me and they best accept that right away. Walking out to the living room, I smile.

Connal and Jake are back in their customary jeans, T-shirts, and cuts. Perfect.

"How's our girl?" Connal asks.

"Good," I reach for their hands. "What's the plan?"

"Gramps' car will take us to their hotel. They have a suite and we thought that would be the best place to meet. Whenever you're ready, they don't have any other plans," Jake tells me, wrapping his arms around me. "All at your pace, baby."

I smile, holding them both close, enjoying the words they promised me when they asked for this relationship.

"I'm ready," I answer and head to the door.

The three of us walk towards the driveway, passing

the guests who are showing up for the wedding brunch. I walk confidently between the guys, we're back in our usual clothes and not putting on airs to impress anyone. That alone causes people to stop and gawk. That, or the two hunks by my side, I think while winking at one of Jake's aunts.

Before I know it, we're knocking on the door to the Scotts' suite. They look confused at Connal's presence but graciously greet us.

"Yesterday," I start after we all get settled.

"Please," Charles says. "We got upset with Jarrett's grandfather last night. He shouldn't have tried to stage our meeting that way."

"He goes by Jake," I nod. "And, thank you. That, well, you know."

"You're a mechanic, I understand?" Mona asks.

"Yes, my Grandpa." my eyes flick quickly to Charles. "He was one and after mom died, we would spend time working on cars. Well, mostly me handing him tools and watching what he did." I smile at the memories.

"What did your Mom tell you about your Dad?" Charles asks.

"I don't remember a lot, I just know she would smile sometimes and say I was just like him. She cried at night when she thought I was asleep." I pause, my throat tightening. "Oh, I brought a couple pictures. I don't have many."

I dig into my purse and pull out the five I brought. Their wedding pictures and a couple of me when I was a child, I hand them over. Mona lets out a soft sob and holds their wedding picture to her chest.

"Um, maybe we can go and get copies made at a drugstore?" I offer.

"Your mother was very pretty, Charlie," Charles says, after several tries. "Our boy looks so happy here. We would very much like a copy of your pictures."

"I saw a place a block down," Connal speaks up. "I can just run them over now."

"I'm sorry, it's been so much. Did I hear your name is Connor?" Mona asks as she hands the pictures to him.

"Connal, ma'am." He smiles at her. "Your granddaughter is very special."

Watching him leave, I nearly miss the confused glance shared between the older couple.

"And you work for him?" Charles asks me while looking at Jake and my joined hands.

"Yes, he lives with us also," I say, not ready to *overshare*.

"I met Connal in basic training," Jake explains. "He was in for four years but I had up'd for six and when I got out, I followed him out to Idaho."

"I don't want to overstep, but how concerned should we be about Charlie being involved with a man tied to a biker gang?" Charles asks.

"It's a club, sir, not a gang. Neither Connal nor I have criminal records," Jake replies in a harder voice. "I fell in love with Charlie the minute I saw her, I'm..."

"I'm not concerned about Connal and can only imagine he will find a new place to live now that you're married," Charles' voice gets louder and Mona and I exchange a glance. "I'm not so naïve to think that this motorcycle group…"

"Connal will stay with us," I insert. "As you said, you don't want to overstep. I don't want you two fighting. Mr. Scott, um, Charles, I…"

"Charlie is quite right, Charles," Mona takes over for me. "Both men served this country and Jake says he has no record. Please."

CONNAL

I wasn't gone more than a half an hour but immediately notice the tension in the room when I return with the photos.

"Thank you, Connal," Mona says when I hand her the envelope. "Oh, let me pay you for them!"

"No, no worries about that," I assure her, crossing to sit down next to Charlie. "Everything okay?"

"I forgot the feeling of worrying for a child," Mr. Scott says, looking between Jake and Charlie. "I know you haven't had anyone to watch over you for a good portion of your life and I am partially responsible for that.

"I knew Jake's grandfather a long time and he assures us you are a good man. I will trust in that, Jake. But Charlie, please know we are here if you ever need anything. We would very much like to remain in touch with you."

"We would like to visit you," Mona quickly corrects him. "Maybe have the chance to get to know you, once this shock wears down?"

"I'd like that," Charlie smiles at her. "Well, I don't want to hurt either of you, but if I may start by using your first names? I kind of need to wrap my brain around grandparents. Also, if you have pictures of my Dad, maybe I can get some?"

"Of course, Charlie, I'll put together an album for you when I get home. Oh! And a medical history, I know that's so important nowadays," Mona exclaims. "And we can talk about a visit? I don't know what your plans are for today, maybe we could have dinner tonight?"

That is quickly decided, and Mr. Scott once again raises an eyebrow in my direction when Charlie says it will be the five of us.

Heading back to Jake's grandfather's house, the housekeeper quickly signals us to follow her. Following Jake and Charlie to Mr. Forsythe's office, he's standing in there with Jake's father.

"Charlie!" Rick quickly greats her. "What news this is! Why, I remember the Scotts from years ago. And to think they would never have known about you if Jarrett hadn't married you."

He gushes on, while Mr. F. takes in the looks on our faces.

"Charlie, I owe you an apology," he says, crossing to her. "When I realized that the names and dates matched, well, I got overly excited and wanted it to be a surprise. It took me a bit to track them down and well... Unfortunately, I didn't take everyone's feelings into consideration and even my housekeeper has scolded me this morning. I am truly sorry to have put you in that situation."

He seems so goddamn sincere, that Jake and I relax a bit. Looking down to gauge Charlie's response, she studies his face for a long moment before placing her hand in his outstretched hand.

"Your execution sucked," Charlie begins, getting a laugh from Jake while Rick's mouth drops open. "But I'm happy for the chance to get to know them, so thank you."

"I owe you an apology also, Jake." He turns to him, grasping his shoulder. "I've always had a soft spot for you and I've ruined this visit."

Jake simply nods, squeezing his arm in reply.

"Most of the family is out on the terrace. Why don't you three change and come join us?" Rick steps forward.

"I think they are fine as they are," Mr. F. looks over his shoulder at his son before turning back to us. "Will you join me?"

Charlie nods and takes his hand, we follow her out. I don't miss Rick's frown aimed at what we're wearing.

"Charlie!" Jake's mom calls out, drawing everyone's attention as she crosses to us. "Darling, I never got to tell you how lovely you looked yesterday."

"Did she look bad on Friday night, Connal?" Jake throws over his shoulder to me, getting a laugh from Charlie.

"She looked hot both nights," I reply. Fuck, she's mine too, and I don't give a damn what any of these people think at this point.

"Thank you, Mrs. Forsythe," Charlie replies.

"Please! You're family now, Charlie. I know we don't know other well and while Muffy likes to call me Mother, please don't feel pressured to call me anything other than Elsbeth," she replies somewhat stiffly, unhappy with our comments.

"Alright," Charlie narrows her eyes at her. "Since I loved my mother so much, I'd never dream of using that title for anyone else."

"Do you know your great-grandparents were at our wedding?" Elsbeth asks next, trying to play up to our woman.

JAKE

"Give it a rest, Ma," I insert, getting annoyed at her sudden attempt to be nice.

"Jarrett! She may very well be carrying my next grandchild, of course, I want to talk to her," Elsbeth responds.

"Jake?" Charlie asks. "Friday night was a blur, I know Tabby isn't here but can we talk to some of your siblings?"

"Of course, follow me," my mother interjects. And people wonder why I don't bother to speak much.

———

"Oh my God! Do we even have time for a nap?" Charlie asks once we're back in the guest house. I shake my head. "My God, Jake, they never stop talking."

I pin her up to the wall. Kissing her for all I'm worth as Connal watches.

"Do we need to change?" he finally asks.

"Fuck that," I growl.

"Give me some sugar Charlie, then let's go," he responds, moving forward.

"Tonight! I want you both in me," Charlie mewls when he pulls away from her mouth.

———

"They know," Charlie says when we're all in the car after dinner.

"No way," I answer, pulling her onto my lap.

"Jake, her grandfather is sharp as fuck. He kept questioning my presence and why "we" bought a house together when you were marrying her." Connal responds.

"Well, you're having breakfast with Mona before we fly out tomorrow; do you want to tell her?" I ask. "I don't give a shit. We'll take care of you, baby."

"I will tell them," Charlie promises. "I just don't want to freak them out right now. I want to know them a little."

"Done."

"Agreed." Connal and I both promise.

Arriving to my grandfather's house, I send Connal and Charlie ahead to the guest house and head to his office. Waiting a moment, his housekeeper, Donna, opens the door. No matter that she's in her fifties, I know the look of a woman who was just getting some.

"Sorry to interrupt, Gramps," I smile at him.

"Fuck off," he growls at me. "You of all of them don't get to…"

"Don't care," I hold up my hands in surrender.

"I'm going to marry her. Quietly, but in the next couple months," Gramps says, looking out the French doors.

"As long as you're happy," I reply, smiling to myself.

"Are you and Connal lovers?"

"No," I reply after a beat.

"He and Charlie?" he asks next. "I've noticed the rings the three of you wear."

"Charlie is with both of us. Our plan, she was," I pause, hating to talk about shit that isn't anyone's business. "She was very, very innocent. We wanted to share."

"And if she has…"

"I gotta whole fucking will and prenup that says his kids from her are mine, that sleeping with him isn't adultery in my eyes. Want to see the video of the wedding where we both kissed her?" I respond, trying to stay calm.

"You really want to act like this is alright?" he snaps at me.

"Don't care what anyone else thinks. She took us as a package. We won't hurt her. We'll protect and love her together…"

"That is so messed up. I can't even imagine how anyone could…" he grounds out.

"Then don't," I start.

"I know her fucking grandparents," he continues.

"When they go to visit her, damn, when she gives birth eventually! They'll figure it out and the gossip will kill us."

"Jake?" Charlie says my name from the doorway. "I didn't want to sleep without you."

I cross to her, kissing her forehead and holding her close.

"Mr. Forsythe," she says looking at him while I hold her. "You apologized to me earlier, and I really appreciated that. Tomorrow, out of respect for you, I will tell my grandparents about our relationship. They can make their decision about whether or not to be in my life. Please understand I am completely committed to Jake *and* Connal. They share such a bond and now with me as well. I..."

"You whored yourself out, I get it," Gramps cruelly cuts in.

"Go pack, baby," I push her towards the door, moving to strike out at my grandfather.

"No! Jake." She attaches herself to me. "No."

Looking between them, I know she won't release me. I flip the old man off and pick her up, carrying her out to the guest house once again.

This time to leave my family completely behind.

CHAPTER THIRTY-ONE

CHARLIE

JAKE WAS NEVER TIGHTLY BOUND TO HIS family, but I know that the idea of complete separation doesn't sit well with him either.

The night of the blow-up with his grandfather we checked into the hotel where my grandparents were staying. The next morning, before he and Connal woke up I called my grandmother and arranged to meet her alone.

I told her everything.

She knew about my father's death during a ski run, but I told her how I survived the crash that killed my mother. Then, I told her about my grandfather's death and foster care. I went on about meeting Connal and Jake and how the three of us were together, about our vows to each other. That Jake's grandfather was disgusted by the thought of our relationship.

I knew that this information was complete overload. It is for me some days.

I asked her to kiss her husband for me and call, when or if they decided to be in my life knowing how I am choosing to live it.

"Charlie," Mona grasps my arm as I turn to leave. "I lost my only child out of pride, stubbornness, and concern about appearances. I want to be sure you aren't being taken advantage of, but know that as long as they are good to you and you are happy, that is all I care about.

"I will talk to your grandfather, although, I think he may suspect something after yesterday," Mona continues. "But his choice will be his own. After knowing you exist, I simply cannot walk away from you. Please, don't leave here thinking this door has closed. I will come out to visit you, even if I'm by myself."

"Thank you," I reply, trying not to cry as I move forward to hug her. Mona's arms instantly close around me as I hear and feel her sob. We draw our heads apart to smile at each other, we're both crying but she is rubbing my back trying to soothe me.

Parting in time to get back to the room before we need to leave for the airport, I realize I only held one thing back from her. I didn't tell her my period was four days late.

———

Another two days go by before I walk into a pharmacy,

still a weird mix of nerves. Heading down the aisles, I finally come upon the pregnancy tests.

Heading up to the counter, I immediately see the clerk's eyes go from the boxes to my ring finger to my cut. I narrow my eyes at her, not interested in her judgment.

Crossing to a coffee shop, I order a tea to go and quickly dart into their bathroom. I pee on two of the tests and head back out to the car, mission accomplished.

I drive straight home before I look at the tests. They both confirm the news I was certain of, so I text my men to come home.

The next hour finds me pacing the living room before I finally call Riley.

"Hello, stranger!" Her bubbly voice greets me. "I'm just leaving campus, what's up?"

"I texted the guys like an hour ago but haven't heard from them, I was just wondering..."

"Something may have come up, let me call Gunner and I'll call you back," Riley suggests.

"They're in church," she says when I pick up her call a few minutes later. "Gunner didn't pick up so I called Betsy. She says it's been a couple hours. I'm about an hour away, do you need anything?"

"No, I'm good. Just never had radio silence from them before and got worried." I let her know. "How are the wedding plans coming? Still in two weeks?"

"Yes, *bridesmaid-of-mine*. No cold feet, still going to wear a simple dress..."

"Because Gunner will tear it off of you at his first chance?" I laugh, interrupting her.

"I can't even pretend that's not true, Charlie." She giggles along with me. "There will be about 40 people at Grams; she's serving cake and cocktails there then we go to the party at the clubhouse afterward. Everyone seems to think I'll morph into a bridezilla at some point, but I'm marrying Gunner. That's all I want."

"Please, you're so easy-going you make me feel like I'm high-strung!" I roll my eyes even though she can't see me. Then both of our phones buzz.

"Ahh, meeting's over! Talk later?" Gunner must be calling her since Connal is calling me.

CONNAL

"Everything alright, baby girl?" I ask as Jake and I head out to our bikes. I can barely hear her over the roar of everyone's bikes starting up but I assure her we're heading home now.

Throwing a thumbs-up to Jake, I'm soon following him out of the compound. I can tell by Jake's posture that he's as pissed off as I am.

As expected, Maddock was furious to be reprimanded when he had warrants served on our homes without probable cause. The uptick in State Police and ATF agents are causing serious issues in supply lines, not only for us but with other MCs.

Riley's one of us now, a hundred percent. But the other MCs—allies even—are nearly calling for Gunner's head over it. That and we still have to deal with fucking Frank.

Motherfucker was still in contact with Deb, sending her money and meeting up for a fuck when he could get away. Jasper's in a hard spot, killing him doesn't fit the crime. But with the shit he knows, we can't have him running to Maddock if we cut him loose.

Cut him loose, without his NGMC ink, of course.

Pulling up to the house hits me differently each time. I've never had a home of my own and even though Jake bought it, he kept his word and put my name on the title next to his and Charlie's. We want to surround the property with a fence, then build a work-shop and add on to the garage. But overall, it really suits us.

Charlie comes to the door at the sound of the bikes and Jake nearly runs to her. I can understand that; needing her touch after this shitty afternoon.

Walking up behind her, I start nibbling on her neck. Jake breaks their kiss and she quickly turns to me. A moment later, she's laughing.

"Good thing we don't have any neighbors!" She pulls us back towards the door. "I ordered pizza, had to promise them a big tip to come out this way but I'm starving and didn't know when you would be home."

"I'm gonna grab a beer," Jake answers. "Either of you want one?"

"Yeah," I answer before Charlie turns him down. I turn back, hearing a car. "Hey, here's the pizza guy now. I got it."

Charlie is quiet even after she slows down around her fourth piece.

"What's going on, Charlie?" Jake quietly asks. "You know we can't talk club business? You ain't mad about that?"

"No! I get it. It's just that I have news..." She walks around the island taking each of our hands and places them on her stomach.

"Did you eat too much?" I ask. Like a fucking idiot.

It's the sight of Jake going down on his knees before her, kissing her stomach, and the soft smile she gives me as she waits for me to catch up, that pulls a war cry from my lips.

"Baby!" I yell so loud, I'm sure Jasper can hear me from his place down the road. I cup her cheeks, pulling her face to mine for a long, slow kiss.

"Thank you, Charlie," Jake says, still placing light kisses around her stomach.

"I took two tests today," she says, caressing the top of Jake's head, smiling broadly. "I was so worried when I couldn't reach you but then Riley reached Betsy and found out about the meeting."

"We'll have to get you to a doctor," I start, grateful I put her on the garage's insurance policy already.

"It's early yet." She tugs Jake up, so she can hug us both. Group hugs are becoming the norm around here, and slowly, getting to be less awkward. "I know there are some vitamins I can pick up. I thought I might ask Emma about her doctor."

"Are you sure? Do you need to quit working? Here,

come sit down," I'm babbling while Jake seems to be taking this in stride.

"I can still work, you doofus." She leads us to the giant U shaped couch we bought. "I'm pregnant, not incapacitated."

"Baby, we're all new to this. Let us catch up a minute," Jake quietly interjects. "We want you to be safe and healthy, that's all Connal means."

"I know, I'm sorry." Charlie squeezes my hand. "And yes, when I can't get on the creeper easily, maybe I can work the desk for a while? Learn how to do the inventory and behind the scenes work?"

"Of course, you'll always have a place there. Don't ever doubt that," I assure her, trying not to laugh at the picture of a rounded belly stopping her from rolling under a car. I make eye contact with Jake and as he knows what I'm thinking, we burst out laughing.

"What?" she squeals. "I hate it that you two can do that!"

"We're happy, baby girl," I assure her. "So fucking happy."

"Connal? I was thinking today, I've never met your family. I mean, I know meeting Jake's family turned into a disaster but do they know about me?" She is back to picking at a callous on her hand.

"Look at me?" I wait for her to look up. "I told my parents I have an amazing woman. One of my brothers, Derek? I told him about our relationship. Everything."

"What did he, I mean? Does he think I'm a..."

"Don't say what I think you're going to say, Charlie," Jake growls at her. "You're our wife. Our love. You don't ever say or think of yourself any other way." Jake's entire body tenses, like it does every time he thinks of what his grandfather said to Charlie.

"He laughed actually," I say. "He came out a few years ago. He's met Jake, now he can't wait to meet the woman who demoted him from the black sheep to the gray sheep of the family."

They laugh. Then we cuddle our woman. In talking, Charlie brings up a point we'd never thought of. She wants our children to have hyphenated names, McKay-Forsythe, and it really touches me.

CHAPTER THIRTY-TWO

FLINT

FRANK AND I HAVE NEVER BEEN CLOSE, SO NO one's more shocked than I am when he asks to speak to me.

"I fucked up, brother," he finally says, after we stare at each other a few minutes.

"Yeah, you did," I reply, accepting a smoke from him.

"Ain't never had a family, not like you did. Arthritis is so bad it hurts to ride anymore. We were fucking kings, Flint!" He slams his hand down on his nightstand, and I can see pain shoot across his face. "You think I don't know those girls despise me? You know how many fucking blue pills I take to keep them bouncing on my dick? To feel anywhere close to how I did when we were young?"

"We ain't young anymore," I quietly add when he stops talking. "No use looking back now."

"And I got shit to show for it," he laughs derisively. "Figured I'd get someone to play house with, take care of me for a few years. Didn't mean to hurt the girl. I was fucked up so bad, I barely felt it when Gunner did this." He lifts his broken arm.

I get frustrated listening to his pity party. That's how I feel about getting older, don't like wasting it around people I don't like.

"We never talked this much before, Frank. What do you want?" I sigh.

"Deb tried to get in with the Savages after she was sent away. No takers there and she can't dance with the scars left on her. Said I owed her, and fuck, some of the stuff I had her do for me, well, I guess I did. I know Jasper has my phone, have him check the recordings on it. Last time I saw her, she said I had to keep the money coming or she'd go to the Maddocks. I got the recorder working in time for that."

"When the fuck were you going to speak up?" I growl, heading to the door.

"Wait!" he yells, and I do. "I'm supposed to meet her tomorrow. Meet her with a couple grand. She lets me bang her and she goes away again for a month or so. I'll tell you where but I need something from you."

I look at him and he knows that I'm thinking of just setting Gunner on him.

"I can hold on long enough that you'll miss the meeting," he cuts me off. "I ain't got much ink, I know the MC gets that back. I got some money saved but I need a partial share of the monthly. Won't ever ask for more and, like me or not, you know I won't fucking rat the Northern Grizzlies out. Deb will."

JASPER

"You knew him from before I was born, what do you think?" I ask, looking to Flint for direction.

"I think he's on the level and I don't fucking trust Deb," he replies. "He knows he's gotta pay something, I think he's made his peace with losing his ink and his cut. If you ain't a hundred percent on this, Prez, then let's go vote on it. Otherwise, it'll be you that they point their fingers at if shit goes sideways."

"I say we vote, Jas," Vice speaks up. "It's not just Frank we're talking about here. Deb will have to be dealt with."

"Everyone here in an hour, times a-wasting," I order. The door stays open after they leave and Emma enters a moment later. "Hey, darlin'. Were you teaching today?"

Standing to pull her into my arms, I just hold on tight to her.

"Yes, I think Noose and the newest prospect will do well," she answers, placing kisses on my neck. "Is it going to be another late one?"

"I'm sorry, Emma," I reach past her to shut the door.

"Why don't you lock that, just to be sure?" She winks up at me, moving to sit on my desk.

"No cheating now, I want to see all of you," I shake

my head at her. She's sliding her underwear down, thinking to hide her body from my sight.

"Jasper! I've been pregnant for like two years," she slightly exaggerates, holding an arm across her slightly rounded belly.

"Please, Darlin'?" I kneel in front of her, lifting the hem of her dress. "I need to start down here, see if I still get you all worked up."

I dip my tongue into her folds, sliding my thumb up to her clit. "Let me get a taste before I worship those sweet tits when I enter you."

Gently massaging her clit, I get her sweet juices flowing and she gradually tugs her dress up. Looking up at her bump, I lay kisses across it and whisper: "Hold on, little one, gonna get bouncy."

"I can hear you, you know?!" She snorts at my comment.

"Come on over here," I pull her to the couch and she slides right down onto my dick. Right where she belongs, her full breasts are at the perfect level for my mouth. The next fifteen minutes are heaven, letting me clear my mind of the shit going on around here, focusing on what's most important.

"I have to get home," Emma finally yawns against my chest. "Bree has work tonight. You know she compared the twins to the Saturday night bar crowd? It was pretty funny. Spit up, crazy behavior, and falling asleep randomly."

"I love you and all our babies, spit up and all," I whisper back, holding her tight. "Drive safe now."

She stands to dress as I get some napkins to clean her off, kissing her again before I walk her to her truck.

JAKE

Leaving the job site, I head back to the clubhouse, answering the call for church. Walking in, Gunner and Vice are looking pretty grim. I nod to them but cross to Connal, Wrench, and Russian.

"Vice never had a poker face," Russian says, as he slides me a glass and the bottle of Jack. "This can't be good and Gunner'll have to clean it all up."

"Patches only," Jasper calls out from the hallway. I shoot my whiskey and follow everyone back.

Less than an hour later, I'm following Flint and Gunner up to Frank's room.

"Need that meet time and place," Flint says as he enters.

"And my deal?" Frank studies each of us.

"Cut and ink stay here," Flint pauses. "Forty percent of your current share for five years, Frank. Best I could do." I blink but don't move. The vote was for thirty. Knowing Flint, he'll add the rest from his share.

"That's bullshit," Frank growls.

"Give Gunner the info. Now," Flint glares back, "or that number drops."

Connal and Roy intercept us on the way out.

"I'm coming with," Roy states. "We leaving tonight?"

"Now," Gunner says. "We're taking Frank's truck,

that'll have her relaxed when she gets there tomorrow."

"Connal, Charlie…" I nod at him, knowing he'll comfort her and keep her from getting angry that I won't get to say goodbye.

"I'll stop by and talk to Riley," Flint grips Gunner's shoulder. "Or do you want her to stay with us tonight?"

"If you could talk her into it, I'd appreciate it," Gunner nods.

Settling into the backseat for the ride to a lodge a couple hours north of us, Roy immediately changes our plan.

"I'll handle her, Gunner," Roy says firmly.

"Mine to do," Gunner replies, though I know his heart isn't in it.

"You don't need Deb's death on you when you go home to that sweet girl of yours tomorrow," Roy returns. "I've got plenty of marks on my soul, this won't hurt none. She won't feel it."

"Roy," Gunner growls.

"Overruling you, now watch the road," Roy shrugs. "Gonna *Netflix and Chill* tomorrow night with my gal, don't want thoughts of you messing with that."

"What the flying fuck do you know about *Netflix and Chill*?" Gunner bursts out, while I laugh at the image.

"Not that it's any of your business, but there's a certain divorcee in town who heard the term from her son-in-law."

"You *chilling* regular?" Gunner smirks at him.

"You interested in knowing how many times a week I can get it up, you little shithead?" Roy throws back.

"*Fuck*. Roy, I need to bleach that image out of my mind now." I groan, Roy's older than Flint.

"Ahhh, he speaks," Roy turns back like he forgot I was here. "How's that wife of yours doing?"

"Amazing," I respond. Gunner nods and I know he understands the feeling.

"You talk to her?" Roy asks next and I nod in response. "Good, tell her that every day. I was married once. We found out she was pregnant and had Stage 3 cancer all within a month. She wouldn't terminate the baby to care for herself, thought she could fight it out. She was too weak towards the end. I lost them both the same day."

My throat feels swollen and I'm unable to do anything but grab his shoulder. Never even knew he'd been married.

"Something you said to Emma once," Gunner's voice sounds pained. "Your wife's father was quick with his fists, huh?"

"Ugly yet smart, Gunner." Roy tries for humor. "You really are the full package. You and Riley trying for a baby?"

"Huh? Oh, no. She's gonna finish her degree. Ri only took the one class this summer, then fall term starts a few weeks after the wedding. She should finish in May. Never thought about a family before her, but I don't want to rush her." Gunner keeps talking, helping to change the topic.

"You, Charlie, and Connal trying?" Roy asks next.

"Uh huh," I respond, looking out the window; not telling them about our news at this stage.

"Haven't heard Royce complain about her lately," Roy looks at me, but Gunner answers instead.

"He probably figured out that Charlie will be running the place in ten years."

"Ten?" I question, knowing the drive she has. "She started working on custom paint jobs this week. Riley is talking about setting up a website about what Charlie and Connal can do."

"Okay, now I gotta ask…" Roy spends the remaining drive drilling us. Doesn't take me long to know he's fishing for who we see stepping up to run the MC. I have ideas but need to test the guys before I'll speak up.

Getting to the lodge, Roy goes in and pays for two nights in a cabin. The rest of the night we alternate sleeping, just waiting for Deb to show up. She's due mid-morning.

We're all on edge when she arrives. She hurries from a broken-down car straight inside. Roy is roughly Frank's size and with the lights off she's almost to him before she notices who's in front of her.

"Is he dead?" she asks softly.

"No," Gunner says from behind her. She spins around and reaches up to slap him.

"You did this, you did all of this. I fucked you whenever you wanted it and you threw me away," she hisses at him.

"Let's get something straight. You were fucking lots of guys. I never promised you shit and told you to cut out the H. That's on you," Gunner says calmly.

"And that rich cunt you're with now, I found her

dad's number. I'm gonna…fuck!" Her back was to Roy and he quickly approached her, sliding a needle into her thigh, near the line of her shorts.

"Come for a little walk with me," Roy quietly says. I nod that there's no one in sight outside and he guides her to the passenger seat of her car. She's stumbling as she leaves. "Unlock your phone now, Debbie."

Roy drives away with her; we know where to meet him. We spend the next hour wiping down every inch of the room, hang the Do Not Disturb sign up and, again, watch for people walking around before we get into the truck.

CHAPTER THIRTY-THREE

CHARLIE

"Are you sure he'll be alright?" I ask for the third time. Connal keeps waking up whenever I do. He knows I'm stressed since Jake isn't home with us. I can't even imagine how Riley is feeling right now, but she texted me when she got to Flint and Bree's house, so I know she's in good hands.

"Look at me," Connal pulls my face up so our eyes are even. "Baby girl, he'll be back and loving up on you as soon as he can. Neither of us wants you to get worked up right now…"

"Well, then don't go riding off without…" I nearly yell before I stop myself. "I'm sorry. I'm sorry, Connal."

"Hush now." He pulls me closer. "Let me see if I can figure out how to distract you."

Moving down my body, he gives me his sexy grin before burying his face in my folds. He tries his damnedest to distract me, I'll give him that.

At work the next day, I keep rolling out from under cars whenever I hear a bike approaching.

"Baby girl?" Connal starts quietly. "I need you to focus. He's going to be…"

"There he is!" I call out, hugging Connal before walking out, watching Jake's approach. Connal follows me, rubbing my lower back.

"Want to take off?" he asks.

"No, you're backed up and you were right," I look up at him. "I wasn't focused, I'm sorry."

Jake parks in front of us and I'm quickly in his arms.

"I was so scared!" I whisper into his ear.

"It's going to happen, time to time," he says, in between kisses. "Connal and I won't do trips at the same time though, ok?

"I left my cell at the clubhouse. I'll swing home and pick up the truck so I can drive you home tonight, alright?" He pulls back from me after a dozen more kisses. I just nod, knowing I have to get back to work.

———

The next weeks fly by and despite some speculation, Riley never morphs into Bridezilla.

"All set?" I ask, after getting word from her gram that it was time.

"Were you this nervous?" Riley looks at me and I nod.

"Times two," I respond, getting a laugh from the bride and Bree.

"Come on, gram is ready to walk you down the aisle."

"Thank you both, for all you've done." Riley clasps our hands.

"Riley!" Bree's unusually sharp voice gets our attention. "No crying. You can get as mushy as you want after the wedding and pictures, but not now."

"Ok! Let's go," she laughs in response.

Walking down the makeshift aisle first, I grin at Connal standing beside Flint and Gunner. The three are in black pants and dress shirts with their cuts on. Jake gives me a big wink from his seat near Wrench. Gunner looks impatient, more than likely because Riley's grandmother insisted she stay here last night. She also threatened to call the police about a trespasser if he showed up and I wouldn't put it past her to do that.

GUNNER

I know they meant well, and probably wanted the girls for themselves but I was not impressed that some of my brothers had a dozen strippers at the clubhouse last night.

Avoided them. Trying to spend time with the guys for an hour before I headed out, passing on Connal and Jake's offer to head back to their house. I knew seeing them with Charlie would make me miss Riley even more. I stayed up most the night texting Riley.

Grinning to myself, remembering the sexts my sweetheart was sending me, even after I told her about the strippers. Today, I just wanted to dart upstairs to kiss her but gram wasn't having that either. Finally, the music starts and after Charlie and Bree make it up the aisle, there she is.

In a mid-length, green dress, my beautiful Riley beams at me while keeping pace with her gram. I just can't take waiting any more though. I walk towards her, meeting her halfway and kiss that lip gloss right off of her.

"You keep your word to me, Alex," Mrs. R warns before placing Riley's hand in mine. I kiss the old bird on her forehead, startling a laugh out of her and covering the fact that I'm unable to speak right now.

Riley loves me. She's binding herself to me and I'm so overwhelmed with emotion I kiss my sweetheart once more—until the Reverend clears his throat.

"Someone likes to have his dessert first, I see?" he starts, getting our friends laughing at me. "Bring her on over here, son, I'll keep it short."

Twenty minutes later, Riley is officially my wife.

Mrs. Riley has a bar set up along with a full dessert spread, in addition to the wedding cake I had picked out. We introduce my half-sisters and a couple buddies from the Corps to our friends. I just can't stop grinning at the thought of Riley Sorenson.

Leaving gram's house some time later, I look across the street and nearly stumble. My father is standing by a truck, watching us. Though not as tall as I am, it's always been crazy to me how much alike we look. Following my glare, Riley gasps, not needing to be told who he is.

"Should we say hello?" she asks softly.

"No, sweetheart," I kiss her forehead to soften the tone of voice I used, then lead her to my bike. Looking back to him, he nods to me before we ride away.

CHAPTER THIRTY-FOUR

CONNAL

JAKE AND I ARE THE WORSE FOR WEAR THE morning after Gunner and Riley's wedding; Charlie takes care of us the best she can, mainly with her pancakes or coffee. We spend the day on the couch or in bed.

Monday comes quickly and as Vice is swamped with work, Jake is on multiple projects while I have my garage closed today. Charlie and I were just about to get down to business when there's a knock on the door. Swearing, but resisting her plea to ignore it, I pull my boxers on and head out to answer it.

"Just be a minute, baby girl!" I call over my shoulder right before opening the door.

"Connal!" Jake's sister Tabby is standing on our doorstep. "I only see one bike, is Jake here?"

"Uh, no," I stutter. "Did he know you were coming?"

"I left him a voicemail when I found out that I…"

"Connal, who is it?" Charlie calls out a moment before we can see her. She's still fastening the belt on her robe and it's pretty obvious she's naked underneath.

"What the hell?!" Tabby's face has darkened and her head is swiveling between Charlie and me.

"Tabby! What are you doing here?" Charlie starts towards her, stopping short when she sees the look of disgust on Tabby's face. "Did Jake know you were…"

"Looks like there are a couple things Jake doesn't know!" Tabby growls at us before turning to her SUV, that looks packed to the gills. "How could either of you do this to him?"

"Tabby…" I finally find my tongue. "It's not what you think. Just come inside and we'll call Jake."

"Oh, I'm calling him alright! Until he answers his goddamn phone this time!" she yells as she slams her car door.

"Shit, Connal." Charlie crosses to where her phone is charging. "Let me try to get him."

She dials him twice before sending a text. "Can you try Vice? See if he can get Jake to call us?"

I nod immediately and walk to the bedroom to grab my phone. Fuck. Of all the damn people to show up.

I stop, hearing Charlie's phone ringing.

"Jake!" She answers as I walk back out to wrap an arm around her. "Tabby's here. She showed up and we didn't have a lot of clothes on. Damn! That's probably her calling you…"

Charlie leans into me, listening to him.

"No, she's in her truck at the end of the driveway. She wouldn't come in. I mean, of course, since she thought we were cheating on you…" Silence on her end. "Okay, we'll see you soon. I'm sorry, Jake."

"He's going to call her then come home." She fills me in before turning fully into my arms.

"It'll be alright, Charles." I rub her back and wonder again why Tabby was on our doorstep. Looking down towards the road, her SUV finally pulls out of our driveway, heading towards town.

JAKE

I feel like shit for bailing on the job. Knowing that Tabs had left me some voicemails, I just never got around to listening to them. Hanging up with Charlie, I call my sister next.

"Jake?" Shit, she's crying so she's going to babble. "Oh my God, I'm at your house. I'm so sorry. I don't think you got my messages?"

"Tabitha!" I snap to get her attention. "Everything is alright. Go back inside and wait for me. I'll explain when I get there." God knows how she'll take the truth.

"You don't understand! Connal and that little whore are sleeping together," she sobs out. "I'm so sorry, Jake, but it's true."

"Tabby, don't call her that! Let me explain. Just don't drive when you're upset," I plead, knowing how she can get. "I'll be there in fifteen minutes."

Hanging up, I race back to the house. Tabby's

nowhere in sight but Charlie runs out when I pull up close to the door.

"She left." My wife wraps her arms around me before I can even get off my hog. "Right after we talked, she took off."

"It's okay, I'll track her down." I'm finally able to nudge Charlie back and, sliding off my bike, I swing her up into my arms. "How's Mrs. Forsythe doing otherwise?"

"I don't know. I haven't spoken to your mom since we got home," she says, narrowing her eyes at me. "Let's deal with this, Jake."

"We will." I nod at Connal as I walk straight past him towards the bedroom. "I think we should deal with it naked. Then it won't seem so bad."

"Jake!" Charlie laughs at me. "Focus!"

"I think you'll find me very focused. How about you, Connal?" I look over my shoulder to see him leaning against the doorway as I work to undress us. Going after Tabby is pointless until she cools down, and Charlie's just getting warmed up.

"Incredibly focused," he says, approaching the bed he grabs the lube from the nightstand. "Want both of us, baby girl?"

"But..." Charlie's face is flushed now and I know she's torn.

"That's what I was hoping for, actually," Connal smirks at her, intentionally misunderstanding.

I pull Charlie on top of me and nearly hum into her mouth as my fingers slide into her warm, wet puss.

Knowing she's ready for me, I shift to slowly enter her welcoming slit.

"You always feel so good, baby," I moan, spreading my legs to allow for Connal to minister to her rosebud. "Relax for him?"

"Please," Charlie begs, trying to move faster on my dick. "Fill me, Connal."

I hold her in place as he enters her and quickly sets a demanding pace. Our hands jockey for position on her breasts and his thrusts drive her up and down the length of my cock. Before long her screams are nearly deafening.

Feeling her tight pussy contract all around me never fails to pull me over the edge. I slam my mouth over hers, pouring my love for her into this second connection.

"Fuck! Oh, yeah, baby girl," Connal shouts from behind her, clasping her hips for a final few thrusts. Pulling her back, he turns her head to claim her lips next. "Love you."

Just as they fall to my side, panting, we hear someone pounding on the door. Charlie groans, covering her face with a pillow.

"We need a gate, Jake." Connal laughs while reaching for a shirt. "A big one."

"I'll get it," I volunteer, pulling my jeans on. "Help Charlie."

I walk, angling to look out the window, getting a view of the sheriff's truck and I sigh in annoyance.

"Got another warrant, Michaels?" I growl at him

when I open the door, zippering my jeans as an afterthought.

"Naw, no warrant," he replies slowly, leaving no doubt there's no love lost between us.

"Bye, then." I move to close the door but he sticks his boot out, holding it open.

"Everything alright, Jake?" At Charlie's voice, Michaels' eyes flick behind me and his frown deepens.

"Seems I could ask you that also, Miss Scott, is it?" he asks her, looking between the disheveled state Connal, Charlie and I are all in.

"Mrs. Forsythe, now, Sheriff." Charlie smiles and puts a hand on my back.

"Well, congratulations!" He smiles right back at her. "See, I knew I'd heard that name recently. Just now, I was taking a nap in my cruiser a couple miles from here…"

"Why don't you get back to that?" I say, putting more pressure on the door until he pushes it firmly open.

"You can't quite see it from the way I parked but a big SUV sideswiped me and tore my mirror off, then hit a tree." Ok, now he has our attention. "Most people, well, most sober people, they hit a cop car and they're nice as pie. But this person gets out before I can clear my head and doesn't she start yelling at *me*?

"Doing my job, I tried to get her ID and make sure she was alright. Then, didn't this crazy *bitch* slap me?" He ends with a growl. "And you can fucking quote me on that because her mouth ain't stopped yet. I got her secured and took a gander at her ID, and isn't her fucking name Forsythe."

CHAPTER THIRTY-FIVE

JAKE

I lean around him and sure enough, my baby sister is glaring in our direction from the back seat of his truck.

"Now, I know all you Northern Grizzlies think I'm a stupid motherfucker. And since you keep trying to slam the door on me, Mister Forsythe, why don't I just lock her up instead of releasing her to you?"

Fuck, he's gonna make me beg.

"Sheriff." Charlie moves to stand between us. "I'm really sorry. We didn't know Tabby was coming and there was a huge misunderstanding."

CHARLIE

Thinking he has no reason to dislike me, I quickly intercede trying to calm him down. His eyes flick back to me and I can see he's trying to get a read on me, but still hasn't made the leap as to why Connal is here with us.

"I've only met her once before, and yes, she is a talker." I give him a small shrug. "Well, most people are if you compare them to Jake. Really, Sheriff, I upset her and then, I can imagine she was shaken by the crash? Are you alright? Do you need aspirin?"

"Come to the vehicle with me for a moment, Mrs. Forsythe," he requests, turning away, expecting me to follow.

"No," Connal snaps, but I follow the sheriff anyway.

Both of them stay on the porch, watching me closely. When Michaels reaches the driver's side of his truck, he stops to stare at me and I do start to get a little nervous about him putting the truck between us and the porch.

"Are you safe here? Do you need me to get you away from here?" he asks in a low voice and it takes me a moment to comprehend what he's implying.

"No!" My hand flies up to my mouth as I almost scream the word at him. "My God, they would never hurt me."

"They?" He frowns at me again. "By 'they', do you mean your husband and McKay, or the MC?"

"Sheriff, honestly, I'm safe here," I insist, looking over as Jake and Connal slowly move down the steps. Turning to have a line of sight on us all, Michaels' eyes seem to flick between the four of us.

"McKay, it occurs to me, you were here the morning the warrant was served?" he asks Connal.

"I live here," he states.

"We bought the property together," Jake adds.

"My truck will need to be repaired," Michaels says after a long pause, still appraising us. "And her SUV isn't drivable right now. Looks like she had most of her belongings in it."

"I'll get her vehicle towed today and you just bring your truck to the garage tomorrow," Connal easily replies. "Charles can handle the repairs and the painting."

Nodding, the sheriff opens the passenger door, slamming it almost instantly when Tabby starts yelling.

Waiting for silence, he reopens the door and gently tugs her out.

"Ah, ah, ah." He puts his thumb over her lips when she opens her mouth again. "One word and I'm pressing charges. Nod or shake your head to answer me. Last time I'm asking. Do you need medical attention?"

Good thing Tabby's hands are still cuffed because she looks like she'd hit him again. Finally, she exhales and shakes her head.

"Good, now, let me..." He reaches down behind her and releases the cuffs before warning her, "Be careful about your state of mind anytime you get behind the wheel in the future."

"Tabby, come inside?" Jake immediately asks and without a word, she grabs her purse from the sheriff and nearly plows me down instead of walking around me. I just shrug at the sheriff, thank him, and follow in her wake.

"Y'all have a good day now," Michaels calls, his

voice laced with sarcasm.

Approaching the porch, Connal reaches out for my hand.

"Let's get this over with." He smiles at me. And indeed, Tabby has already started in on Jake about kicking my ass to the curb. They both turn when Connal and I enter. She looks furiously at our hands intertwined, while Jake walks towards me and kisses me.

Passionately. Intensely. My knees start to buckle as the stress leaves my body, luckily Connal has moved up behind me. I arch my neck to the side to give him better access then Jake's mouth slowly moves down to the other side. Connal quickly turns my head, giving me a quick peck.

I moan before I remember. My eyes fly open to see Tabby staring at me wide-eyed and her jaw hanging open.

"Baby?" Jake draws back from me, giving me his sweetest smile. "Why don't you and Connal go get the SUV towed and I'll talk to Tabby." I reach my fingertip up to touch the area his dimple usually appears. Taking the hint, he widens his grin.

"I love you," I whisper, looking once more to Tabby before I go to grab my wallet and keys. Tossing Connal his T-shirt, he puts that on and grabs his cut.

CONNAL

"Today's been interesting," I laugh.

"Barely half over." Charlie smiles back. "Do you

think they'll be okay? I know how much Jake cares about her."

I shrug, no way to know.

"Wonder what she's doing here?"

"Oh, shit!" Charlie looks at me wide-eyed. "I talked to Emma yesterday, I asked her about her doctor and she told me that her doctor was retiring. That the new OB/GYN was due any day!"

"Oh, shit is right." I shake my head at the timing. "Guess Jake will start listening to his voicemails after this. Though technically, he did ask her what was holding her back home."

"She said she looked forward to getting to know me better." Charlie's head is all the way back and she's staring straight up. "So, Tabby, my 'new' grandparents, Jake's gramp, your brother, Mack, Mrs. Riley, Rogers, and the MC."

"We haven't been shy about it anywhere we've eaten, baby girl." I grab her hand. "Hardly consider it a secret around town anymore, but I know what you mean about Jake and Tabby. We'll find a way to help him through this, okay?"

"Of course."

Over an hour later, we've moved Tabitha's truck into the garage; Charlie thoughtfully grabbed a duffle bag and phone charger that were on the passenger seat. Entering the house, Jake is on the couch, looking exhausted.

"Where is she?" Charlie crosses to him and straddles on his lap.

"Guest room," he responds, pulling her into his

embrace. "I need you, Charlie. I know we have to talk, but…"

"Bedroom," Charlie whispers, giggling and grabbng his shoulders as he quickly stands. I cross to the fridge for a beer before getting comfortable on my favorite corner of the couch content to let them have their time together.

"Where's my truck?"

I turn my head to see Tabitha watching me, I was pretty zoned out not to hear her get so close.

"At my garage. Charlie grabbed that bag for you." I indicate it sitting near the door. "You really hit the sheriff?"

"He deserved it," she answers and looks like she'll say more until we both hear Jake yelling out his release. Looking from the direction of our room back to me, she starts to open her mouth.

"Do you ask any of your other siblings for details about their love lives?" I cut her off and she blushes. "This works for us."

"Gramps found out, didn't he?" I give her a nod in reply to her question. "He was furious when I announced where I was moving. Up until Blaine's wedding, I still wasn't sure if I'd take a position in San Francisco or here. But I really liked Charlie and figured I'd give small town living a whirl."

"Your grandfather doesn't want word to get out, the *all-important family name* and all. Want a beer?" I ask when I go for one.

"Have anything stronger?" She laughs and I point her to the right cabinet.

"Tabby," Charlie's voice comes from the hallway.

"I'm still processing this, Charlie," Tabitha quickly replies, cutting her off. I move to stand in front of Charlie as Jake wraps an arm around her, cradling her stomach in his palm without thinking.

"HOLY SHIT!" Jake's sister doesn't miss the caress. "Is she pregnant?"

"Weren't telling anyone yet," Jake acknowledges it. "Guess you'll be her doctor now, in any case?"

Tabby shoots back her drink.

"Are there any other bombshells any of you want to drop on me? Just fucking tell me now!" she explodes, staring at each of us in turn as the silence stretches.

"I was the one who broke the vase when we were kids, I always felt bad that you got blamed," Jake says in a low voice.

"You? I was sure it was one of the maids." She frowns at him. "That's why I stopped insisting it wasn't me."

"Sorry, Tabs." He smirks at her.

"Do you have any idea whose child it is?" Tabby turns to Charlie.

After a moment, Charlie nods. My eyes flip to Jake and he looks as confused as I am.

"Theirs," our wife replies firmly. I smile as I reach to place my hand on her stomach, below Jake's.

"Ours," Jake and I say, looking back at Tabitha.

EPILOGUE

MICHAELS

WISHING I HAD SLEPT MORE THAN A COUPLE hours on my day off, I shake off the happenings of the past twenty-four hours and walk into Roy's Diner to find it nearly deserted.

"You ever go home, Margie?" I call out to get her attention and she waves to indicate the coffee machine is brewing fresh liquid bliss. The diner is empty except for young Joe Madda, wearing his Northern Grizzlie's prospect patch, down at the end of the counter.

"Hey, Sheriff." He nods to me.

"Still going ahead with that?" I shake my head at him. Heard he did well on his GED exam so I picked him up a couple months ago. Talked to him about trade schools, community college, or the Military, that I'd help however I could.

"Yes, sir," Joe replies, looking back down to his meal. I handed him over to Flint, so I can't help thinking that anything that happens to, or because of him, will be on me.

Taking a seat in the booth furthest from him, I wait on Margie.

"I put your usual order in, Sheriff," she addresses me as she pours my coffee.

"You see any newcomers in here today?" I ask her, getting an appraising glance in return.

"Guessing you're talking about Jake's little sister since I don't imagine you care about Dorothy's Aunt Bea." She rolls her eyes at me. "Any reason, you never just ask me straight out?"

"Just making sure you're staying sharp." I laugh at getting busted, again.

"She's taking over Will's practice," my sometimes-spy informs me, surprising the shit out of me.

"She's a doctor?"

"Here just in time, too, from the glow I saw on Charlie's face the other day," Margie adds. "Emma's about half-way through..." Margie rattles on, listing the pregnant women in town.

From her license, I only knew she was pushing thirty, from Massachusetts, and lies about her weight. Every inch of her rounded hips and thighs were high-lighted in those jeans she had on. Fucking jeans that probably cost more than all of mine combined.

"She's a pretty little thing, isn't she?" Marge asks me suddenly and I nod, remembering the fire in Tabitha's eyes when she slapped me. I had it coming, but man, I never saw *her* coming.

ABOUT M. MERIN

Born and raised in Chicago with a serious case of wanderlust, I've also lived down south and out west but I eventually moved back and live in Oak Park with my two great loves: my husband and my Norwegian Elkhound.

I first published on Amazon in February of 2018 and what an incredible ride it's been since then!

Stalk the author:
My webpage: www.mmerin.com
My email is: merinbooks@gmail.com
My facebook page is: https://www.facebook.com/merin.book.3
My newsletter is: http://eepurl.com/dpHl9T

MORE BOOKS BY M. MERIN

Northern Grizzlies MC Series

Jasper

Flint

Gunner

Charlie

Michaels

Betsy

Shade

Chains

Wrench

———

Black Hills Shifters Series

Slate's Surrender, Book 2

Gabe's Destiny, Book 4

———

Ever After Series

Dark Ever After

Julia's Journey

Defending Our Ever After (Coming in 2020)

Royal Bastards MC Series

Axel, Flagstaff Chapter Book 1

Declan, Flagstaff Chapter Book 2 (September 2020)

TNTNYC Mobbed Up Anthology

The Reluctant King (October 2020)

Rogue Enforcers Series

Kale, Rogue Enforcers (December 2020)

Standalones

His Touch

Made in the USA
Middletown, DE
15 September 2021

48389213R00198